GRINDSTONE 4 LIFE

"The Unauthorized Truth"

AUTHOR:

AQUIL ALI

DEDICATION

It took 20 years to write this book, delayed one time or another by a jealous significant other that didn't want me reminiscing on the best times of my life. Granted, it's also the most traumatic with "All" the shit I've been though. I'm Telling you "Now," my story is based on true events of my six-year reign running an illegal after-hour *"Go-Go"* Club known as the *Grindstone.*

The biggest delay was when I suffered a stroke back in 2013. Losing my ability to move, I found myself abandoned and homeless by my so-called "wife." All I had left was my thoughts and dreams in that Mercy Hospital bed, trapped in a wheelchair typing with only one finger on a laptop, rehabbing through the pain, writing our story when we were "Hustlers" on the *Strip* in that City we love… Philadelphia!

To my Crew,

It's been a pleasure hustling with all of you in the thick of night, elbow-to-elbow in any fight, checking foes together, stomping though this thing called *"Go-Go,"* putting in that "work." I'm proud to say all of you are family to me. For those of you who think I've wronged them in anyway … you already know "I didn't tell one single lie!" about this "Game." Except for your real names … If, we've given your "nickname" to you… I'm not changing a thing!

To my Squad,

Ladies, I know you've paid me in so many ways for my silence, but the more I developed your stories, it quickly occurred to me… all of you have endured a lot, which makes you "Superwomen" and don't let anybody tell you different. You will always be my "phenomenal survivors," loved as my homegirls and cherished as my friends … WITH THAT BEING SAID… you "all" are the "Freakiest Bitches" …I KNOW!

To my Haters,

I'm glad you bought the book!

TABLE OF CONTENTS

CHAPTER ONE

"Who's the Boss?"

It was 1996, in West Philadelphia, on *52ⁿᵈ & Master Streets.* It's 3:00 in the morning. The 19th District Police are everywhere with red, white and blue lights, illuminating the cold, dark, busy thoroughfare, with hundreds of people lined up in the street, waiting to see who they would bring out the of *"Go-Go"* after-hour spot, in handcuffs. The *Grindstone,* a mysterious private social club, had the ambiance of *"Harlem Nights,"* offering *"Go-Go"* Girls, gambling, booze and *Mrs. B's* delightful soul food dinners.

Authorities searched and questioned every patron inside. Their number one question was *"Who's the Boss?"* Each patron was questioned, one by one, and had to show ID. Officers poured out top-shelf liquor and ice-cold imported beer. The search produced two matching 12-gauge shotguns, equipped with laser-sights, a couple pistols, several knives and countless bags of illicit drugs. Several patrons emptied their pockets to avoid charges. Little did they know, *Five-O* wasn't concerned with their petty contraband. *"Who's the Boss?"* they asked again.

"The Kingston dread, arguing with police answered, *"I just play the records Mon."* He couldn't explain why half-naked girls were jumping off hard pricks during lap-dances, or *"tricks"* scrambling in the dressing room pulling their IDs out of their dance bags, that's also hiding small caliber pistols and knives. "The big raid was here, and plans to make big money for tonight, was over.

The Club's DJ had the most to lose. His personal DJ equipment would not be confiscated by police if he could only answer one question, *"Who's the Boss?"*

Amongst the patrons sitting at the bar, was an older lady named **Mrs. B.** She's dressed in African attire, sipping Colt 45, when the police asked her, "**Who is the Boss Miss? We know you know!**" She simply replied, *"I'm a grown ass woman. I don't know shit!"*

Mrs. B. was puffing on a **Newport** cigarette. She slowly put it out and calmly walked out the of building, untouched, with $7000 secretly stashed away in her purse. That was the night's bar and food revenues. The Police figured that out when the **donut patrol** finally checked the empty register.

The pressure was on **DJ Max**. He's a neatly dreaded, tall man from Kingston, Jamaica. *"Mon, me not know who the Boss is!"* he replied in a thick Island accent.

"Maybe you will, if we confiscate your shit," threatened the young Irish **Boot-Cop** that would love to jump around to some locked away **House of Pain** records. **DJ Max** almost lost it when the officers confiscated every crate of classic wax. *"Still don't know who the Boss is?"* asked the cops, wrapping-up amps, microphones and the infamous bubble machine which gave a nice effect to the stage for water shows.

The Officers turned on their flashlights to light their way through the Club. They noticed two bedrooms fully equipped with incandescent mood lighting and mattresses covered with rubber sheets. The female officers chuckled saying *"They thought of everything."* There're dried-up flowers that littered the floor, half melted scented candles and potpourri for stank panties. The rubber sheets are good for quick clean-ups after *dates* and used condoms in the waste basket gave away the illusion that dancing wasn't the only thing going on at the *Grindstone.* They grabbed the stashed *night stick* by the date room's door, with the words *"Trick Daddy,"* written in blood.

Meanwhile, the officers continued to check IDs on the patrons, discovering these people had come from all walks of life; from Rap stars to everyday *"Hustlers"*. Some were scared about their warrants, others were more petrified that their wives could find out and started to give in by, confessing the only information they knew. *"The Boss's nickname is Q."*

The State Police Liquor Control Board coordinated the raid with the help of the Philadelphia Police Department. The officer in charge was *Special Agent Lt. Mary J. Smith*. She's an older, dark Italian woman with a serious chip on her shoulder, especially for any entity that exploited young females. She stared at the patrons like they didn't deserve to walk the earth. Her distaste for this Club of ill-repute showed like the stress wrinkles in her face; marks of a scorned divorcee. The frustrations of raising two daughters on a cop's salary are deep and raw.

Agent Smith is a *South-Philly Sicilian,* and a crusader-type for all exploited women, especially teenage girls that sell their bodies for cash. She's making every dancer show their state ID, hoping that at least one of them is underage. She couldn't wait to save a young impressible teenager's life out the grasps of these *"Pimps."*

The patrons filed out one by one after being searched and identified. She was accusing them of undermining the minds of minors, even though no one was proven underage. Thinking that the **Ladies of the Night** are having to do despicable things to make a dollar, she thought of her own two daughters showing off their bodies and having sex with strangers.

"Who's the mastermind of this place?" asked **Agent Smith,** as if she's the Champion for Prostitute's Rights.

Finally, the police officers found a light switch. The fluorescent light exposed the array of drug paraphernalia that was tossed under chairs. The drugs were collected for evidence, including the good stuff. **The Strip** always has the best dope, and they were stealing some of the bags for their own personal research.

"They were having a good ass time huh?" asked **Agent Smith.**

They searched the kitchen. The menu on the wall read **Mrs. B's** soul food dinners. At that moment, they realized the older lady from earlier was in fact **Mrs. B!** and most importantly, that she left with all the money from the Club, because nobody gets in her way when it came to her knowing her rights as an *"Old-head."*

The remaining patrons were now unable to leave. **Agent Smith** ordered them to their knees, angrily thinking **Mrs. B** was the ring leader that got away. **DJ Max** chimed in the argument between *Agent Smith* and the other Officers.

"She's not the Boss Mon," he stated to the high-strung cops with his thick Jamaican accent. The other officers are interviewing pleading patrons, agreeing the *Boss* of this *"Club of Sin"* is a male.

The *Boss* was described as a very dapper-dressed, black man, between the age of 25-30 years old. Some called him *"The Black Hugh Hefner,"* but all would agree no one there knows his real identity, however, confirming that *Mrs. B* is his mother. *"Son of a Bitch"* said *Agent Smith*, missing the opportunity for leverage by not arresting the *Boss's* beloved *Mom Dukes*.

"Lock everybody up! Let them figure out who's the Boss at the Barracks!" shouted *Agent Smith.* The guys by the front door with security shirts on, obviously working here, are whining about getting locked up. *"Who's the freaking Boss then?" Agent Smith* asked again. Nobody said a thing.

Frustration started to set in. The cops started to rough-up some of the security guys until they flashed their own badges. The security guys were Police Officers from the 12th District. The off-duty cops are generously paid by the Club, to keep the peace, at $50 an hour.

Agent Smith went off when she heard the news. *"How embarrassing would this be if your commanding officer finds out?"* says the disgusted *Agent Smith.* City corruption has no boundaries. The fellow *Boys in Blue* have been caught red-handed, making money on the side.

"Heads are going to roll if this gets out,
Lieutenant," said *Officer Mack,* secretly trying to persuade his
commanding officer on the scene to allow them to get away
with this embarrassing situation, which is compromising their
image of Authority while spooked criminals watched to see
"who's Black" and *"who's Blue."*

"To have two Cops working security in an illegal
"Go-Go" Club? I can read the headlines now," whispered
Officer Mack. "Shit!!!" said *Agent Smith,* wondering if she
should ruin their careers. Their own fellow Officers caught in
the act, moonlighting at the *Grindstone.*

"Get the fuck out of here!" said *Agent Smith,*
reluctantly letting the two officers go. They didn't know the
Boss's real identity either. Useless accomplices! They could've
saved the State's budget reporting Intel about their off-duty
activities. These two *gum shoes* weren't snitching about
anything. They didn't ask questions about receiving under-the-
table dirty money. They're able to walk-away with dirty hands.

Among the Security staff, is a colorful guy named
Big Country. He's describing his job description as the *MC,* the
guy who talks on the mic, while watching the girls backs, when
they're on stage. He's foolish to think he could flirt with the
irritated *Agent Smith.*

"Oh! You should know who the Boss is then,"
Agent Smith stated with authority. *"No, I don't! I just keep the*
party going baby," replied the flirtatious *MC,* admiring her
Moorish figure with sexy, olive skin. She probably has long
flowing black satin locks hidden in the hair bun she's wearing,
he thought.

"You ever thought about shaking what your Mama gave ya?" said the Tubby-Bear, swiftly getting a slap for messing with an *Eggplant Pizza Nigger,* from Packer Avenue. *Big Country* was rubbing his face as she said, *"Shut the hell up!"*

Suddenly, someone fell out of the tree in the backyard of the Club. The screaming individual literally fell two stories. The half-dressed male was hiding in the tree since the raid began. The suspect, with his clothes and shoes in hand, jumped onto the tree from the 2nd floor window, eventually falling while trying to climb down. Officers heard him screaming in pain and the suspicious, fleeing black male suffered from a bruised back. He was apprehended after he landed on the concrete steps in the rear of the building. Law enforcement assumed this person of Interest to be the owner of the illegal Club. Police drew their weapons and quickly handcuffed the fleeing suspect. Falsely reported as *"Stable."*

The young overzealous cops beat him with *Billy-clubs* (of course, hidden from the report.) They cracked him on his back and legs, stomping him repeatedly. Half-naked and bleeding, they blamed his injuries on the fall. With no witnesses in dark alleys, the *Boys in Blue* weren't playing any games.

Agent Smith is thrilled, thinking she finally got her *"Man."* The Officers radioed the Lieutenant with the bad news. *"Negative on the identity of the Boss,"* squawked over the walkie-talkies while the *Patty-Wagon Boot-Cops* slap each other high-fives, proud of tap-dancing on an unarmed *Black-Buck* escaping from the scene.

The suspect in custody is questioned inside the ambulance by *Officer Mack.* The arrested detainee's ID read

Harry Williams, a hospital worker that frequents the Club, spending time with the **Ladies of the Night. Mr. Williams** explained, he was receiving a private lap dance, when he heard a loud bang.

The startled **Mr. Williams** fled out the back window, not knowing they were the police. The truth is, he was balls-deep inside one of the main dancers at the **Grindstone**. She's the one that told him to hide. He chose to play like Spiderman. She witnessed him ultimately falling and getting his ass whooped by the cops, which only stopped because she yelled out the window.

She's the **Captain of the Squad,** named **Jazzy,** only 19-years-old; a tall amazon, with long sexy legs and seductive eyes. Many believed stress made her look older, helping new dancers make money, teaching them the *"Game"* while carrying herself like a seasoned vet. **Jazzy** started dancing at the very young age of 15, trained by **Ghetto Exotic Dancer Icon** named **Snuggles,** taught to be a **Dancing Beast** on *"Go-Go"* stages all over the city, learning **the *"Game"*** from the best.

Jazzy rarely has sex for money. She loves to dance. The **Squad** calls her a *"Coochie-friendly Jump-Off,"* with her huge appetite for a sexual connection with the **Crew**, passed around to whomever needs her the most. *"Tricks"* would describe her sex as *"real,"* thinking that she loves them *"personally."* The only thing **Jazzy** loves is her mom and kids.

"Proving you can't turn a hoe house into a housewife" said every failed relationship that even tries.

Agent Smith interviewed **Jazzy**. *"Who's the Boss?"* she asked. *"He's not here and I don't know where he is!!"* she replied. **Jazzy** started to pull out her dancing license provided by the City of Philadelphia, figuring, flash her credentials then, be on her way. Little did **Jazzy** know, she just implicated herself to identifying the **Boss**.

Jazzy is livid! she can't leave! Her kids and cancer-stricken mother flashed in her mind. Her mother's words rang in her head, *"You need to quit this dangerous lifestyle, Betty Jo!"*

Betty Jo is **Jazzy's** real name, which she can't stand or could ever get used to. She won't ever try to like this fucking name that her mother loved so much and was passed down from generations. Her mother is simply the strongest black woman she's ever known...the only person that could call her by that name and not get cussed out or beat up in some cases. Schoolyard brawls over her birth name inspired the boxing classes.

The arresting officers had a ball making fun of her name. They were taken aback that a rough & tough dancing amazon was named **Betty Jo**; laughing at the **North Philly** Dancer-Boxer. with a dumb hick name.

The **Defiant Brawler** was only feminine when she made love. Every other time, she's a brawling, sass-talking thug, that just happens to dance. **Jazzy's** tattoo of two boxing gloves on her arm lets **Agent Smith** know to watch this one at all times!"

"Betty Jo, I understand you know the Boss of this Club?"

Agent Smith chuckled as she said her name. *"I know him so what?" Jazzy* replied, lighting a cigarette, reminiscing his touch, voice and the size of his deep-dish, which is perfectly sized for a deep peach-gobbler. Having a huge crush on him from the start, the heartless lover from *North Philly* criticized herself for being in love with a man that's not hers. In her mind, one day he would be.

Jazzy began to drift off in deep thought, recalling his slow, powerful sexual stroke, that makes her climax every time the Casanova bass whispered in her ear when they smashed.

"Betty Jo!!!" shouted *Agent Smith,* yelling to get her attention. *Jazzy* gets wet panties just thinking about the *Boss.* Then it dawned her; the pitiful *side-piece* doesn't know him as well as she should.

The one and only *Aquil Q. Bashir.* She didn't know he had been a talk-show host on *WDAS AM/FM,* a historically black-owned radio station in Philly. He was well known and respected by many.

His friends called him **Q** or *"Q-Deezy,"* depending how long you've known him. He has a knack for talking anybody into doing whatever he needs them to do. Growing up in his mother's Daycare, he sold 25 cent lemonade for 2 bucks at age three. Living next to a Texas highway on-ramp, he was clocking cold drinks in 105-degree weather. At age seven, he swam in the Georgia creeks with the deadly Water Moccasins. He was picked up by a Tornado in Oklahoma and given a crash-course lesson in the wonders of flight at age nine. He learned not to drink the water in Mexico, smelling the

Gringo-Kush at age ten and was raised as a Nomad across North America before the age of twelve."

The *"Voice of Overbrook"* had a natural flair with the ladies in high school, college, and beyond. He turned school loud-speaker's announcements into sexy dedications for a dollar and was called the *"Candyman"* for doubling his investment slinging "sweet-goodies" in the hall at age thirteen.

Aquil Bashir was business-minded from birth, being the oldest heir to a successful dental practice that was destroyed by divorce. He was made to be the man of the house at age fifteen and became an enforcer of his *"Gangsta"* Mother's real-estate rackets, bagging and tagging delinquent tenants and collecting rent, strapped with his father's 357 Magnum, a worthy equalizer used to manage 10 properties. Before the storefront was the *Grindstone,* it was the home of teenage *Red-Light* parties with *Double Trouble* instigated DJ battles between *Jazzy Jeff vs. DJ Irv*, *Master of Ceremony* for classic battles between *Rappers, DJs and B-Boys*; all for the love of *Hip-hop.*

He was mentored by radio Icons like *Georgie Woods, Butter-Ball* and *Jocko,* and groomed by *E. Steven Collins* to be the Young Black Voice of a generation. He became a radio activist and role-model, commanding more than $36,000 a year salary at age sixteen, when average teen-agers were making $3.80 at minimum wage in the 80's. He quickly became *"Mr. I Got what you need,"* making side deals with the elite moguls and stars on dark back-stages. He was also employed at night Clubs like the *Phoenix* as a *Bag-man* for promoter's revenues.

The young hustler understood early that everybody has a price or a vice, selling **weight** to celebs, while sweet-talking their groupies with his baritone voice. He seduced his listeners on the radio the same way. Working television on **Channel 17 "Kid Time News"** and **B.E.T.'s "Teen Summit,"** his path to Stardom was clear.

Envisioned as the next **Arsenio Hall**, his future dreams and ambition was side-tracked for the **Cream.** His resume on the streets spoke volumes. He is **"The Man!"** The **Boss** of his own exotic criminal empire. The talented decisive leader of a **Crew** called the **Grindstone!** Personified in rumor like ghetto folklore; men wanted to be him, and women wanted to fuck him.

Back at the Raid...

"Betty Jo!!!" **Agent Smith** shouted. **"The name is Jazzy, Bitch!!!"** she snapped. She noticed **Jazzy's** body language as she is trained to notice the smallest detail. **Agent Smith** immediately noticed that **Q** had this bitch turned out and getting any information out of her was utterly useless.

"Can I go now?" asked **Jazzy** after noticing that **Agent Smith** is getting restless questioning countless people in the middle of the night. Her response was simple.

"No! You'll be spending the night in jail baby! Take her to the barracks!!" announced the very proud dark-Italian flashing her badge.

Jazzy started to struggle with two male officers. Her toned, dancer's body is a handful for the out of shape cops. Their coffee drinking, cigarette smoking, donut eating ways have caught up with them as they're getting out of breath, still trying to handle *Jazzy's* diesel ass.

The only thing that calmed her ass down is *Agent Smith's* gun. Just the sight of this huge 40 Caliber proved to be very effective against any further aggression out of the tough-girl. The cold-steel of *Agent Smith's* firearm pressed against *Jazzy's* temple was just an unfriendly reminder, life is short especially if you continue to act a fool.

"Arrested for what?" asked *Jazzy. Agent Smith* responded, *"For being a stupid bitch!"* Knowing a night in jail has scared the toughest chicks, *Jazzy* won't be any exception.

"Tell me where the Boss lives!" she pressed the gun harder against her temple, threatening to shoot the forgetful *Q* who likes to box officers of the law.

With the cold steel handcuffs barely fitting around the wrists of the ex-boxer, *Jazzy's* goosebumps were telling signs that she's in way over her head. The sad fact was, she didn't know where he lives. She only slept with him in motels and *"date-rooms;"* playing the clueless *"side-jawn"* wasn't an act.

They escorted her to the Squad car waiting outside the Club; the crowd outside gasped at one of their favorites getting locked-up. *"Tell Poppy I ain't tell them shit!"* said *Jazzy* in protest to the gawking crowd. She would never turn on the love of her life; even if it's just imaginary in her head.

Jazzy is extremely loyal and knew she'll be rewarded. *Q* would be very grateful, and they will ride off into the sunset together, just like in the western movies her mother made her watch. Reality started to set in that very instant, noticing his new bitch sitting safely with the head of security, **Storm,** in his car.

   "Charmaine Rosa James," is a dark-skinned, very attractive, young woman, with a beautiful, voluptuous body to match. She could be mistaken as the famous rapper, **Foxy Brown's,** prettier sister. The 18-year-old **Star-maid** made more money being a bartender than most dancers made **"tricking."** Rumor has it, that she's turned down thousands of dollars to have sex for one night. She thought the **Ladies of the Night** needed their whole **"Game"** revamped. She's a therapist to the weak and the voice of reason to the deranged.

   Haters could only wish for her swag, class and, of course, **"Game"** in handling these thirsty, horny men out here. Men would kill for her hand in friendship, let alone to be her man. She's crowned the **"Baddest Bitch in the Hood"** on every "Nigga's" lists in **West Philly.**

   Ballers and **shot-callers** would line up at the bar flashing money, to get her attention. Trust, she noticed, plotting to have every one of them fill up her tip cup. Since the **bad little mama's** arrival at the Club, drink sales have tripled overnight; she promises **"I'll Be Good,"** seductively lip-syncing **Foxy Brown's** lyrics, played every time she opens the bar.

   The **teenaged bombshell** had men, and dancers in awe of her. She was taught by **Q-Deezy,** how to make drinks. The quick study also taught them to mix-up themselves, in one night. **Charmaine** was encouraged to wear the tightest outfits, to highlight her sexy body, as she's best known as the *"First-lady of the Grindstone."*

The raid is winding down, and the officers finished confiscating the last of the DJ equipment. The enraged *DJ Max* is beside himself. The overzealous rookie cop thought of spraying him with pepper spray, as she was having his prized processions packed up like contraband and tagged as such. That's when the tears filled his eyes. He was about to lose hundreds of dollars-worth of *Classic Wax. Agent Smith* asked *DJ Max* one last time…

"Where's the Boss?" The pressure of losing everything was too much for him to bear. His DJ equipment is everything. The cordless microphones were his pride and joy.

Those alone could make him snitch out his own mother. *"Well?" Agent Smith* forcefully asked. *"Can we talk outside?"* whispered the *Ja-faken,* born in *Camden, NJ,* not *Kingston.* A whole lot a people got their real stories told when the IDs came out. *"Why?"* she asked. The tired Agent didn't understand at first until she noticed one last patron fitting the description of the *Boss.* A soft baritone voice said, *"I'm the man."*

"You're the man, huh?" Agent Smith replied. *"Yes, I'm the Boss!"* he re-stated. *"You're under arrest sir!"* snapped *Agent Smith. "Were you here the whole time?"* she asked with a confused look on her face. The arrested Club owner didn't want to let on that he hid under the stage when the raid started.

The crafty *Boss* snuck out of his hiding place when he heard the officers were about to confiscate *DJ Max's* equipment. *"Nobody deserves to have their livelihood taken away,"* he thought, and just like that, the infamous **Q** surrendered to the police.

The police escorted the **Boss** to the awaiting Squad car outside the Club. The block is filled with luxury cars and custom hot rods with blaring sound systems. Onlookers started playing music when they escorted **Q** away, playing one of his favorite songs *"Quiet Storm"* by **Mobb Deep** featuring **Lil Kim.**

The sidewalks are filled with hundreds of onlookers, cheering as they brought him out while **Lil Kim's** verse boomed in the background. They cheered, not because the fallen **Boss** is getting arrested, they cheered out of admiration for his reputation, style, and demeanor despite the fact, he's getting locked the fuck up, adding more "Stats" to his developing **Street Cred.**

Out the corner of his eye, he noticed his right-hand man, **Storm,** a friend since the 10th grade. People thought he looked like the rapper, **Apache,** with the hit song *"I need a Gangster Bitch."* **Storm's** a rugged tough guy who ran **Q's** security force since the dollar-party days at **Overbrook High.** He was a heavyweight champion wrestler at their Alma Mater. As one of **Q's** closest friends and most trusted employee, he's sitting in a car with **Mrs. B.** and **Charmaine**

He knew they were safe with his **Brother from another Mother**. *"Thank God they weren't arrested"* thought the relieved son, and boyfriend, feeling like the *"Game"* is over.

Mom Dukes never liked the feel of handcuffs.

"Last time I felt Police shackles… in the 60's for Revolution" declared the **Boss's** giver of life. *"**That was 17 hours of complete and utter torture and hell. The Good Doctor had to use clamps!**"*… *"Mom!"* said the embarrassed son, at the memory of telling the story of Aquil's birth!

A "Free Q" chant started to resonate through the crowd.

Agent Smith looked disgusted. *"How is this fucking guy admired by so many people?"* thought the arresting Lieutenant. **Q** noticed **Agent Smith's** distaste for his cheers. *"What you think? I'm some kind of monster or something?"* he whispered to **Agent Smith,** shaking his head.

The cautious Agent wanted to smack the devilish grin off his fucking face but knew that might start a riot; restraint was on every police officer's mind that night. **Agent Smith** tucked **Q's** head ever so gently in the Squad car, and they were gone just as quickly as they came. The **Boss** was now in custody and going to jail for the very first time. *"DAMN."*

CHAPTER TWO

"The Crew"

They arrived at the police station at about 7:30am; just before the start of the 1st shift. The officers handcuffed *Q-Deezy* to the bench in the main office area. *Agent Smith* had the officers escort him to her desk; a meager workspace needing a good cleaning, complete with an overflowing office waste basket, and coffee stained cup rings on the folders that contained files of the city's after-hour *"Go-Go"* spots all over the city. In the distance, a few shackled detained prisoners are waiting for the *meat wagon* to cart them off to the *Roundhouse.*

"What is your name? Please give me your last name first." Agent Smith asked with authority.

"Bashir B-A-S-H-I-R" he replied. *"What's your first name is it 'Mr. Pimp'?"* she jokingly asked, barely pronouncing his name right.

"I never 'Pimped' a mother fucker in my life" shouted *Q. "Oh, really? Explain the sex rooms and used condoms then!"* she replied with a judgmental stare. *"Who knows, why people like to fuck in my Club...Nobody is 'Pimping!' And Everybody's Grown!"* he swiftly corrected the Agent.

"What is your first name?" She asked with a condescending grin. *"Aquil A-Q-U-I-L"* he replied. *Agent Smith* continued to take down his address and other pertinent

information to file the report. She then fingerprinted him and took his mug shot. It's official, **Aquil Q. Bashir** is now a known criminal on record.

The charges were as follows: Conspiracy to a prostitution ring, selling liquor without a license and firearm charges. The confident **Boss** began to laugh. ***"What's so funny Mr. Pimp?"*** she asked. ***"These are some serious charges!"*** the pencil-pushing Agent stated with disbelief, knowing the felony charges can draw 8-year sentences.

"You ain't got nothing on me, Ms. Cocky Cop!" replied the **Boss** with connections she couldn't even imagine; urgently waiting to make his one phone call. ***"I got four words for you cop! I want my lawyer,"*** smiling at this confused cupcake, trying to call the shots on the scene.

The frustrated Agent agreed to cease with the questions, due to police policy. **Agent Smith's** slam-dunk case was going to be a little harder than she thinks. The **Boss** of the **Grindstone** can't wait for the cops to feel the power of his connections. Every telephone ring in the busy police station heightens his anticipation.

The undercover police officers, that made the illegal liquor buys, entered the room. The handcuffed **Boss** is looking as a regal ***"Gangsta"*** facing his accuser, while they looked like shameful snitching groupies.

They're **Officer Brown** and **Officer Riley,** remembered as happy patrons, that had nothing but admiration for The **Ladies of the Night**, and drinking at least a case of "Budweiser" a night for the last 2 weeks. The undercover cops were good customers, *"tricking,"* and some more shit, trying to find the words to apologize.

"You've paid for my silence," quoted the **Leader** of the **Grindstone,** reciting the **Rule #5** of the **Crew's** oath to its members, holding true to the pledge even after finding out, they're undercover pigs. **Agent Smith** is busy with paperwork, writing up statements and running identity checks on the **Boss** & **Betty Jo,** dreading the mundane dotting of the I's and the crossing of the T's.

The undercover **rats** clambered to reveal their deepest inner-feelings. *"We didn't want to shut you down my man,"* said the **flat-foots**, with star-struck eyes. *"We love the Grindstone and Mrs. B.'s food,"* they said sorrowfully. *"We were pressed by our supervisors, and they insisted that we do our jobs or find new ones!"* said **Officer Riley,** revealing the depths of his pain to the hand-cuffed **Boss.**

"No problem my man, you got to do your job, right?" he responded. They quickly exited the room noticing **Lieutenant Agent Smith's** glaring eyes, wondering *"What the hell are they talking about?"* just blatantly kissing his ass. Fearing a write-up, the two officers instantly went from groupies back to officers of the law.

"Does everybody wanna to ride this guy's jock?? Damn!!!" said the overbearing goody-two-shoes.

Agent Smith's" frustration flared up again. *"Let's be professional people, he's a fucking criminal!!!"* she shouted in disgust. Little did she know, the undercover officers took a blood oath, vowing to never expose the lust of another in this *"Fraternity of Freaks,"* by telling its members' identities, especially to the law, knowing a lot of the freaks in *Philly*…are cops!

When the police allowed the one-call to his lawyer, the *Boss* had other plans. He called the one important person he's been sending fat envelopes to for months; the same man that offered protection from raids, investigations and any other government problems. He calls none other than, City Councilman, *Mike Mutter.*

Councilman Mutter is an influential government official, who longs for power, prestige and fat envelopes filled with hundred-dollar bills. "The councilman from the *52nd Ward* rarely gave out his personal number, but in the case of one of his biggest *street* contributors, he didn't mind. The call was short and sweet.

The *Boss* knew the charges were weak and that the councilman had his back. The only words he uttered were his location, and the name of the arresting officer, *Special Agent, Lt. Mary J. Smith.* Then he hung-up the phone, patiently waiting to see what his protection money was going to buy.

"Time to cash in my chips" said *Q* with an eager look on his face. The second-hand seemed to move as slow as a ticking time bomb. The impatient *Boss* began to daydream, while he waited for his get out of jail favor to kick in, thinking about his new girlfriend *Charmaine* and *"How she's gonna to react, and what would she say?"* about everything. One thing is for certain, she's not going to like this big illegal lie!

His brain started to wager a bet with his gut. *"Would she ride or would this relationship die?"* Butterflies starts eating at his nervous stomach. The gravy train is over for her *"Gold-digging ass,"* assumed the vulnerable new boyfriend, feeling subjugated to the facts; there's not an inch of room about the *LIE* that's wrapped around his neck.

   Aquil risked his unsanctioned support with his estranged-wife, Denise, for their two daughters he's supporting. They'll be looking forward to their usual allotment of financial support. *"Daddy's money is always there. Child support?"* He scoffed at the idea. The father of two enjoys putting wads of cash in his wife's hand during their separation, as a *"token of thanks"* for having his kids. The kids he can't deny the striking resemblance... the slightest glitch ...Baam!

   "Please Stand! For the Honorable Judge Nailanigger Balls to the Walls," said the brother that's been there from the beginning. She wants problems cause' it pains her to look at his face... *"The funny thing is our kids look just like me"* said the proud father, knowing his likeness will live forever!

   He questioned if the   locked down the Club. Busted locks draw crack-heads like roaches-to-sugar on the *Five-Deuce.* He also wondered if his cash is accounted for; the number-one rule in weighing money... keep the thumbs *"OFF"* the scale. Too many times people get forgetful about...what's mine and what's his... a zillion thoughts seemed to clash in his mind at once.

   Finally...

   Agent Smith's phone rang. Evidently, she's hearing an earful from the caller. *"Yes sir!"* she said with a disgusted stare directed at the **Boss** of the **Grindstone;** the powers of the councilman's influence at work. *"It's not WHAT you know, it's WHO you know in this city."*

She hung up the telephone, disgusted and appalled, that her own supervisor had so much concern for her prisoner. She was instructed to charge him with a lesser charge of selling liquor without a license and to *"release him immediately!"*

This was the moment that their rivalry started. **Agent Smith** vowed, at that very moment, to expose this well-connected criminal, *"so, help me God!!!"*

It's 10am after his release. **Q-Deezy** is waiting outside the State Police barracks for his **Crew** to pick him up. The arriving **Crew** members included his business partner and 2nd right-hand man, a handsome 33-year-old, well-dressed man named **Quintin Hooker.** He's a legendary playboy and a **bag-man** for the **Brotherhood;** a strong- armed collections expert, and an armed robber of *"Hustlers"*, to help fund the Temple's collection plate. He's also a **Militant Soldier** for the **Movement,** freelanced on several capers, stick-ups and kidnappings, all for the **Cause.** Any struggles being association with the Club was squashed by the **Captain** of the **B.B.O**. aka **Big Boys Only,** added *"protection for the complexion."*

He's the person that exposed **Q** to Philly's *"Go-Go"* night life with a boy's night out at **Fox Valley.** **Quintin's** popularity was enormous. He tripled the **Grindstone's** patronage in a matter of weeks, utilizing guest lists from his Grown n' Sexy parties at **New Alternatives Night Club.**

Quintin looked just like *R. Kelly* and, some say, he acted just like him too. The only difference was *R. Kelly* can sing! Everybody knew you could trust *Quintin* with your money and your life, but never your woman, especially a wifey with whorish ways.

The *Ladies of the Night* described him to be too well-endowed to have sex and being thirsty for any sexy female, has gotten him in a bind or two. The *Grindstone* dancers would feel like they *"bit off more than they can chew!"* The charismatic womanizer could seduce the pants-off most women, from 18 to 80, with his personality, reading women's minds... always one step ahead a female's thought. *Quintin* is best- known as *"A Hustler's favorite Hustler."*

Storm, the Apache look-a-like, made a name for himself in the streets of *Philly*. *Storm* is a grappling brawler from *Hill Top.* He's a devoted friend, through thick and thin. As a life-guard at the *Kelly's Pool,* he orchestrated the "*Freakiest Adult Swim*" *in Philly*. Countless unplanned pregnancies were conceived on his watch, for a $50 cover charge at the pool.

Storm and *Q* have been friends since *Brook.* He talked many bullies out of *"messing"* with his home boy. They were elbow-to-elbow, when things got rough. After the first to swing, it was, *"Fuck it! What we talking for!"* expressed by the Champion Wrestler, chin-checking foes with *Tyson* blows.

Marvin "Storm" Towers is a faithful young husband, with character that spoke volumes about his will power, being around naked women every night; a world record for any man, with the abundant offers that poured in his lap! ... The Homie never wavered. Staying true is very special to him. *"It means I kept my word"* stated the loyal hubby, that's always accused of cheating.

His Indian blood didn't mix well with alcohol therefore, **Storm's** only vice is his Pepsi-Cola. He's the sobering voice of reason for the **Crew.** While they smoke the **choke,** he's the one designated to remember *"all"* the lies.

The next Crew member is Storm's cousin.

The Club Manager, **Moose,** is a 19-year-old, 6ft. 5in., Star-football player from **William Penn High School**, waiting to enter college. **Moose** started as a bouncer, but quickly earned **Q's** trust, helping to run the Club.

The promising athlete is strong as an ox, bench pressing 600-lbs with ease. He got his nickname from **Mrs. B.,** when he happened to be standing in her way. He seems to overshadow the world with his gigantic size, *"big as a Moose."* The offensive line-man weighed his hopes for an NFL career against being part of the **Crew;** his allegiance to the late hours and the late-night treats, distracted him from practice. The **Gentle Giant** is not to be fucked with when he gets mad. That's when you'll witness *"The Black Steve Austin,"* like his semi-pro wrestling, big brothers.

Stephen "Moose" Brown struggled with shifting from being the *"Man"* in high school because of athletics, to lying about being drafted in the *"NFL Draft,"* duping *"Gold-diggers"* into giving him free sexual favors. He was too busy to train for the walk-on Squads in the league. Dumping loads on *"Go-Go"* girl's titties sounded like more fun than receiving broken legs in Tampa Bay, from a calling NFL instigator,

Warren Sapp. He's best known as the *"Big Gentle Giant,"* at the *Grindstone.*

The next Crew member is Quintin's cousin.

The *"Master of Ceremony, Big Country"* is the Club's *MC* and backup DJ. He's a colorful, wise-ass that loves to mess with everybody, with his fast wit. The 6ft., burly teddy-bear is in his early 20's. He seems to wear the same checkered shirt that reminds *Q* of a country picnic table. The nick-name seems to stick.

Big Country is a self-proclaimed *"Pimp,"* a "*hack*" and "*drug-runner*" for the *Ladies of the Night. Kenneth Big Country Casey* aka *Big Country* wasn't a high school crush, as an over-weight kid. Making up for lost teen-age fantasies, he's found his niche with the *Ladies of the Night.* He could get a dancer paid, by hyping the crowd to tip their last dollar.

The erotic *Maestro* could mess-up a dancer's night, in terms of making money, by simply not saying a word. He could be a dancer's best friend, if she'd tipped him right, for gladly enforcing Stage Rules at the Club. It's hard work cock-blocking horny men's desires, paid by lost $1 bills that fall behind the stage, unknown to the dancers. Either way, he got paid.

Another Crew member is Moose's former classmate.

Big Twin is an attractive, 6ft. 3in., 18-year-old young man, still struggling with high school for the third year in a row. He's *Moose's* classmate and childhood friend. The big guy kindly vouched him into the clique. The good *"church-*

drummer boy" was hooked on his first visit at the *Grindstone.* Trying to make ends meet, at a very young age, *Big Twin's* high school sweetheart, Trisha, was pregnant with their second child. His biggest struggle was working at a *"Go-Go"* Club, instead of finding a *"real job,"* per his soon-to-be wife. The *Grindstone* was his only escape from the pressures of husband life.

David "Big Twin" Fredrick enjoyed being around sexy vixens every night, making him question his marriage; forever feeling trapped by a woman with a plan. *Trisha Parker's* not playing about getting married, being 8-months pregnant by a *"slacker,"* wondering why things aren't falling into place for her.

The next member is Charm's high-school friend, Junior.

He's an adorable, teen-aged handyman and server. *Junior's* the son of a master carpenter, having all the tools to build the Club. He's known as the brick-layer to the clique. He's the *Crew* member that helped *Q* build the *Grindstone,* when his first partner, *Cez,* got locked up.

Lionel "Junior" Franklin struggled with the peer pressure from the *Crew* to be a lady's man like them, but they didn't know about his homosexual tendencies he was desperately trying to keep secret from them. He's secretly gay, but *Charm* treated him like family.

In the beginning, only *Charm* knew of his secret lifestyle. *Junior,* despite his sexual preference, is utterly infatuated by her beauty, settling for friendship, which is typical for most men that knew her. *Junior's* infatuation for *Charm* made him a victim to her every whim. Growing-up, he was best known for being everybody's favorite young boy on the *Deuce.* During the Club's off hours, he tried his hand at reading people's future, with tarot cards and a ouija board, calling himself Jacques the Beneficent.

Another member of the Crew was an ex-patron named Big Gene.

He's a fugitive from Jamaica. The tall 6ft. 3in., (*hiding his age*) 43-year-old, dark-skinned man, looks just like **"Shaft,"** from the 70's. He's always making people very uncomfortable with his mean demeanor, yet, he's another **"Gentle Giant"** in the *Crew.* He's a lovable, nice-guy, until you get on his bad side. He's been there with **Q** though gun battles and free falls.

As a patron, **"Eugene Parker"** struggled, as an older gentleman, with trying to find love, looking in the wrong places. He's living a lie, with an alias, 10 years younger than himself; fighting with his innermost demons of his past that haunts him every day. Big Gene's forever the workaholic, and he prides himself for never missing a night of work.

He's best known for always being there for homeless dancers needing a place to stay, and never pushing-up on them or asking for sexual payments for a solid favor. He's a true friend to the *Squad* and the *Crew.*

Another Crew member knows Q from his radio days at the station.

DK aka **Super D.** is in his early forties and stands about 5ft. 3in. He's the former bodyguard for **Diana Ross** and several other celebrities. During his days of protecting the

"Ultimate Diva," he learned how to *"cloak and cover."* He was taught to be a shadow in the spotlight and trained to be an effective combatant in close situations, quickly and discreetly handling any problem, while the star gets carried on his back.

He's accredited for saving the recording artist **Rick James'** life, per the people in the industry. He was the side-kick for *"The King of Funk Punk,"* delegated to take care of the star's dirty-work, from copping dope to hiding the dead bodies of overdosed groupies, to crossing paths with mobsters to negotiate gambling debts.

He's a stone-cold, crazy mother-fucker, especially if you try to harm any of his clients. Despite his size, he's a very effective bodyguard, with a fetish for pain, enduring gunshots to vicious beat downs, considering them a turn on. He's also a very loyal friend to **Q.** His greatest drama at the **Grindstone,** is that his estranged daughter, **Kali,** is one of its dancers. They're reunited by working at the Club.

The absentee father realized who she was because, coincidentally, she looks just like her mother. He's been in constant battle whether to reveal his identity, or continue being anonymous with lustful eyes, struggling with nervousness being around with his estrange daughter, **Kali,** in close encounters, i.e. dressing rooms, stages etc.

DK did personal security for her and the rest of the dancers at bachelor parties, blaming himself for not being there as the father she desperately needed as a child. Now, her DNA-hopeful, secretly guards her body, reluctantly condoning her freakish profession with an inappropriate hard-on. **DK** is best known for being *"The Diva Protector."*

The Crew arrived at the Police Station...

They're excited that **Q** was freed and only facing misdemeanor charges at best, relieved his payments to the city councilman wasn't in vain. He's delighted to see the Crew surround him like they're returning *"Hannibal,"* ... freed from *"Caesar's"* grasp, coming home from *"Rome."*

"Where's Jazzy?" he asked with a distressed look, not knowing her criminal record as well as he should.

"She should be out any minute," replied **Storm,** looking at his watch, calculating the time prison computers register that the bail is paid in full.

Jazzy's his *"Bottom-Bitch,"* meaning she was the most important dancer in the clique. She lives at the Club on the weekends, and reigns over the girls during off hours. The **Crew** needed *Jazzy's* influence to keep the girls in line. She reveled in her position and ruled the dressing room like a **CF-CF** prison guard, controlling the natural order of things.

Jazzy's stomach filled with nervous butterflies when the Turn-Key opened the gate. She's thankful her **Crew** is right outside. **Q** and *Jazzy* locked eyes and had a whole conversation without saying a word. This was the first time the **Crew** meant family for *Jazzy.*

The sun's out and shining bright with a cool breeze. Belmont Avenue is buzzing with rush-hour traffic. The **Crew's** starving and awaiting **Q's** orders to ride out to their favorite breakfast-spot. The famished **Boss** didn't eat the cheese sandwiches provided by the C.O. His stomach is having a conversation with his back, obliging the Crew with the order, *"Let's Eat!!"*

The *Crew* loaded in the cars after hugs for *Jazzy* and high fives for *Q-Deezy.* They arrived to *"Spiro's"* restaurant at 40th and Girard. The sassy waitress, *Pearl,* knows the *Crew* well, from the pretty-good tippers, to the ugly-pretenders, but loves the *Boss* the best. He always makes everybody leave a tip or get called out as a ratchet cheapskate.

Q-Deezy always gets to order first. The cautious leader sits with his back towards the wall in the rear of the restaurant. If anybody in the *Crew* had to speak to him, he could see who's asking the question. Spontaneous *"Dozens"* may pop-off, if you ask a stupid question. All in fun, the *Crew* is hella-tight.

Storm and *Q* sat together along with *Jazzy,* who's rubbing on his privates under the table. *"Don't tease that thing girl,"* whispered *Q.* *"I won't, you Moby-Dick Monster,"* *Jazzy* replied while she positions her wet panties. *Jazzy* then excused herself and went into the bathroom.

Storm's ready to report the damages, give messages and, of course tell *Q* the mindset of *Charmaine.* The food is delicious, as usual. The *Boss* wanted to enjoy his meal first, thinking his news was all bad. The anticipation of informing *Q* of all the events that took place last night was burning a hole in *Storm's* head. The long-time friend waited for the newly freed *Boss* to finish slopping his biscuits in the cheese grits.

Jazzy is still in the bathroom with a $20 bag of blow, given to her by *Junior;* peas in a pod, those two. *Jazzy's* biggest vice is her coke habit. It's the main reason, the *"Bottom Bitch"* wasn't the *"Main Woman"* in the *Boss'* life. She was too busy using drugs to numb the pain of losing her kids to her Mom who has health issues.

The bottom chick returns from the restroom, as *Storm* and *Q* finishes their meals. Once again, a high *Jazzy* is a complete turn-off. The disheveled dancing addict, tried shoving a dollar in the restaurant's juke box, finally selecting *Patra's "Pull up to my bumper,"* and starts jiggling in the middle of the diner, without shame, trying to entice every man in the room, then abruptly spins and falls in *Q's* lap.

"What yawl talking about?" she asked with a slurred voice and bugged out eyes. *"Business!"* replied *Storm,* hoping her actions wouldn't start a fight. They needed to discuss last night's events, and not be distracted by *Jazzy* trying to put two words together while she's high… desperately trying to cuss out *Storm* and sidetrack *Q-Deezy* from learning about *Charmaine's "Golden-shovel"* tactics.

"Where's your new bitch now?" she asked with sarcasm. *DK* quickly stood up and tried to calm *Jazzy* down. The annoyed leader of the *Grindstone* knows their secret relationship isn't going to last. She's catching feelings … she's un-able to keep her emotions in check, after experiencing multiple orgasms with him. They didn't just bump the nasty, *Q's* been making her feel like they've been making love.

"Why the fuck she's not here Q?" *Jazzy* yelled with disgust, grabbing his face with affection, while a tear rolls down her cheek, providing everybody front-seats at the

breakfast-counter, with an award-winning melodrama, nixing *"Jerry Springer"* on the TV, for the reality-show unfolding over coffee and pancakes inside the diner.

Jazzy's high… DK take her ass to the car!" A struggle ensued, and *DK* had a problem getting her under control. *Big Moose* kindly picked her up like a new-born baby and carried her ass out to the car. The cry-high baby needed some air. She was made to sit in the car's seat until she got her shit-together.

"Amazon… time-out?" joked *Storm* and continued their conversation.

"Man, I didn't know if you wanted Charmaine here or not" he explained. *"It's Cool man... How did she react to the raid?" Q* eagerly asked. *"She's a rider for sure Dawg!"* he proudly explains. *"Mom-Dukes got away with all the cash register money, and Charmaine collected all the dancing fees from the chicks that didn't pay." "She calmed your Mom's down and turned in ALL the funds"* explained *Storm* with a happy grin, needing to get paid badly. *Q's* AMAZED at *Charmaine's* skills of controlling the real silent partner of the Club … *Mom-Dukes,* who always remembered a forgotten loan the *Crew* hasn't paid back yet.

The total amount in the envelope is a little under $9000. The delighted *Boss* quickly counted the money with a smile on his face, thinking last night's take was confiscated by the police. The *Crew* did better than expected. They secured the Club, and having cash in hand, he gladly paid payroll and separated money for stock that needed to be bought… thanks to the hating ass cops.

Storm chimed in on his thoughts. *"She's a good girl dawg, don't fuck it up with this Jazzy shit!"* Good advice fell on deaf ears when the *Boss* counts money. *Storm* handed *Q-Deezy* his cell phone. He placed the device on his ear thinking *"This can't be safe."*

"Who's this dawg?" frowning at the "walkie-talkie," his nickname for cell phones he doesn't trust. *"It's NOT the CIA, It's your girl"* *Storm* replied and then walked away. *"First-time anybody's call her that!"* thought *Q.*

Q's surprised to hear a crying, concerned woman on the phone. It's *Charmaine.* Contrary to popular opinion, she was scared to death. Up all night, doubting if she'll feel his touch again, the *"Gold-digger"* had to shake off this foreign feeling her *"damn"* self. She started this relationship contemplating on just playing her part, while she spends his money ... eventually getting bored, and then *"dumping his ass."*

The raid exposed feelings she didn't even realize she had for him. Just yesterday, she was in love with her baby-father. Now, the trophy ex-girlfriend was crying out of genuine concern for *Q-Deezy* ... and this was no act. *"She likes me?"* he thought, listening to her whine for him to come to her father's house. Thoughts of caressing *Charmaine's* fat beautiful chocolate ass replaced any thoughts of *Jazzy's* drug-addicted flat-ass, real quick!

"This shit is real" thought the convinced new boyfriend hanging up the phone.

Outside the restaurant...

The **Crew** began to pull off in their cars. **DK** and Big **Twin** had to go home to their wives. **Quintin** didn't even eat, deciding to get faded on the ride over. **Storm** drove **Q** and **Jazzy**" from the restaurant. **Charmaine's** blowing up **Storm's** phone trying to clock her new lover's arrival. **Q** didn't take the call. **Jazzy** usually has a small tantrum about awkward moments like this, but on this day, she sat in silence needing to get to her kids.

Jazzy realized something the moment the handcuffs were placed on her wrists. She could be lost to her ill-stricken mother and the kids in a moment's notice. She doubted *"all"* her life's decisions. She's usually looking for pleasure from a **Crew** member to mask the pains in her life; the apparent "rape" in "Fox Valley," running away from a life of sexual-slavery from its owners and entering a world of *"Go-Go"* on different terms.

She's the last thing on **Q's** mind, and even though **Jazzy** would've usually seized her opportunity to spend some time with her beloved *"Poppy,"* on this day, her babies took first precedence. Not even, the seductive strokes of her *"Poppy's"* cock was going to interfere with **Jazzy** reuniting with her kids.

Q, on the other hand, was very eager to meet up with his new chocolate girlfriend. Where **Charmaine** lacked in years, she makes up for in beauty. He loves it when men would fall out for her fine-ass, making celebrities like the very married **Will Smith,** best friend of her older brother, ask for her number.

The very attractive and voluptuous young mother of one, gave birth at the tender age of 16. She got caught up in a loving moment allowing him to plant his seed, because she was jealous of another girl trying to steal her boyfriend.

The problem with this beautiful blessing of a daughter, is her baby-father; a small-time hustler from the neighborhood named **Munchie.** He's a 5ft. 9in., average looking, light- skinned, very abusive brother, with a serious issue that his baby-mama now works at a *"Go-Go"* Club.

Charmaine, pregnant with their second child, secretly started working at the Club to earn abortion-money, thinking having another kid with a broke, controlling mama's boy wasn't a good idea. One-night of drinking *"Old Granddad"* whiskey at the **Grindstone** fixed that problem. She's no longer pregnant and free to date a *"baller"* like **Q.**

Storm arrived to **Jazzy's** mother's house, even though she basically lived at the Club three-to-four nights a week. She found herself evicted from her mother's house for good. **Jazzy's** mother was done with her missing-in-action ways. Last night's arrest was the straw that broke the camel's back. **Jazzy's** Mom boxed and bagged her belongings and sat them out with the trash.

"My Shit!" screamed **Jazzy,** snatching bags of clothes from the garbage-men rolling down 13th Street. When the wind blows, there goes **Jazzy's** written rhymes about **Erie Ave.,** and the rest them *"Cats"* rolling dice against the bricks of *"Max's,"* home of the *"Biggest Cheese Steaks,"* right next to *"Eagle's Bar"* where stick-up kids rob negros for high stakes!

The **Crew** knows exactly where they are … quietly retrieving **Jazzy's** shit and loading it in the trunk, fearing the biggest threat on the block ... *Jazzy's* Mom, *"Corporal Louise Jackson,"* a correctional officer on medical leave, and now a full-time, frustrated *"Mom-Mom,"* raising *Jazzy's* four kids.

Young *Betty-Jo* got caught-up in a statutory rape romance with a 30-year-old man, burdening an already full household with baby after baby, purposely conceived, to make her *"Old-head"* know this unlawful relationship can end with physical bars*,* or the ones written on paper blowing down the street.

The same curtain closed on the 2nd floor when teenaged *Jazzy* was pushed-out to hustle in these streets. She had to hold it down when her *"African't,"* unemployed baby-father moved in. He's closer to *Ms. Call me Louise's* age, at 39 ½ years. For the tenth year in a row, she's committing the deepest betrayal having sexual relations with that *"Man,"* that's having babies with her youngest child. *Jazzy* got duped to *"kick in her share"* by half-way *"tricking"* with the dope-boys on the Ave.

When that same curtain closes, *Cpl. Jackson* cracks the whip. *"Either eat this 'Black Butter,' or clean the entire house;"* knowing how to use a lazy-loafer, sleeping in the basement all day. *"Slick Erie Ave Rick"* chose to play house with his kid's Mom-Mom. *Slick* didn't pick-up a broom. He would rather crack his back for hours a day, sparring with Mama's hormonal sex drive.

Slick got cocky at a pinochle-game once, having diarrhea of the mouth, telling *Jazzy's* Mother's business, and caught a beat-down by her family for lying about the absolute truth. Loose lips sink ships in the *Hood.* Right in front of their whole entire family, Mama's dirty laundry came out.

"You fucking my man Mama?" asked the betrayed *Jazzy,* screaming at the embarrassed Mother by the 2nd floor window, watching her baby-father get carted away by police, called by *Cpl. Jackson,* sounding all official, making the situation the 911 operator's number one priority.

"Slick Erie Ave Rick," battered and bruised, amazed the police didn't arrest his attacker, *Ms. Jackson,* who already put the fix in his ass, is going to jail! All he did was smile when the police took him away for screwing a minor, escaping the middle-aged monster sliding the curtain closed on that same damn window.

"Mom!" screamed the thrown out *Jazzy.*

Moose is restraining *Jazzy* from going into the house. They didn't want to sit there while *Jazzy* and her Mom have a *"Don King"* sized argument. They're like *"Tyson and Holyfield"* when they get to fighting. The *Crew* got lucky that day and retrieved what she deemed worthy and left everything else. She no longer felt the need for the boxing trophies from her Coach Dean, training her for the Golden Gloves Finals, that being her only ticket out the *Hood* at age 13…another dream aborted because Mama thinks she's a man.

"Men can screw WHOEVER they want!" said the scrupulous *Ms. Jackson,* heeding to no boundaries, living life in the past. Payback is deep-rooted to the bone, thinking *"all men ain't shit!"* while flashing threw teenage crush paraphernalia and other harsh skeletons of her childhood; of a

younger Mama, having 5 kids by 7 different daddies. Now that she's older, she belittles every move her daughter makes.

"Miss Judgmental is the first to point the FINGER!" says the teenager with too many fucking kids!

Depression started to set in for **Jazzy**. She longed to hold her babies today. **Jazzy's** thoughts started to crowd her mind. *"What will Child Services do?"* another frantic thought that flashed in her head, fearfully thinking the worst all the time, depending how mad her Mother gets.

"Mom is going to tell them all my Shit!" Jazzy thought sorrowfully about the mandatory drug-test for **D.H.S.** It's the ace card that's **Ms. Jackson** always plays. *"One call from Mama, and it's a wrap!"*

"Take her to the G-stone Storm!" ordered **Q.** *"The Club?"* asked **Jazzy**. *"You chilling Poppy?"* She's begging already, while she tries to unzip his pants, a go-to move to ease the pains in her life, suggesting sucking all the juices out of **Q-Deezy's** body, with an eerie sense of desperation, spawned by her current situation. *"Chill Baby-girl!"* he said, knowing he'll need his full strength to properly satisfy **Charmaine's** sexual appetite; nothing but focused, penetrating attention for his awaiting girlfriend.

In the past, **Jazzy** would've straddled **Q-Deezy** right in the backseat. Home-Boy flipped like a light-switch. Usually he's weak to her sexual demands but, not TODAY. He hungered to explore **Charmaine's** smooth warm thighs and her heavenly hips. Those nipples are still growing and forming everyday ...not to mention a plump, fat ass.

Jazzy's feeling defeated. She can't stand rejection, especially after getting tossed in jail *"plus"* eviction. *Jazzy* wanted him to console her about her Mom, kids and most importantly, getting locked up. She just wanted to smoke a fat cigar filled with weed and lay on her *"Poppy's"* chest, then get pumped hard to forget any memory of last night.

"But No!!!" she scoffed. *"This Nigga wants the 'Gold-digging' BITCH!"* she screamed while, **Big Moose** watched their light argument from the front seat. It's another episode of *"Day's in the Hood,"* where the busy **Boss** is supposed to care about the *Jump-off's* feelings, smelling like Cell-59 at the Barracks. She's crying about her *"dysfunctional "MOTHER!"* bailing out her baby-father cause' she can't *"cum"* with nobody else but *"HIM!!!"*

"Yeah whatever, I'll be back!" the **Boss** responded knowing he wasn't.

Jazzy paused in her tracks, surprised **Q** turned down oral sex. *"He never says No!"* she thought, confirming this new relationship must be serious. *"No!"* ...man, alive can ever resist the *"Drain-gone,"* ...those sounds alone that devours a long-hard shaft of a man are legendary in the **Hood**. Those *"Super-head"* -type skills which make boyfriends, baby-daddies and *"tricks"* put her in their top five. Her slow, methodical strokes with continuous suction on your manhood would have a Porn Star climaxing prematurely. She was called the *"Gobbler"* behind her freakin' back since **Ben Franklin High.**

They arrived at the Club...

The block is quite different during the daytime. The *"T&D" deli* on the corner seemed to attract everybody from the crack-heads cracking "forties" to the busy working folks needing their morning "Joe."

The folks from *"Bible-Way" Baptist Church* are cleaning the block from all the beer bottles and other party trash from the weekend's late-night activities; getting *"sick and tired"* of cleaning after the party-goer's mess. Compensated helpers provided by the *Grindstone*, (various "smokers,") cleaning all the Club's street trash, usually squashes the Church's "Beef."

Everybody knows who they are, from the working "Joes" who saw them and said, *"What a Life!"* they're making a living partying with naked girls, to the Church folks who loath them for the same reason; right or wrong... all eyes were on them when they pulled up.

The buzz about last night's raid even had the corner-boys nervous. They watched in envy, surprised *Jazzy* and *Q* were released so quickly. The whole *Squad* pays the cost to be *Bosses.* Only broke "mother-fuckers" go to jail. The jealous haters peddling "nickel-bags" on the corners didn't understand this!

In *Q's* drug-slanging days, he bumped heads with these same fools, arguing over selling better product to their clientele. They alone provided the crack on the block and called themselves the *"Operation."* Q switched from selling crack to showcasing *"cracks of that Ass,"* just two years ago.

Now, their resentful looks are signifying their disgust for a *"Hustler"* that just won't quit. Even a mysterious fire couldn't stop him. They secretly fire-bombed his family's apartment building, which ended his drug-dealing days for good.

Guilty of drawing heat to his family's once thriving Dental business, he vowed to never sell another "cap." His parents' pending divorce killed the corporation, but the fire was the raggedy-nail in the coffin with the "*Royal Family*" of "*Paramount Dental*" barely getting out alive.

Aquil and *Mrs. B* rose from the ashes together, elbow-to-elbow, selling chicken dinners out the Bar-B-Que pit in front of a hidden, burnt-up, massive, 20-unit apartment structure, covered by $5 pictured art for sale. They made the money to start rebuilding the property with duct tape, and bubble gum. Now, it's thoroughly financed by sweaty back-sides, wearing G-strings, at the *Grindstone.*

Jazzy stepped out the vehicle, feeling the church lady's beliefs. She's labeled a *hoe,* just for walking though the Club's entrance of the ominous black and purple, 2-story building, with a sign that reads: *Grindstone Private Social Club.*

"Come and stay awhile Poppy please? I really have to talk to you," she's pleading her last hope to change his plans. *Q-Deezy's* not hearing any of it, reluctantly walking into the Club with *Country,* unlocking the new metal door; another idea of *Quintin's.* Everything is cleaned-up by a neighborhood crack-head named *Clint,* who's never stolen anything from the *Crew,* if he can *"keep"* what he *"sweep."* The hard-working crack-head had to clean up a complete mess from what the cops tore up looking for evidence.

"Did they find it?" asked the **Leader** of the **Grindstone** entrusted with a family artifact, secretly stashed in the building... *"My apologies sir, but the police have taken it"* winked the long-time family servant, addicted to cocaine, serving the *"Young Master's"* bidding for a $10 "rock."

"Would there be anything else sir?" asked *"Food Stamp Clint,"* in his *"Alfred"* accent, wishing *"Bruce Wayne"* pay his ass with a tip; offering his excellent services to the *"New Joker,"* building a sneaky surprise for the despicable *"Villains"* that come though unannounced.

Everybody in the **Crew** thought the missing new partner, **Quintin,** was busy under some skirt. In fact, he's been burning the midnight oil with constructing a metal death trap for anybody trying to bust-in, or escape; both functions rigged to a button. Everybody must get buzzed though two metal doors, surrounding them in a bullet-proof metal box, rigged with tear gas... the secret weapon against *"Gung ho"* niggas of *"Gotham."*

Big Moose and **Storm** are instructed to make the liquor/beer buys, a job that's usually handled by **Q.** They must take a trip to New Jersey and illegally buy the "re-up." Smuggling liquor over State-lines becomes an issue when you're buying over $1000 worth. The chinks in the Garden State liquor stores don't mind the Keystone-State tags in the parking lot ... *"if the cash is real."*

"The deal will always be real!" says the slanted-eyed brother from Asia, checking every American dollar.

Today is a day of delegating his normal tasks. *"Biggie Small's"* said it best... *"them cat's that hold guns can do jobs too."* Playing gangster isn't going to cut it today. New Jersey State Police plays no games. They're judges like locking up *"Rum-Runners"* with ancient post-prohibition laws. Even legitimate bars can't buy out-of-state. They can lose their liquor license, plus they're awarded heavy fines; for speakeasy smugglers like the *G-Stone Crew,* 5 years plus a 10-year probation.

   Quintin and *Big Gene's* assignment is Home Depot for more building materials for repairs they need to put the finishing touches on the death-trap. Colorful ideas like electric-shock and fall-away floors are being discussed, while they walked excitedly out the door with a better budget.

   Q laughed at the fact that after all the begging and attempts of sexual sabotage, *Jazzy* is crashed out on the couch upstairs in the VIP area. *Junior* retrieved a blanket to cover her with warmth. The snuggled gesture is complete with a smile spelling *"satisfied"* in any language.

   Junior always knew just what the *Ladies of the Night* needed. He had a knack for knowing what to say to them in times of crisis, and most importantly... he kept their secrets intact. He already had the weed rolled cigarettes packed with the *"lucky"* already *"flipped-up"* and, of course, some hella-fired *"nose-candy,"* treating the *"Bottom-Bitch"* like a resting *"Ghetto-Diva."*

   "June-bug" has heard it all when it comes to the *Ladies of the Night.* He talked a few of them out of suicide, walked them though unwanted "Beefs," and some out of quitting the "life" all together. He's considered the *"ear"* of the *Crew,* and meddles in dark magic on the side, trying to

make a buck on the gullible ones stupid enough to believe *"Jacques the Beneficent"* in his bag, giving out words of wisdom.

No need for a chauffeur, the *Boss* is now in possession of his own vehicle. It's a nice ride, but not too flashy. *"Players"* know you better not have these rats out here thinking you got some real cheddar, starting with his *1988 "Buick La Sabre,"* with a glossy, candy-red paint job. He turned on the *"Bose"* system with his *"Outcast's"* CD and allowed the streets to fill with some *"Southern Playeristic Cadillac Music,"* and headed to *Charmaine's* house with a big-ass smile on his face.

CHAPTER THREE

"Welcome to My Stable"

     Q-Deezy arrived at **Charmaine's** father's house located in **Southwest Philly** at 58th and Rodman Street. It's 12 in the afternoon. The block is deserted. The neighborhood kids are already in school, and most of the adults are working folks. **Charmaine's** father's house is next to *"Nick's"* barber shop, which is slightly busy during this time of day. The sun's shining brightly and today's temperature marked the 3rd day of a Heatwave. His anticipation to hold his horny girlfriend overwhelmed his senses. The smell of sweet nectar fills the air, thanks to their neighbor's rose bushes.

     He opens the unlocked front door. Breakfast aroma of mackerel and grits occupied his nose, and noise from a running shower, alerted him that **Charmaine's** in there, obviously getting ready for his arrival. The steam fogged the bathroom mirrors, cause by the heated water-flow, which intensified the feverish passion, already deep inside her, disbelieving she's *"sprung"* and longing for *"HIM"* to take her *"temperature"* with his *"dip-stick."* All the while, **Q** is quietly watching the un-expecting **Charmaine** take a shower.

     Charmaine's washing with fancy soaps with scents that rivaled the finest flowers, massaging her vagina just a taste before her *"Love Doctor"* arrives. Little did she know, he's already there, watching and quietly undressing to enter the heated shower with a ready-hard point to make.

She's startled and pleasantly surprised. *Q's* 10-inch manhood stood at attention, engorged with excitement. The best news of the day was that nobody's home except for the hot and bothered *Charmaine,* with no interruptions, not even her two-year-old daughter. She began washing him, wanting to wash-off *"any"* other women's juices from his stable.

Charmaine's young, but not naïve. He must have another woman, because of his current profession. She heard stories of his sexual escapades with his *"sexy stable"* from her buddy, *Junior*, who repeats the vicious rumors, which are denied by her new lover, battling the *"truth"* about his *"greedy-nature,"* fed by the visions of the naked vixens every single night.

All the guys in the *Grindstone Crew* had one. This was their way, *"not"* to pursue each other's concubines, baby-mamas, exes and current "*side-jawns*." Most of them followed the rules, but some didn't. With jealousy and baby feelings in their hearts, they start spreading vicious rumors like the *"word"* of a dirty kitchen to a nest of roaches, feeding off the crumbs of the main *"hand"* that feeds them.

Charmaine threw caution to the wind one night in the Club, weeks before, after spotting her baby-father, *Munchie,* driving down the street with a white bitch from work, in her Maxim; kindly pointed out by the friendly employer, convinced that her baby-father can get cheated on *"too."*

"They're all gonna be so jealous," became their laughable joke after the quickie, weeks ago. *"I'm your only 'Bottom Bitch' in your Stable...Daddy!"*

In the shower...

Charmaine kissed him with her big juicy lips, soft and supple and perfectly matching his. He begins to caress her secret spot on her neck, traveling his steaming red-hot tongue to taste her chocolate breasts. Shock waves run though her body, as he teases her soft, ripe nipples that's hard as a raisin, while her moaning gave a great indication that every move is the right move.

"Lucky Charm" is wet and ready, poking that beautiful chocolate ass out with no hesitation, thinking the *"quickie's"* exploding orgasm was a fluke. This wasn't a fluke, when he penetrated her tight wet *"fanny,"* causing a massive orgasm, once again, just like the last time, making her legs weak, loving his size... He's way bigger than her baby-father. The dark-chocolate vixen is loving the pain.

They proceeded to go downstairs to her basement bedroom. The bed's the perfect height to hit all the right spots, screaming from the ecstasy with every stroke, taking his time, savoring every inch, she's as deep as the ocean, watching her make cute "love" faces, digging for her "G-spot," allowing her time to catch her breath, before another wave of intense mind-blowing orgasms.

Nick's barber shop next door heard the screams and was tempted to call the cops until, she hollered

"I'm Cumming baby!!!" letting the eavesdroppers decide for themselves, that she knows her so-called attacker, figuring out quickly... she's alright. The mothers waiting on their sons' hair-cuts next door listened with envy as the naughty couple disturbed the quiet block with their ravished ways.

Outside the home, *Charmaine's* baby-father, *Munchie,* arrives to secretly see if she's having company since their break-up. He had every intention to scare off any *"new sucker,"* trying to date his *"girl."* Little did he know the *Boss* would be *"banging"* her back out! *Munchie* entered the backyard to glimpse into the basement window, hopefully, to watch a secret peep-show of an unsuspecting *Charmaine.*

He's eager to sneak-peek his naked ex after a bubble bath or settle for a strip-tease while she gets dress. The over-protective boy would often do this, even when they were together; she just never knew half the stuff he did.

The screams of passion didn't even deter the baby-father from looking. *Munchie's* heartbeat raced, and his eyes witnessed the unthinkable, as his baby-mama was having sex with another man. He's thinking, *"That's not her because she never wails like that"* with him; he only heard how *"it hurts!"* because fore-play was a foreign practice with him. On this day, she loved it ...screaming and begging for her *"Big 'Boss"* to penetrate her, *"again and again."*

Munchie watched *"HIM"* caress her whole body, swallowing her juices like a viking when he ate the *"coochie,"* another thing *Munchie's* reluctant to do. *"That Dick-Sucking Bitch!"* returned the favor and sucked her erotic juices off

"HIS" excited shaft. *Munchie* rarely experiences that favor, even on his birthday. Watching the *"Got-Damn Bitch"* climax again and again, *Munchie* secretly stood there in horror, noticing *Charmaine's Boss* is twice as big as him, taking both hands to hold his *"meat."* Feeling defeated, he started thinking that she'll never be the same again. Not knowing *Q's* real age, he's convinced that *"This 'Old-head' is turning my baby-mama out!"* while his heart-stopped from the horrifying sight.

A jealous rage is his normal reaction after some guy would try to talk to her, but this is way too much to take. The horror-stricken baby-father suffered a panic attack and passed out, right there by the basement window, while the new couple fell asleep, sexually satisfied.

After two hours, *Munchie* regained consciousness. He stumbled to his feet watching his beautiful voluptuous baby-mama lay in the bed with another man. *"That cheating Bitch!!"* he thought, hurt by his ex-girlfriend's unfaithful deeds, even though he cheated on his baby-mama on a regular basis during her pregnancy.

"Payback" is finally here, strangling the blood right out of his heart. *Munchie* thought his influence would never end. Even his own father threatens him, that he'll be the better boyfriend, if he doesn't stop the *"bull-shit."* His daddy warned him this day would come, that a *"Baller"* would snatch her pretty-ass up, willing to spend *"bank,"* and *"bounce"* his cute baby-girl on the knee.

There was a time, *Munchie's* young, impressable fiancé would *"never"* give herself to another man. Now, his greatest fears are being realized and it's the *"Old-head 'Pimp' from the Club"* enjoying all the chocolate *"CAKE"* he wants. She's no longer impressed with *Munchie's* wackness, who can't even blow-out a candle right!

"It's the 'Pimp's' fault…. That damn Q!" said the blaming *Munchie,* while he runs off and fetches his father's gun.

Later that night…

"Wake up baby it's 9pm," reported *Charmaine,* kissing *Q's* face to wake him up. The day seemed to melt away during their hibernation. It's only three hours till opening the Club. His *"Main Squeeze"* checked her voicemail messages. She quickly realized that *Munchie* watched all the events that took place in her bedroom. *Charmaine* felt violated. Even though she's been with him for more than three years, She never wanted to hurt his feelings in this way, but he asked for it… sneaking by her window like that.

Charmaine has never felt this way before. *"It just feels so good baby,"* said *Charmaine* surprisingly. She wasn't going to let the jealous ways of her baby-father deter her new-found pleasure of *Q* making her climax at will.

Q laughed at the revelation, knowing *Munchie's* digressions of the past. The new couple used to talk for hours about his cheating ways. They shared a laugh knowing he deserved every sultry sight. *"He actually said you're bigger than him,"* she said after reading the countless texts on her phone. *Munchie* explained via voicemail *"I now know how it feels to be cheated on and I'm sorry!"*

Charmaine was now being reminded that *"she's his life"* and *"one true love,"* but his pleas fell on deaf ears. She's excited by the drastic changes made in her life; making her own money and a great sexual connection with her employer, a surprising bonus. Just taking a chance on doing something else other than *Munchie,* felt so exhilarating*. "The Spell is Broken!"*

Once the fascination that *Munchie* alone wasn't her life because his meager revenue can't quench the *"Magic" Charmaine's* growing need to look absolutely flawless, and no longer would his small dick hypnotize her into thinking his sex was so good and realizing that getting wet and heated is a far cry to a full-blown orgasm, *Munchie's "Hex"* got lifted after two exciting moments with the *"Old-head 'Pimp' from the Club."*

The new, excited couple shared another shower. This time, with no hot, steamy love making. They're pressed for time, because her father is due to arrive from work shortly. *Charmaine,* at 19 years of age, wasn't allowed male company, especially *"ones"* fucking her in the shower.

The new *"power-couple"* quickly washed away their earlier deeds, a hard task to do, with flashbacks of him caressing every inch of her body, controlling his mind like crack. She'll be his newest addiction. While her alluring aroma still filled his nostrils, the sweet taste of nectar between her legs savored in his mouth, chasing the voluptuous sweet-sticky thing to the basement bedroom.

They stood in her bedroom naked, dripping wet, watching the clock, drying and grooming themselves. The feeling is electric, watching each other with a starving passion, wishing they had time to do it again. The bedroom dresser mirror reflected the obvious, the so-called *"Pimp and his Bitch,"*

and the *"Not"* so obvious…

Munchie, staring in the window, is back to confront his cheating baby-mama, but, found himself about to watch Part-two of *Charmaine* and *Q's* Live sex show. *Munchie* is ready! The look in his eyes looked like a rabid dog, strapped with his father, *Joey's* 32 caliber pistol. The crazed ex-boyfriend couched down, exposing his daddy's weapon, letting the startled lovers know he does mean business.

"Get ready don't beat ready!" thought *Q,* calculating *Munchie's* next move, who's smiling, knowing he's got the drop on the infamous "*Q-Deezy*," who was about to *"Fuck the shit out of his girl, again!"*

"Note to self, Never leave your gun in the car!" thought *Q,* wishing he could pop-off a few shots with his Ruger 9mm in his ass for this stalking *"bull-shit, busting-up Round Two of that sweet Ass."*

Munchie's still crying in a jealous rage with blood shot eyes. *Charmaine* started screaming at her unwanted visitor. *"Munchie what the fuck!"* she said, then dared him to shoot. *Munchie* pulled out the shiny "32 Caliber" from his waist. One minute he was pointing the gun at them, the next towards his own head. *"Why are you peeking in my window? You stalking-ass dude!"* she snapped.

Q's beginning to get tired of *Charmaine's* stoking the fire on this situation. *Munchie* began to kick and yank on the basement window's protective metal bars. *Munchie* became enraged, sparked by her hollering. *"Fuck you motherfucker! You cheated on me at least 10 times!"* shouted *Charmaine.*

"I love you!" confessed the *"Bi-polar"* ex-boy-friend. *Munchie's* tight-roping the thin-line between love and hate, feeling played like a sucker in front of the *"Old-head."*

Q and *Munchie* locked eyes. *"I'm gonna kill this 'Pimp' Mother fucker!!"* *Munchie* shouted. He pointed the gun at *Q. "Biggie Smalls'"* lyrics blared from the clock-radio, that was set to play *"Power 99"* for an alarm. *"I tote chrome for situations like this... I'm up in his broad...I know he don't like this."*

The song played, right on cue, like a movie musical score. The tension could be fileted with a knife. *Munchie's* bloodied hands revealed his conviction. *"I want my family back!"* shouted *Munchie,* in his crazed suicidal rage. He didn't notice *"The Family Robber"* retrieve the wrong underwear and pants, left there just weeks ago, by *"Him."*

"Don't move Mother Fucker!" yelled *Munchie.* His attention was back on the *"thief"* who stole his woman; threatening to kill the man fumbling with the sweatpants *"He"* left there just a week ago.

"He's not that big after all" joked *Munchie,* apparently the *"Boss'"* dick doesn't get engorged when a pistol is waved around.

The memories of the earlier events flashed in *Munchie's* head. He snapped mentally after seeing his baby-mama suck another man's schlong. It's the same mouth that kisses his daughter to sleep every night; the supple lips that once placed passion marks on his chest for everybody in High School to see. Reality was a cocktail of destruction, too heavy to bear. This made *Munchie* very unstable. He didn't like the strip-tease with another dude in the room. *Charmaine* stood defiant and began to get dress.

"Fuck you Munchie I gotta go to work!" *Charmaine* stated after looking at the alarm clock. *"I knew that 'Pimp' would change you Bitch!!!"* snapped *Munchie* as his rage turned towards his baby mama grew."

"Who you calling a Bitch! …. Little dick Mother fucker?" *Charmaine* snapped. *"You saw how a real man gets down! How's it feels?"* asked the revengeful baby-mama.

Charmaine was taught by her father, never allow any man to call her a *"Bitch."* Unfortunately, he didn't teach her *"not"* to argue with a jealous crazed ex-lover, holding a loaded gun, after smoking a blunt laced with *"Wet."* The drugs were kicking in for *Munchie,* choosing to cop a bag of PCP, instead of seeking medical attention for his panic attack. Heart-break can kill like a murderer…when another *"mother-lover"* is screwing your girl.

"CRASH!!" the sound caused by a grown ass man, crying snot bubbles, peering in…

The window's metal bars snapped from *Munchie's* crazed tantrum, snatching the reinforced iron off the basement window. *Charmaine* looked to *"Q-uick Draw"* gesturing *"You better grab your hot shit,"* referring to his latest personal protection, the "9mm Ruger."

He spoke with his eyes, confirming the worst. *"I'm not carrying 'Roscoe,'"* his pet name for the firearm stashed in the glove box in his car. Then suddenly, *Munchie* broke the glass and snatched the lace curtain down. The busted lovers ducked, thinking they're should be gunshots. N-E-X-T *"Munchie the Maniac"* was coming in, and there's nothing they can do but.... *"Roll on his ass!"*

Shotokhan-Ninjitsu training came in handy to disarm his ass. *Charmaine,* still butt-naked, smashed *Munchie* over the head with a metal lamp. *Q's* grappling techniques dislocated his wrist, and the *"Un-wanted Ex"* found himself cracked on the noggin and laid-out. The karate-man, *"Q-LEE,"* scrambled to the fallen gun, but it's empty!

"No Bullets?" said *Q-Deezy* feeling bamboozled. *"I Told you this nigga is a fucking fraud!"* ridiculed *Charmaine.*

The immediate threat was contained. *Munchie* was knocked out by the lamp. *Charmaine* searched his pockets. The robbery rationalized by his on-going debt with child support for the baby, and damages to her father's window, but *Munchie* only had $3 in his wrinkled jeans.

"Barely, enough for a bus pass!" said the calculating *Charmaine,* wondering why he even came over anyway with *"chump-change"* in his pocket, feeling thoroughly embarrassed about the *"Fallen Mucho-Loco,"* better known as *Munchie,* having another psycho episode, without a haircut.

"Ay Charmaine!!!!" yelled her father, *"Mr. Tracy Nathel James."*

Mr. Tracy James is a 5'5,'' dapper, suave 50-year-old correctional officer, and a single-parent of three. The man has two personalities, one is a loving father, the other is *"Sgt. James,"* that is not in the mood for any drama, especially after working double shifts at the *"Curran-Fromhold Correctional Facility;"* better known as *"CFCF Philadelphia County Prison."*

"Shady Tracy's" reputation labeled him as a *"hard-ass,"* with prisoners and subordinates alike. Fellow correctional officers feared his write-ups and reprimands. He could ruin a prison guard's career with a stroke of a pen, and is a stickler for policy and procedure, but the sergeant's stripes on his ego seems to dissipate when he comes home.

Sgt. Tracy N. James is still in his prison guard uniform arriving to his home though the rear entrance. He often does this just in case he's followed to his residence. In the past, ex-inmates have wanted to inflict harm upon him and his family, that's why *"Shady Tracy"* never uses the front door. He quickly notices *Munchie's* lifeless body, half-way hanging out the basement's window. *Sgt. Jones'* first reaction is, if the father of his beloved grand-daughter is dead as the doorbell.

"Damn… you kids are at it again!" said *Mr. James*, disgusted that the familiar assailant is tripping again. *Munchie* has snapped off in the past, but never *"WHEN"* the hard- working father is home. *Mr. James* despised him with a passion. *"Magic-Munchie"* is conveniently a vanishing attacker

of his baby-girl's abuses, but today is different. *Munchie's* still on the scene to answer for *"his"* erratic behavior.

Q is standing in the basement, half-dressed, with his heart still pounding a thousand beats per minute. *Mr. James* and *Q* locked eyes, recognizing they met once before when *Charmaine* invited her father to the *Grindstone.*

At that time, his greatest fear was that his extremely beautiful daughter was an erotic dancer. The reassured father was very relieved that she's only a bartender there; noticing the chemistry between *Charmaine* and *Q* before they even knew it. Clicking with the mild-manner Club owner is *"MUCH"* better than the *"knuckle-head"* that lays at his feet.

"Damn Charmaine what happen to Munchie's... Stupid Ass!?" questioned her father. *Q's* relieved that *Mr. James* knows of *Munchie's* psycho ways. *"Well is he dead?"* asked *Mr. James.* His words fell on deaf ears, shocked seeing *Munchie's* lifeless body is too much for *Charmaine* to explain. *"Pop"* checked *Munchie's* pulse.

A thousand thoughts ran through her father's mind. He didn't want to wonder how his youngest child would fair in prison, being the daughter of the infamous *"Shady Tracy."* This wouldn't be a bad thing for his enemies that's always lurking around every corner behind the prison's walls.

He finally confirmed signs of life. The relieved *"Turn-Key"* attempted to wake up *Munchie,* who is knocked out cold by one vicious blow, administered by his one true love. This betrayal will never be forgotten*... "Clowned in front* of another *"Man"* and you taking *"sides?"* …will never be forgiven.

"What's the gun for?" asked **Mr. James,** noticing the *"New-Guy"* holding a weapon.

"This gun's not mine…it's his!" attested the new boyfriend. *"What he try to do kill yall?"* **Sgt. Jones** asked grabbing the gun and the unconscious **Munchie** by the collar. **Charmaine's** father switched from a concerned father, to *"Curly from South Philly,"* a kidnapping murderous accessory that knows how to discard a body.

The ex-boyfriend's fate hung in the balance because of his jealous tantrum. **Sgt. Jones** knows half the young men in prison doing life-sentences for situations like this. He's no fool. *"Curl the Casanova"* quickly realized what this *"Beef"* was all about, uncovered by how scarcely dressed the new lovers are, the tore open condom wrappers and by the underwear scattered about… *"Yeah!"*

"Munchie saw something he didn't wanna see…huh?" he chuckled. **Charmaine** felt embarrassed. She didn't want her father to know about her mid-day activities. **Charmaine's** house was notorious for hooky parties with her high school friends. The teenaged-clique was called the *"Wrecking Crew,"* who included **Junior, Boo** and **Anwar** for the guys; **Renae, Rhonda** and **Big Sexy Rasheeda** for the girls.

Munchie, and the birth of her now 2-year-old baby changed all that. He's been controlling the teenager's life like her father, but **Charmaine's "Pop"** is a firm believer in *"It's not what you do…It's how you do it."* He would often preach this daily,

"The moral of this story is: Don't let every Tom, Dick and Harry run through your panties!"

He's a realist to the fact that his daughter is sexually active. The pregnancy two years earlier exposed that. He is no longer naïve to his daughter's exposure to the real world, knowing she'll be the focal point for men's desires, and more importantly, she can handle herself.

Munchie begins to wake up. He's in disbelief that the woman who used to comfort and love him, rendered him unconscious. This is the same young lady that used to fight every female rival trying to steal him. Those days were long gone. *Munchie's* thoughts were interrupted by *Sgt. Jones'* authoritative voice. *"What the fuck Munchie!"* he snapped. *"You're going to fix my shit!!!"*

He scrambled to his feet, grabbed his father's gun from *"Pop's"* hand, and scurried away like a thief in the night, not wanting to face the angry music. He's defeated once again, the first time when his own heart failed him and now, his baby-mama knocked him out. 0 for 2 versus the *"Conniving 'Pimp' from 52nd Street."*

"Punk-Ass bitch!!! I told you this Mother fucker was a fraud!" said the sarcastic *Charm,* with malice, exposing his ugly truths. *"Pop's,"* relieved that the situation is over, ordered the new couple to clean up *Munchie's* mess while he rolls himself a well-needed *"Joint-Ski."*

Q called his *Crew,* using *Charmaine's* phone. He wanted them to secure the perimeter of the home and bring *Junior* with his tools to fix the broken basement window. *Sgt.*

Jones is very impressed by how fast things got fixed. His home is now protected by two *Grindstone* disciples.

The first *Grindstone* Soldier is *Big Gene,* who lives the closest to *Charmaine's* house. He posted up at the rear entrance. The other *Grindstone* Soldier is *DK.* He's excited to oblige the *Boss* whenever he calls, knowing they'll be properly compensated for their efforts. He also reveled in the fact that his *"vow of loyalty"* would be recognized with every answered command, clicking his steel-toe boots as an added effect for his newest convictions. *"Yeah whatever!"* Shady Tracy chuckled.

"Pop's" ecstatic that his house is back in order. *Charmaine* is fully dressed in a sexy, dark-purple, tight- fitting Cat suit, showing off all her voluptuous curves, stopping traffic from the front-steps, hearing the car horns blowing *"beep-beep"* for the block's finest *"Star."*

"Damn Charmaine...You look like a Music-Video girl or something!" her father proudly stated, puffing on his *"Joint-Ski,"* trying to take a Polaroid picture like she's going off to the Prom.

"Thanks Dad!" she replied feeling validated in being a grown-ass woman handling her business, but she's hanging on the arm of a *Boss* ...Now... not a kid.

Meanwhile, down the alley behind the house, *Munchie* lays motionless in his dark hiding place, watching *Big Gene* stand post, feeling annoyed watching his former friend *Junior* helping the new *"Power couple"* repair the window. *Junior's* the one who introduced *Munchie* to *Charmaine.* `He's cringing at the fact that *Q-Deezy* possessed all his friends.

Even his own father filled out an application ...of *"riding this man's dick! Begging for jobs and what-not."*

Big Gene's a very effective deterrent from *Munchie's'* violent ways. He didn't return on this night, after watching the tall mean-looking Jamaican fella with the long leather trench coat, barely concealing two Mack 11's attached to his shoulder-gun-holster standing guard. This made the little ex-boyfriend have a seat behind the bushes.

The fugitive from Jamaica has found himself in this position before. It's not the first time he had to protect others with them same tools of destruction. In his hometown of Kingston, his hands are still stained emotionally with guilt, killing rivals over drug territory on the Island. Now, this mysterious killer works for *Q-Deezy*. Even *Q* doesn't know how treacherous his pass is!

The front of the house is thoroughly protected by *DK's* demeanor, which rivaled some of the notorious *Gangsters* portrayed in the movies. A short leather jacket didn't have to conceal a damn thing, his weapon of choice is already in his hand. His trusted stainless-steel ice-pick is the only weapon needed. *"Super D"* fantasized about poking *Charmaine's* longtime attacker, falling victim to her every whim too.

The *"Power couple"* emerged from the house, *"dressed to death,"* looking like a *"Gangster Boss 'Pimp' and his '1# Lady."* *Charmaine's* outfit glistened as the passing cars' headlights shined upon her garment; shining like a piece of candy, a tight ensemble showing off her plump *"camel-print"* with no fear of retribution. She's rolling with the *Boss,* a refreshing change from her crazed baby-father, who would never allow the *"hoochie-mama"* clothes.

Q's outfit is a matching purple 2-piece suit. It's the same color as *Charmaine's* skimpy outfit, feeling like the 1990's *"Go-Go"* version of the infamous *"Foxy and Jay-Z."* *Charmaine* sported a nice all-natural short hair style with cute pinned curls, and he sported a *"Godfather"* hat with purple *"Gator"* shoes.

The *"Power couple"* knew matching colors had a purpose. They coordinated *Charmaine's* new work outfits to the colors of her *Boss'* vast suit collection. He wanted to *"tag"* her with new outfits after their first sexual episode at the Club, so the weeks that followed their quickie, they were secretly dating and shopping; this lead to his thinking then, that she was a *"Gold-digger."*

The anxious *Boss* was getting tired of purchasing the finest of fabrics for a woman that didn't take their relationship seriously, but tonight is different. They no longer had to hide their newfound relationship from *Munchie's* family, who lives around the corner from the Club, or his gossiping neighbors telling his Mama everything they see. *Charmaine* embraced her newfound freedom. She didn't have to entertain *Munchie's* low-life friends, questioning their loyalty to him after enduring their lustful eyes. They even knew deep down, *Charmaine* deserved a better man. The newly enlightened lover couldn't wait to admit she belongs to another, by wearing his colors.

The *Boss* and his *First Lady* waited for *DK* to thoroughly inspect his car. *DK* was formally a personal bodyguard for Delegates and Dignitaries. Trained by the United States Army, his *"skills"* for finding bombs were deemed useful after all. The vehicle is free of sabotage and explosives.

"You've searched for explosives too?" he questioned *DK* after he exposed *Munchie's* secret about an empty gun.

"If he can't get six bullets...He ain't placing no bombs!" said the "*Boss*," feeling the same way his *First Lady* feels. *"That Nigga's a fraud!!!"* said the liberated baby-mama repeatedly throughout the night.

Q started the engine to the *Buick La Sabre*, purring like a frisky kitten. *Charmaine's* finishing her make-up in the beauty mirror, wearing perfume that is over-powering the car's air- freshener. The *Boss'* nostrils are being tantalized by *Charmaine's* body oils. Her make-up is flawless, not needing much foundation, just eye-liner to emphasize her *"bright"* beautiful eyes, while possessing flawless natural skin. The enhancements seemed unfair for anyone trying to match her beauty.

Even her own cousins tried to bump her off her throne, back in the day when she rocked long natural hair that flowed down her back; no weave needed for the *"Foxiest Girl"* in High School. Just like the song on the radio plays *Black Rob's* rap song *"Whoa,"* the lyrics describes her well as they rode off to pick-up her friend *Renae.*

"Renae S. Franklin" is one of *Charmaine's* closest friends. They went to school together since the pre-school's sandbox. She's a 4ft.11in., dark-skinned, sexy 20-year-old; an

unexperienced dancer looking for someplace to *"shake her ass"* and make some money. She's funny-looking, but sexy at the same time, possessing a perfect pair of D-cup breasts, with a petite build.

The *Boss* knew she'd be a welcome addition to the Club, seductive and mysterious with a shy persona, another victim to *Charmaine's* whims. She had a crush on her since puberty and down with whatever *"Charmazinn"* has in mind, fantasizing of a sexual encounter with her, along with *Charmaine's* new beau, who seems to encourage that kind of behavior more than *Munchie* ever would.

The *"Gangsta Pimp"* would be a useful partner in crime in terms of making *Charmaine* act out *Renae's* most secret fantasy. *Ranea* surprised the *Grindstone's* new power couple with two more potential dancers, *Tracie* and *Mamasita.*

"Tracie L. Smith" is a 5ft.7in., big-breasted, brown-skinned cutie with a *"Rump-shaker's"* juicy, enormous ass that jingles every time she walks. She loves attention from men, explaining to the couple that working as an exotic dancer is better than waiting for one of her male *"Sponsors"* to give her some money.

The *"Around the Way"* girl nicknamed *"Tee-Tee,"* is a mother of 2 kids, desperately needing to feed and clothe her children. Her baby-father is locked up for armed-robbery. She needs this break, feeling blessed to have the *Boss* and *Charmaine* coaching her the rules of the *"Game."* The thick-ass neighborhood freak knows *Charmaine* from school. She's an honorary member of the *"Wrecking Crew"* because *Ranea* likes her crazy-ass.

"Veronica 'Mamasita' Luiz" is a 5ft.3in., skinny Puerto Rican, formally-*"Pimped"* street-walker. She's 100lbs. soaking wet, fortunately a cutie in the face, but she couldn't fill an A-cup bra with her boney ass, desperately in need of some good-old rice & beans.

The young *Mamasita* is built like an under-aged girl, 18 years of age and legally old enough to act out any *"Schoolgirl"* fantasy, dressed in her former cheerleading outfit. She didn't need thongs back in *Edison High,* but tonight, she's asked to *"add"* them to her uniform permanently.

Ranea found the cute Spanish renegade running away from the *"Pimped"* life. She scooped her up at the laundromat hallway, *"tricking"* with the *"Old-heads,"* washing their clothes, now willing to try the *"Go-Go"* life like a free-agent switching teams. *Ranea* was told to keep an eye out for new talent. *"Like birds of a feather, hoes do flock together,"* wondering if she's gonna be all the way *"down."*

Ranea and her friends filled the backseat of his Buick. It's 11:45pm., 15 minutes before the Club opens. *Q-Deezy* looked at his watch, pleased they're on time. He adjusted his rear-view mirror evaluating his current situation, taking it all in, "three scoops" of different flavors hitching a ride to this thing called *"Go-Go".*

"What did I do to deserve all this sexiness at one time?" asked *Q,* flirting with *Ranea* with his eyes in the rear-view mirror, astonished of what a little make-up and spritz can do. They all chuckled at his jokes. While the heated

leather seats warmed up all that *"Pussy"* by the pound, the funny *"Gangsta"* headed for the Club.

It's a cool Saturday night, the car radio pumped the clearest sound, though its Bose speakers, *H-town's* R&B hit song *"Knocking Boots,"* while the ladies enjoyed a fat blunt rolled by *Charmaine.* The enthusiastic girls were feeling eager and frisky.

The nervous *"new-comers"* decided to pop *"E-Pills."* The exotic weed mixed nicely with their Ecstasy high. *Charmaine* wasn't down with any pills. She drinks *"brown"* liquor and smokes *"green"* weed, and every now and again she'll snort a line of coke. She describes her cocaine recreational habit, as the *"White Bitch on the side."* Simply put, *Charmaine* has these girls eating out the *"palm of her hands."* She's controlling their minds with her finesse; the girls are feeling excited that one of their own is putting them all the way down.

They arrived at the *Grindstone,* pulling up to the front door entrance. The *Boss* jumped out the driver's seat and entered the Club. *Big Moose* replaced him as the driver. The colossal man was instructed to park the car and escort the ladies in.

The ladies in the backseat looked apprehensive being in the car with such a massive man. *Charmaine* quickly hugged her *"Teddy Bear."* As soon as he parked the *Boss'* car, *Moose* gave them a moment, allowing them their privacy, and posted outside the vehicle.

Charmaine turned down the radio and began to reveal her true intentions. The *Boss Lady* carefully explained that her *"hook-up"* wasn't free. She demanded 50% of their tips, after expenses, which included admission, transportation, make-overs and even the blunt they were smoking on...cost money.

Ranea quickly had to persuade *Tracie* into going with the flow, needing money for her kids. She's known to be snappy, especially when the *"ghetto-bird"* feels taken advantage of. *Ranea* needed this *"thing"* to go smoothly for her sake, wanting her opportunity to seduce *Charmaine,* enjoying their private dance practices teaching *Ranea* how to *"lap dance." Charmaine* aroused *Ranea* when she touched her, demonstrating the groping hands of *Grindstone's* patrons. The close encounters sparked some old sexual desires when she fondled her silver-dollar sized nipples. *Ranea* would never forgive *Tracie* if she messed this up.

Mamasita, on the other hand, is fine with the money breakdown. She usually would have to give *"all"* her money to *Serrano,* her former *"Pimp."* The Puerto-Potty has been through hell and back with him, walking the cold *"tracks"* looking for a *"trick"* for 40 bucks, then getting her ass beat if she didn't make $500 a day; he wanted her to sprint on the *"Track"* with *"quicksand"* prices.

"If I have kept half the money from all those dicks I sucked!" confessed *Mamasita,* fantasizing about every *"trick"* she's slept with, every dark alley with the aroma of piss, twitching and switching on the *"Track,"* needing more *"Goya Beans"* to get her ass fatter.

Charmaine's demeanor changed when she looked at *Tracie. "You Bitches don't understand how much* money you could make?" snapped the **Boss Lady.** She knew these scrambling *"chicken-heads"* have never made a thousand dollars in one night. *"How long you wanna be broke Bitches?"* cracked **Charmaine** with the truth ringing in their ears… asking the girls one last time,

"Who's down and Who's not?"

Tracie frowned her face. She didn't like *"Pimps,"* especially a female one duping her on the whole thing as a *"hook-up."* She knows *"Charmaine Rosa James"* from school too, sitting behind her in Biology class for years, confused on how her former classmate flipped to a new person overnight.

"This is some Bull-Shit Charmaine!" shouted **Tracie.** The high-school friends been so-called tight, since the 9th grade. They shared their deepest secrets from confessions of each other's loss of virginity, to sharing tampons in the gym's locker-room.

"Now, you wanna "Pimp" us?" said **Traci,** astonished she didn't just hook them up.

Charmaine and **Tracie** began to argue. **Ranea** tried to calm the heated debate down. **Tracie** always thought **Charmaine's** full of herself anyway and she wasn't about to get *"Pimped"* by the *"voted the most stuck-up chick"* in the school-yard.

"You foul girl!" said the insulted **Tracie,** trying slam the car door. **Moose** caught it in mid-swing, while grabbing the heated rump-shaker to calm her down and escorted her off the block like this week's trash.

"Voted the most ratchet Bitch" tossed off the block!

Ranea and *Mamasita* remained in the car, faithful to their new *"Queen,"* listening to every word. While watching *"Tracie"* get swept away by the executive protection against all comers, openly hanging outside in clear sight,

Mamasita gets spotted by a familiar face.

Serrano, the Colombian *"Pimp"* notices his *"Skinny-Bitch"* in the back seat of the Buick. His "Mercedes-Benz" out-shined everything on the block. The purring European engine eased beside the vehicle. The front tinted-window rolled down revealing a very upset individual. *Serrano's* been looking for his missing *"Chiquita-Banana"* for 2 weeks now.

If *Mamasita* had been in another's *"Pimp's"* car, she might've got shot. He smiles at the voluptuous *First Lady* talking tough in the front-seat. He recognized the *"kitted-up"* ride. It's *Q's* classic whip. Pleased the *"Go-Go"* man got his property, this small misunderstanding can get fixed *"real"* quick.

All *Serrano* must do is claim his *hoe* and be on his way. That's the Code.

Moose returned to the *Boss-man's* vehicle. *"Move along!"* said the massive body-guard for the *First-Lady.* *Serrano* burnt donuts in the asphalt with his rubber tires, making a dramatic scene on the block as he parked.

Mamasita started shaking like a runaway *"wet back,"* fearing for her life. She can't go back! *"sucking pee-pee's all day"* without a penny in her pockets. Funny thing is, *Mamasita's* not offended to please every man… she can find.

The *"Spanish-Nympho"* loves that shit! but hates when she can't put food in her own mouth.

Even her molesting step-daddy knew to spoil her, giving the young *"Veronica"* whatever she wanted, until *Mamasita's* mother shot him dead for teaching her baby how to give oral sex. She learned how to survive in the streets from her Mami, on the run for her Papi's murder; dwelling in the shadows of the *EL Train* ...Yeah, she came up rough, left abandoned to walk the *"Tracks"* ...alone.

After, her Mami's felony arrest, Social Services dropped the ball on *Ms. Luiz's* teenaged daughter. *Mamasita* was continually being raped by the male counselors and the teenage boys, so she ran away from the rooms. Tiring of their broke pockets too, *Serrano* pulled up to her one day in his shiny Benz, and rescued the young *Mamasita* from the molesting blow jobs for cigarettes. She got duped by a slick *"Pimp"* acting like a boyfriend with deep pockets.

The handsome Colombian half-breed bought her every sexy outfit she wanted. Dining at fancy restaurants, arm and arm, with real napkins in their laps, *Serrano's* trying to fatten-up his prey. However, turning into an Indian-giver overnight, *Mamasita* had to payback all the money for the lavish gifts. Feeling obligated to pay the sadistic *"Pimp,"* she found herself performing oral sex all night on him and his Amigos; 12 hours straight of dripping semen all over her face, *"Bukkake"* was payback for the juicy steak at *"Ruth Chris"* and 2 outfits from *"Exotic Zone"* on *"South Street."* ..."Damn!"

Mamasita immediately felt duped because these horny fucks wanted it every night. Worsening the deal, the fantastic, juicy steaks were out the window, replaced by 3 wings and some fries without a drink. The fancy outfits were stained by the Spanish, freaky-mechanics with dirty hands; so, not seeing a dime of the money, she left.

The short response got the reaction... she was hoping for.

"Queen Charmazinn" called **Storm,** who was posted on the front-door, banning **Serrano** entry to the Club. With a phone-call, the whining *"Pimp"* got checked at the curb, watching his freed sex-slave go dance to freedom. No need for a conversation about who's *hoe* this is... walking with a **Big Moose** escort.

The girls felt proud of their *"Queen"* with the armed entourage. **Serrano** glared at the Spanish *hoe* but didn't say a word. He wanted to snatch her up by the collar and order her back to the *"Tracks"* like the good hooker she *"is."* His lost property wasn't having none of *"THAT!"* She's down with the **G-Stone** now and proud of it ... buzzed through the Club's 1st door, right past her former *"Pimp."*

The **Boss Lady** had her answer. *"One more thing ladies"* announced Charmaine as she smirked.

"Welcome to My Stable!"

"BUZZZzzz...." Though the 2nd door.... (speakers playing) *D*

"Don't dis shit make you wanna... Jump! "Busta Rhymes" fills their ears

CHAPTER FOUR

"No Doe…No show"

The ***Grindstone*** is packed early on this warm, Saturday night. Security concerns are at an all-time high. ***"Whose idea was this to open the Club a day after the raid?"*** asked **Storm** wondering if it was ***Quintin's*** or ***Q-Deezy's*** decision, always questioning the new partner's choices. The newly acquired business ***"partner"*** is the fast-talking, charismatic **Quintin,** who seems to talk **Q-Deezy** into risky situations. **Storm** disagreed with the ***"new"*** 7 days a week schedule the most.

The decision has already proven to strain relations between the ***Grindstone*** and ***Bible Way Church.*** The new schedule was believed, by **Storm** and other **Crew** members, to be too excessive. They thought a day off would give everybody a well-deserved break, their other concern was the neighbors complaining about all three Clubs' booming systems.

Quintin quieted their concerns with promises of elaborate sound-proofing to muffle the booming bass sound, in theory, but was unable to appear because of other expenses. Renovations and revenues, needed to service a more upscale clientele, swallowed the budget for sound-proofing… for now. Like a politician, he could spin his words beautifully, promising block captains, community leaders and the Church nothing but ***"Hard Dick and Bubble Gum."***

"Mr. Grown n' Sexy" was brought in by *Q-Deezy* to upgrade the Club, providing a loyal clientele he'd cultivated over the years, hosting up-scale urban events. The *"Go-Go"* business was new to "Quinton." His expertise was devoted to putting more butts in the seats, while *Q-Deezy* oversaw the entertaining erotic show.

Quintin capitalized on the fact that they're friends beyond the Club. They first met as landlord and tenant. *Q's* family owned half the block, including the *Grindstone. Quintin's* ten years older, but respected his younger business associate's vision, seeing the potential in a speak-easy on the *Strip.*

"Storm's" posted at the front door; his main task is collecting the $40 cover charge from the whining, reluctant patrons paying the price hike, which is *Quintin's* idea.

"Do you wanna eat Shrimp or Lobster?" verbalized the promoter of the *"In-Crowd."*

"This will separate the men from the boys" preached *Quintin* as he tried convincing his new *Crew.*

Moose returned to the collection booth, after escorting the girls inside. This was another new addition to the Club, designed to keep all monies out of the security guard's pockets. There would be only one person collecting the cover charges and dancing fees. The cash would be secured in a locked booth, secretly stopping front doormen's side hustles.

"I gotta pay again?" whined the *Butter-face* with the fat ass, lying about *"tricking"* in somebody's Jeep.

The dancing fees are now $25 due upfront by non-**Squad** members. Dance fees were due again upon re-entry to the Club, implemented to deter dancers from taking their **dates** to their cars. **"Dates"** was the term used to describe a **"cash for sex" interlude.**

Tonight's disc jockey is **Big Country.** He'll be performing two tasks this evening, **MC** and **DJ.** Dancers are encouraged to tip the **"Teddy Bear,"** usually, $5 a song, and the more seasoned dancers would tip him $10 per set; a **"set"** being at least three consecutive songs.

Requests were only offered to tipping performers. Non-tipping ones got two choices, a fast or slow record. Dancers had to sign the **stage list,** keeping the stage rotation intact. Some of the ladies loved the stage. Others could go a lifetime without the spot-light. The rules were clear: **"All dancers must perform on stage when their names are called."** The rule made sure someone is always on stage.

The vibe was right inside the **Grindstone,** the beers were ice cold, and the women, red hot. The **Ladies of the Night** were freakier than usual, rhythms and beats seemed to affect them differently. The first floor doesn't usually fill up with patrons this early.

The raid inspired an influx of people who would miss the Grindstone if it closed for good. The growing clientele was delighted to find the Club still open for business, despite the pigs. **Philadelphia** started this **"Pimp Shit"** in the **"New World"** back in **1860. The City of Brotherly Love** has always been known for its **"Black Butter."**

The word of yesterday's raid spread though the City like the news of a passing loved one. Everyone that ever wanted to visit the *Grindstone* are present. Tonight, regulars didn't even bitch when quoted the new cover charge; glad to see their after-hour spot still open. *"Where else are you gonna find Good Homemade BBQ burgers… 3am in the morning?"* said *Mrs. B.,* putting a work of art in everybody's platter. After, one bite most folks let Mama keep the change.

The dancers started to turn in all their $1 bills for bigger bills at the bar, a calculated effort to keep tipping customers with an ample supply of change, politely asked by *Big Twin* and *Junior*; while stubborn amateur dancers liked $1 bills littered all over their body, instead of a $20 bill hidden away in a money bag.

Big Country provided the soundtrack for tonight's events, playing sultry love-making slow jams, providing the right tempo for sensual lap dances. *Country* described a *"Bump N Grind"* as a *"lap dance."* The cost, $5 per song, the *Ladies of the Night* were being summoned in every direction to render another dance. Tonight's patronage was almost to its capacity. This was a rare occurrence; they don't usually get this packed until 2am., after the regular bars closed.

They're *"Prime-Time"* … The *Grindstone* is *"Everybody's After-Party."*

Charmaine was swamped at the bar. Don't even think about getting a drink for free, she needs that *"Doe,"* pouring drinks right, and don't forget the tip jar while *"YOU"* stare at her ass. She gestured to her *"Boss-Lover"* that she needs his assistance; she loves feeling his *"rock-hard pole"* rubbing against her big booty, wrapped in a purple, velour cat-suit, behind the cramped bar.

Junior and *Big Twin* begin taking orders from the tables to relieve the bar, selling cigarettes, cigars and various treats, dressed up like the gentlemen of the 1920's, complete with derby hats.

"You don't know if you wanna be a spiritual advisor, or a drug-dealer," joked *DK* passing by *Junior* aka *"Jacques from the Hood"* hustling Tarot readings on the sly, plus the $20-bags of the *"Baddest White Bitch"* you'll ever snort up your nose.

Charmaine's outfit drew all the clientele to her, not making the connection of wearing the *Boss'* colors. Just wanting a glimpse of her sexy curves, her tip jar was spilling over. She's paid to bend over and grab another *"Heineken"* deep in the freezer, earning currency that outshines *"peep-show"* performers.

She didn't even have to give guys back their change. Every time she'd turned around to the cash register, they just kept telling her *"thank-you"* and *"keep the change"*... payment for wearing that outfit.

The *"Star-Maid"* needs a security-escort to the restroom; especially on packed nights like this one. Normally, her employer delegates her escort for bathroom breaks to security personnel, but tonight, this will be handled personally by her *"Boss-Lover."* The hardest task in the Club is escorting *Charmaine* though a crowd of thirsty-ass men. Her tight outfit is a target for probing hands. She hated to be touched on the butt, loving when her *"Karate-man"* protects her body, applying wrist locks and Jiujutsu secret strikes to deter those, who's trying to violate her body... another attribute that turns her on!

"On a slower night, they might've knock boots on the bathroom sink." Describing their secret passionate embraces in the same bathroom for weeks.

Outside of the bathroom located on the second floor, **Charmaine** had to urinate like a race horse, thanking her *"hero"* with a kiss; agreeing with his naughty thoughts... promising *"Later"* the sparks will fly, keeping his balls empty...her apparent strategy to keep his *"dip-stick"* only in her *"engine."*

Jazzy interrupted their moment with a jealous look, passing by the sexy, color-coordinated couple in the hallway, right between their embrace. The rude intrusion wasn't appreciated by the feisty **Charmaine,** controlling her nasty remarks to go relieve her filled bladder.

"Don't fuck up the mood of this party," said **Q,** reminding her to *"get"* the money and *"forget"* the drama.

Jazzy obediently strolled downstairs, knowing the code best. *"Country"* began calling her name to dance on stage. He started playing the record **Jazzy** requested, **Monica's** R&B hit song *"Angel of mine."* The lyrics spoke for her, while she suffered through a broken heart, feeling replaced by the barmaid with the *"big booty."*

"He's never let me wear his colors," reflected **Jazzy,** wishing for love with a defeated gaze directed at her beloved *"Poppy."*

Big Country's baffled at *Jazzy's* choice. She never picks love songs for a set. Rap or Reggae was her usual selections to gyrate on stage, but revealing her true feelings through song, only the *Boss* understood the secret dedicated performance. The patrons had no idea of its significance. The audience didn't know *"Who's her Angel?"* The *Boss* watched her sensual dance and vowed to stop playing with her emotions. Mouthing the words *"You're Tripping,"* shaking his damn head.

Charmaine, inside the bathroom, washed her hands and gazed into the bathroom's mirror, evaluating her reflection. Only she sees her imaginary *"flaws."* They were more mental than physical, wondering if she *"CAN"* trust an owner of a *"Go-Go"* Club?

"Why was Jazzy hating?" *Charmaine* asked her reflection when her woman's intuition started kicking in.

"Does that Bitch got something to tell me?" she asked herself. These suspicions seemed to trigger old familiar feelings. She's been through this before; no longer will she play the fool. *Munchie's* cheating was typical workplace love-triangle shit, but this, on the other hand, was the *"deep-end"* of the pool. *"Ms. Spring Water"* was with a *Boss* now, *(his loving nick-name for Charmaine.)*

The scorned teenager used to criticize *Munchie* for the women he chose to cheat with. These carefree and naked vixens would prove to be her greatest challenge in keeping a relationship intact. They didn't catch feelings and let themselves be known by the girlfriend. These sneaky bitches are too slick for *"THAT,"* Weeks later, she'd Jack bitches by the collar *"TRUST!"*

"None of these bitches gon' fuck my 'Man!" she says, fixing her cleavage in the tight outfit in the magical mirror on the wall, talking *"LOUD"* to her woman's intuition, with common fucking sense.

Charmaine exited the bathroom to a line of waiting girls wanting to use the restroom, sucking their teeth, gesturing that the *"Bad Mama Jama"* took too long to just pee. In their minds, she was up in there snorting coke, because the smell of marijuana wasn't in the air, gesturing back at *"Go-Go"* girls that the delay was her *"tight- ass"* outfit's fault, confidently switching a *"Gibraltar-of-Ass"* down the hallway.

On the second floor, down the hall from the restroom, is the VIP area. It's equipped with a better décor and a bigger stage with a 10ft brass pole, soft-leather couches for $20-dollar lap-dances, and a 100-gallon fish tank with six *Piranhas* in it called the *"Deep-Six,"* fighting fish for dollars against snakeheads and oscars.

The VIP area cost an additional charge for access, another idea of *Quintin's*. This special area came with bottle service, an occasional crap game and a 100-disc CD changer playing different music than the first floor, with totally naked girls grinding on the *Real-Ballers* of the Club under intelligent laser lighting.

Charmaine noticed *Ranea* lap dancing with The *Philly* Hip-hop artist *Cool C.* who has the hit song, *"The Glamourous Life."* *"Renae's"* in awe that she met one of her favorite rappers ...Dancer turned Groupie in seconds.

"This is my Girlfriend, the Boss Lady!" proudly announced *"Cherry,"* grinding on his excited *"Mic-stand."* The star-struck dancer was really enjoying herself; easiest money she's ever made. The clueless rookie kept her countless tips on the floor, right in front of her. *Ranea* gestured to *Charmaine* to pick up the large pile of cash. The *Boss Lady* obliged without hesitation, knowing that 50% of it belongs to her. The money was covered in red paint. *Ranea* was unaware the huge pile of cash was stolen money from a bank robbery tagged by paint bombs.

The groupie-rookie hasn't danced long enough to *"Check your money,"* the first thing often taught by seasoned vets. Too many times, gullible amateurs have gotten deceived by fake money or the wrong denominations. *Renae's* star-struck attitude made her more trusting than usual, allowing the star to *"finger"* her pussy for *"Marked-Money."*

Charmaine didn't want to tell the groupie her discovery, remembering the rule to never *"snap"* on a customer until you talk to **Q.** She whispered in her friend's ear to *"Take a break." Ranea* could not believe **Boss** Lady would *"bust her groove"* like that. First, she thought *"Charmazinn"* wanted him for herself. It wouldn't be the first-time *Charmaine* stepped in on a scene, taking her man's attention away, accompanied by the fact that he wouldn't mind the switch.

"Damn Baby it's enough of me to go around!" Cool C. confirmed, flashing himself to the ladies.

"No baby, she's just gonna go freshen-up a bit," explained *Charmaine,* deflecting the real reason. *Ranea* wanted to grab his exposed shaft and show this hip-hop rapper a thing or two, but she was dragged away from her future *"Baby-Daddy."*

The *Boss Lady* escorted the reluctant *Renae's* rookie-ass to the dressing room. *Ranea* is trying to understand, after weeks of preparation of how to seduce a *"Baller,"* why would she snatch her off a *"bona-fide shot-caller?"* *"Charmaine'"* quickly closed the dressing room door. *DK* is posted in the VIP area, noticing *Charmaine* snatch the naïve *Ranea* off the Celebrity and then scurry into the dressing room.

DK immediately asked the *Boss Lady* were they alright, entering the dressing room ready to switch to *"Super D"* in a heartbeat, *"Just say the word!"* he explained, letting her know this situation can get handled *"Right Here. Right Now."*

"Could you go get Q please?" asked the shaken *Charmaine.* Her mouth is responding that everything's cool, but her body language is telling a very different story.

DK nodded his head and went downstairs. *Charmaine* revealed her findings, that their large sum of money is covered with red paint. *"So, what?"* said the confused rookie. *Ranea* didn't know she's dancing for *"Blood Money."*

Q and *Big Twin* are at the bar pumping out drinks. They're swamped when *"Super D"* came downstairs to relayed *Charm's* message to come to the dressing room. *"I can't, do you see this line?"* snapped *Q,* popping another $7 *"Heineken"* for an impatient customer.

"Stars and their Egos" said *DK. "dead eye"* serious. The *Boss* asks *"Who tripping?"*

"Can't keep Cool C." is beginning to grow impatient. It was during *"their"* lap dance, *Renae* was saying everything he wanted to hear. First, it was, she was an avid fan of his music, handsome looks and the *"Dookie"* fat gold chain he's sporting. The second thing, she wouldn't mind if they fucked all night in a hotel room and wake up to breakfast, and the third is, *Renae's* not charging a dime for an all-nighter without condoms. He loves groupies wanting a *"meal-ticket"* baby.

He had no intentions in taking her to the *"Hilton"* or *"Hyatt."* He isn't trying to prove *"What Ballers do."* The famous recording-artist is thinking *"We're going to fuck in my Jeep"* like *"L.L. Cool J.,"* and eat some *"Taco Bell,"* and that's only if she's lives up to the *"hype."*

Cool C. knocked on the dressing room's door. This isn't allowed by its sign.

"No male patrons can touch, stand near or enter the dressing room."

"Renae!!!" he shouted, not knowing her dance name is *"Cherry." Charmaine* immediately knows *Renae's* been getting too familiar with the B-list rapper, questioning *"How does he know your Gov't?"* She knows *Renae's* a *"sucker"* for entertainers, growing up with every rapper's" poster on her wall like a hit-list of who she'd like to fuck.

"Queen Charmazinn" went into instant *"Pimp Mode."* *"You ain't fucking anybody you meet outta here for free!"* she roared, revealing the *"so-called"* hook-up came with unforeseen consequences. *Ranea* would be on a short leash. No longer, would she be in control of her own *"Punany," Renae's* boyfriend's nickname for her sweet vagina, that's always extremely tight and deep.

Cool C. would've been pleasantly pleased, she has complete control over her *"walls." Ranea* prides herself that she can adjust to any size *"Baloney-Pony"* to *"Gigantic Bratwurst,"* making any man proud of his sexual prowess, but *"can she give up random sex with cute guys?"* Ultimately, that's the question.

Ranea could easily renounce all men for one passionate night with her only lesbian infatuation, agreeing to the *Boss Lady's* rules, focused back on her *"Game"*, she repeated after *"Queen Charmazinn."*

"No Doe No Show!"

Charmaine felt empowered she could persuade *Ranea* to discontinue her *"one-night stands,"* hoping she knows, *"Pussy is like gold and the price for it fluctuates,"* depending on how you carry yourself. *Ranea* agreed to stop giving it away for other reasons.

"Did you know 'Cherry' is so good with chocolate?" asked *Renae.* The dancer named *"Cherry,"* grabbed Charm's exquisite ass and kissed her childhood crush in the mouth.

"Cherry's" her alter-ego tonight. Her hands ravished *Charmaine* like the *"wishful"* hounds' downstairs, squeezing her *"Sweet Ass."* Being friends for years wasn't the reason *Charm*" didn't want this new-found attention, *Ranea* has a questionable reputation of fucking anybody on a whim. Granted, It was the same character- flaw that qualified her entrance, to her *Stable.*

Charmaine had an idea *Ranea* may have wanted her through the years. She made her feel eerie a time or two. From friendly seductive stares her way… to generous favors, her suspicions were repeatedly dismissed; she's always running after the next guy. *"Renae likes dick! Not chicks!"* is her defending *"chant"* since *Sayre High School.*

"Bitch did you hear anything I just said?" asked *Charm,* looking astonished, wiping her lips like they were touched by a kid with a cold. *Charmaine* didn't have time to mentally process what just occurred.

"Yo Renae!" the towering rap artist shouted through the cracks of the door jam. The dressing room door was barely on its hinges from all the girl fights.

"Are you coming bitch? We about to leave!" said the *"Hennessey"* drinking *Cool C.*

His rowdy entourage wanted a change of scenery, so the up-town *"Go-Go"* after-hour named *"Nite on Broadway,"* was the next stop for the drunken whirlwind, going off at the dressing room door, banging like a spoiled privileged brat.

"HOOH…HOO!" the secret call to arms for the *"Hill-top Hustlers."*

DK became annoyed with the drunken rap star. *"No male patrons can touch, stand near or enter the dressing room!"* The sign wasn't an effective deterrent for the rapper. His intoxication was caused by the Club's efficient bottle service.

The *"Lansdowne Hustler's"* temper flared again by the 5ft.3in. security *"Super hero." Chris* stood 6ft.5in., looking down on this short-stacked man with the bleached-blonde hair. He didn't know *DK's* brass-knuckles have *"KO'd"* better; nick-named *"Super D,"* he has been in this position before.

"Stars and their Egos" he whispered, reminiscing about an insider motto of his body-guarding days.

The egotistical B-list rap-artist didn't know who this security *"Action figure,"* but his entourage knew exactly who he was, hearing legendary stories, told to them by industry folks and fellow bodyguards. They were told a long-time ago, *"Don't judge this Book by its Cover!"*

"Super D's" steel-toe cowboy boots have squashed many battles. The *"Short Bodyguard "Phenom"* is a deceiving *"Catastrophe,"* waiting to happen. *"Not so Cool C."* ordered him to go in the dressing room and *"bring Ranea out!" DK* tried to help the horny rap-star. As soon as he opened the dressing room door, he stormed in and grabbed his groupie like a *"microphone."*

"We out! You coming little Bitch?" teasing the 4ft.11in. groupie-dancer in heels.

"Little Bitch?" *"Cherry's"* deal-breaker, without *Charmaine's* influence. Words like little, shorty or tiny dries the *"Punany"* right up! She didn't mind the word *"Bitch"* all day. That she can be, depending on which *"Bitch"* you wanna see. *Ranea* declined any cashless advances made by the Entertainer.

"No Doe No Show fool!" said the enlightened dancer. *"Cherry"* was back on her hustle, autographs and pictures don't pay bills here.

The *"Hill Top"* native is feeling duped, *"Mr. Glamorous Life"* shouted *"Fuck You Bitch!"* remembering the glory days when groupies flocked his dressing room. Now-a-days, it's arguments with little bitches.

"Alright now! You got to go!" said DK, already knowing what he's going to do to his unruly patron. **"Motherfucker you haven't had a record deal since the 80's."** "Super D" had a knack for "pissing off" people that thought too highly of themselves. His facial expression frowned at the jab to his "rep." "Super D's" wondering "What warranted this "Prima Donna" attitude anyway?" It's time to upper-cut his ego.

"You're a fucking has-been," teased DK, positioning himself to "Hip Toss" the ignorant star patron.

Cool C. tried to **"Pimp smack"** the seasoned street-brawler from North Philly. DK is old-school, he knows three things you don't ever do to a **"grown-ass"** man. One is spit on him, two is put your foot upon him and third but not least, never try to slap him like a "Bitch!"

The ex-bodyguard flipped the hip-hop "**Goliath**" on his head. Security had gotten word that a disturbance was unfolding upstairs, rushing upstairs to diffuse the problem. The rap-star's" entourage is standing in the way of an onslaught of G-Stone's security. Four of their six-man entourage, unfortunately, got tossed downstairs head first!

The 60th Street rap-artist-thug attacked "Super D" with a swing-and-miss. The savvy street-fighter flipped his "Big-Ass" on the floor. The last two of his security details gathered their fallen benefactor, gracefully bowing out of any further "**Beef**." Security responded to a full alarm, but DK resolved it with a simple assault. This was typical behavior in any Club when hard-liquor and "**baby-feelings**" are mixed together.

Cool C. has bigger problems...

Real name, **"Christopher Douglass Roney,"** is being sought after by Authorities for the January 2nd shooting of a Female Philadelphia Police Officer in a botched bank robbery in "**Feltonville**." He used different after-hour spots to "cloak" his whereabouts during the night. Places like the Grindstone provided a perfect hide-out for suspected murderers.

Nobody believed the rumors about Cool C.'s involvement in this horrific crime on the news, but his connection was being realized by everyone in the dressing room. The tall rap-star lay helpless in a pile of "marked money."

"I thought yawl didn't get any money from that Bank Robbery?" asked the Boss, helping Cool C. and his entourage find the missing contents of his pockets, after the hip toss applied by DK.

"That's mine too…" said the discombobulated rap-artist, pointing at "Cherry" and Charmaine's tips that's laying on the floor. In an instant, the Boss played the "**Judge and Jury**" about the stolen "**marked money."** He ruled in favor of the girls because, there's are no refunds at the Grindstone …. **"No Doe…No Show!"**

CHAPTER FIVE
Lines are Drawn

The street lights outside the Club welcomed **Cool C.** and his entourage with open arms. His entourage knew they escaped an ass-whipping at the least. The revelation about the marked-money and the erratic behavior of the once beloved rap-star, left them feeling helpless; staring at the end of an era, not to mention their long overdue pay checks.

That blood money is what bought their freedom without harm inside the **Grindstone.** Being tossed on their heads was a small price to pay, compared to **"What could've happened,"** thought the **"out of work"** security detail.

Big Gene of the **Crew** towered over the entourage with his mean demeanor, looking like **"Shaft."** He's a not-so-friendly reminder that they can get their chins checked at any time; shoving them on their way up the street.

Cool C.'s the only one that didn't know how serious his situation was, getting out with their heads still intact. His entourage didn't know they're protecting a guilty man, more importantly a **"Wanted"** man, running from the cops.

Agent Smith and **Officer Mack** are parked outside the **Grindstone** in an unmarked police sedan. They're astonished that the Club is even open. The officers felt defied. **"These fucking guys have the audacity!!!"** grunted **Officer**

Mack. **Agent Smith** would've bet her next pay that the **Boss** was smarter than to open up the night after a raid.

"The Balls on this guy!" said **Agent Smith**. She's about to call for Back-up when, **Officer Mack**, at that very moment, noticed *"Public Enemy #1"* ...

"Christopher Douglass Roney" aka "Cool C.," leaving the Club.

A Cop-Killer is a bigger concern for the Agent, but she knew not to apprehend him without proper Back-up. The *"dead-man walking"* and his entourage jumped in his black jeep and sped away. The officers followed him, instead of kicking in the doors at the **Grindstone,** and, just like that, the heat was drawn away.

"Storm" is posted on the front-door as usual. He's the one that noticed the drama unfold and immediately radioed **Q.** *"Your Favorite Snowflake is here!"* he said with sarcasm, questioning the partners' decision to even open this soon in the first place.

Q rushed to the front-door. *"Where they at dawg?"* asked the anxious **Boss**. **Storm** was shocked that he could move so fast in alligator shoes. *"They left....and followed the 'Ice Cold Cop-Killer,' instead of raiding us!"* explained **Storm**. He didn't understand the decisions of his friend from the 10th grade.

"Why?" he asked. One word can convey a whole conversation between them. *"Money!"* he replied. **Q-Deezy** knows to *"Get all you can...when you can!"* Nevertheless, **Storm** is convinced that **Agent Smith** has a *"serious hard on for us!"*

They both knew the unwritten rule: *"Never open the day after a BUST."*

The other Clubs on the *Strip* are afraid of the *Grindstone's* police issues. They're many after-hour speakeasy, *"Go-Go"* bars and gambling houses in a one-block radius alone. Not to mention, every other *"Shady"* establishment throughout the City. Everybody thought they were being *"Ballsy,"* threatening the whole entire *"Game."*

There's a *Jamaican* dance-hall spot owned and operated by a *Kingston Rude Boy* by the name of *"Tee."* This after-hour spot is a favorite for party-goers who enjoy Reggae, smoking the finest weed and drinking after-hour alcohol. There's usually no drama, just Island bass. On the 1st floor, is a Jamaican restaurant. The aroma of *Jerk Chicken,* mixed with *"Skunk"* weed, attracted the *"potheads"* with the munchies. The transformed basement has cute Caribbean décor and is large enough to hold 200 party people grinding against the wall.

They're known to draw large crowds on the weekends; half of the people in line couldn't even get in. Those that did, swapped places with the over-heated party-goers. Summer nights are brutal from the heat and second-hand Marijuana smoke. While, the *"Selector"* plays the hardest hitting Jungle beats to sweat, party and grind to.

Dance-hall Freaks wind and grind better than the *hoes* down the street. They only locked horns with *"Go-Go"* girls if they're *"tricking"* the same dude. Judging each other on *"how"* to do the same thing.

One asking for *"money up-front,"* the other knows her *"trick's"* name, **both fucking to get paid!** They're green-eyed of the *"dancing tricks"* that's stealing the "*bread-winners*" from their beds. The exotic dancers are *"envious"* of their *"normal"* lives and *"real"* jobs. Every one of them wearing sexy see-through outfits trying to catch the same *"John,"* battling for his attention.

The *"Go-Go"* girls just loves his money, the *"jobless-freaks"* love guys with money, saving *"their"* men from the late-night heist called *"Go-Go."* This can be an expensive habit, spending the household budget on the *hoes* down the street, who's trying to fulfill the supply and demand of their man's freakish nature, while the ratchet freaks don't think mankind deserves the effort. The dancing Jezebels under *"black-light,"* fooling *"suckers"* with the ability, *"Glamour,"* dancing all night, keeps the body tight, showcasing their sexy figures on stage, popping and gyrating all in effort to please a man.

"What's so enticing about these loose women?" speculated by every woman that passed by. It was quickly becoming a known fact: If you were caught coming out the **Grindstone** by your mate or family member, you were instantly labeled a prostitute.

The judgmental *"9 to 5 Freaks"* proudly worked for minimum wage; jealous of the fact that they didn't have the kind of body to really get paid. The hard-working women wished they could play with their husband's pricks all night long. The *"Go-Go"* girls did it for them tax-free.

"Bitch your welcome!" were sentiments from the heart. *"It's better he's getting a $5 lap dance, than a 'Gold-digger' taking 'all' your man's money."*

"Gold-digging Freaks" battle relentlessly for men's pockets too. Slinging pussy out of both pant legs to get their rents, car-notes, and hair salon visits paid. That bitch don't care! She's spending all his money, acting like a *"Good-girl"* until the *"big bucks."* *"How disrespectful are these Bitches!"* said the wives, discovering *"she's"* been driving *"their"* man's vehicle, making him hide his wedding ring acting like this *"shit's"* personal, playing daddy to their kids while, dodging *"Child Support"* for his own.

"They'll make your man leave your ass so he can pay her bills better," good advice from a wise *hoe.*

A *"Gold-digger"* has a *"one-track"* mind, while the *"Street-walkers"* are on the *"Track"* all the time. They didn't have time to talk, grind and dance. *"Wham bam…Thank you Man!"* will do, serving *"quickies"* in dark-alley ways, back-seats of cars or by the hour motel rooms; like the *"Blue Moon."*

"Pimps" want high volume, quick turn-over profits, working the **"Tracks."** Under the bridges at *52nd & Jefferson St.,* were common sites in the summer, but when the hawk of the winter hits… They come in… out the cold.

A *"Street-walker"* with dance skills blends well inside a warm Club like the *Grindstone,* offering emotionless sex equivalent to a hand-job, you can do yourself. *"Where's the motivation?"* when the *"Pimp"* gets all the money, having hookers turning *"tricks"* like their dead inside.

They battled with the *"Go-Go"* girls, attempting to *"trick"* for $30 bucks for a *"lap-fuck,"* damaging the going-rates for sexual favors. These offenses are often being reported to the **Crew** by **Jazzy** and other **Squad** members, after the **Squad** trashed their asses in the dreaded dressing room.

The dressing room is where everything goes down. Exposing *"outsiders"* who want to do harm to the **Grindstone** or its **Crew** is the **Squad's** oath. Pledging to live by a code; *"**Never ruin the mood**"* is the number one rule, pulling *"violators"* to the side and straight back to the dressing room. It is the place where all *"Beefs"* are settled, while trying not to disturb the party, going on downstairs.

"Fuck your man better! He wouldn't have to pay me!" often said during girl-fights as they *"throw 'dem bows."* They couldn't handle the truth. *"Shots- fired"* to their egos, discovering their man's car parked outside a *"Go-Go"* spot. *"Maybe Nigga's ain't Shit?"* ...Especially at the **Grindstone.**

Housewives despised dancers, like salt to a womb, when their men got caught patronizing the **Ladies of the Night,** while *"Wifey's"* giving childbirth or at home, tired with the kids. Sexually frustrated spouses Storming out their houses right into the arms of *"Go-Go"* girls with flawless hairdos and caked up make-up*. "If you're caught stealing, that'll get your ass kicked."*

Justice is swift *"Have security carry them out!"* said **Jazzy**, a knockout artist from *"Broad and Erie,"* usually sets the tone, deciding if their dance bags gets *"tossed"* or both, thrashing guilty thieves lying on a stack of bibles, ...anything to avoid a beat-down.

Street-walkers vs. *Grindstone Squad* started over an unpaid lap-dance. A so-called *"Pimp"* felt disrespected, getting cursed-out by *Jazzy* over a $10-dollar debt. His *"Girls"* jumped to his defense. *"Don't touch my Daddy!"* yelled his *"Tricks."*

He refused to pay her for a lap-dance. The *"Brawling Bottom-Bitch"* of the *Grindstone* turned-down his offer to be *"Pimped"* by him. She's already getting *"Pimped"* by her *"nose-candy"* habit. The offended dancer blamed the refusal on having to take care of 4 kids, but addiction already had her under contract.

In an angered rage, she socked the *"Pimp"* in his condescending mouth. His bitches leaped on her back! They better react or face a beating themselves for *"not"* protecting their *"Pimp." Jazzy* made them pay heavily for that mistake. Precision combos are thrown by the dancing boxer from *North Philly,* beating three *Street-walkers"* like a light workout on a punching bag. Their *"Pimp"* watched in horror as his *"Bitches"* get out-matched then stomped on by the other dancers in the *Squad.*

The brawling *"Amazon from North Philly"* earned her stripes years ago. She didn't forget the 3-minute punching drills learned at *"Joe Frazier's Gym"* on *Broad Street.* The body blows worked well on his malnourished *hoes.* The *"Amazon"* sold all her *"wolf"* tickets.

She proved his *"harem"* couldn't protect their king. His pride couldn't let it go, he kept promising idle threats and broken *"Gangsta"* promises. His critical mistake was trying to *"Pimp smack"* the *"Amazon."* That's what got his ass knocked-out with a hook to the body, and an upper-cut to the chin, while security broke up the scuffle like an impartial referee. There's no need to stop the fight, he got KO'd for a $10 debt, free-falling towards the stage, knocking his front teeth out.

Meanwhile, one block down, on **Master Street,** was the **Cherokee,** a former religious banquet hall with a larger stage. It could easily hold up to 1,500 patrons. The sheer numbers used to cloak the actions of horny men. Dancers would get groped and raped without security even knowing it, until, it was too late. They didn't even seem to care about it at the **Cherokee.** Safety is always the *"number one"* concern for *"any"* dancer, but at the **Cherokee,** especially!

Grindstone didn't appreciate the Club's intrusion, even though they had their own clientele and dance roster when they moved on the block; only charging $10 for entry, while the **Grindstone** was trying to get $25 a head.

The *"Cherokee Hustlers"* are in the *"Game"* to sell their real product... Cocaine. The face of the Club is **Roscoe,** a 60th Street hustler trying to take over the *"Go-Go Game,"* charging the *"Corner boys"* extra, allowing them access with their *"work,"* while selling weight of his own in the back room. The married womanizer got his payback, getting shot on stage hosting a two-girl show by his own shady past. Security concerns tightened after that fiasco.

James "Roscoe" Scott acted as paranoid as *"Tupac"* trying to figure out his own shooting. The gunman wasn't playing any games with the *"Go-Go"* Club-owner... could've been a former dope boy that he betrayed, setting him up with the NARCS to catch a drug case ...or the disgruntle ex-security guard from *"Prince's Lounge"* on a shooting rampage killing everybody that had something do with his niece getting raped. Maybe it's more personal, like his wife's brother fresh out of jail serving revenge on his cheating brother in law, or it could've easily been the *Operation* trying to collect on an old debt.

   Grindstone Security vs. *Cherokee Security* never had any real *"Beef,"* sharing the same threats i.e., police, stick-ups and, of course, dancers' *"Beefs."* Many of them were from the same *Brotherhood*, working celebrity personal protection details, to Club security for the entire City together, but, after *Roscoe's* shooting, some questioned if their security could even protect themselves.

   The *Grindstone* enticed their dancers and patrons with a calmer atmosphere. *Cherokee* dancers used to come to the *Grindstone* for *Mrs. B.'s* soul food platters. Her savory delights reminded them of their own mothers' cooking. The late nights took a toll on *"all"* the night-owls that frequented both Clubs.

   The *Cherokee* dancers immediately noticed that the *Grindstone* caters to an older and calmer crowd. The staff is polite, and security is always just a holler away. They wanted in and this would cost them a double dancing-fee of $50.

   The *Crew* was trying to persuade them to come dance earlier. The cut-off time for non-*Squad* dancers was 2am or pay double, so they were trying to convince *Storm* that they just wanted to order food platters from **Mrs. B.,** but he wasn't hearing none of that.

"*$50 ladies, have your ID's out, open your purses and pass your dance bags to security for inspection!*" ordered *Storm*, knowing that weapons could easily be smuggled inside in a dancer's bag. He already knew once they saw the type of clientele that the *Grindstone* has, they'll *"definitely"* want to stay anyway.

The *Grindstone Squad* always arrived on time; half of them lived there at one-time or another. They resented *"late"* dancers trying to *"reap"* the benefits of their hard labor, heating up horny crowds, one lap-dance at a time, while the *"latecomers"* get tipped walking through the room. *"They're Dirty Cherokee Girls!"* said the resentful *G-Stone Squad. "Payback"* for the greedy bitches arriving from across the street.

A line was drawn a while ago. The *Grindstone Girls* vs. *Cherokee Girls* acted like rival gangs. The *Cherokee Squad* would taint patrons against visiting *G-Stone* dancers. *"Don't tip that Bitch!"* would echo in their ears, vicious lies told on them that would hurt their pockets, hating-ass rumors that would shut down dates, lap-dances and tips, throwing pennies on stage for laughs, anything to start some shit! This started dressing rooms brawls and free-falls, tossing bitches on their dance bags.

Security must search dancers at both Clubs very thoroughly. *"You never know with these grimy bitches,"* sentiments from a *G-Stone* dancer exploring new turf, discovering overlooked weapons on dancers, *"praying for the best while preparing for the worst,"* both Clubs used their *"Beefs"* against them, keeping each in-house dancer roster intact, but the rivalry spawned many of battles all over the City.

The *G-Stone Squad* represented well in night-clubs on their *"Go-Go Nite,"* defending themselves in Dance battles to repping" their home Club like gang-territory. Battling for bragging rights and more importantly *"Money"* thrown on stage.

"Winner takes all!" announced the *"Studio 37's"* MC *"Big Keith"*

The *Squads* loved competing against one-another, like a *"Freakish Relay-Team,"* best *Pole* dancer against *Grindstone's* best, *Kalifornia,* who likes to twirl around in a pole-dance off, like a sexual acrobat, while *Tupac's "California Love"* plays during her *battle set.*

Jennifer "Kalifornia" Bell trained other *Squad* members as well. They practiced the pole just in case they got called-on to defend the *Grindstone's* reputation. She's a great teacher, giving away trade secrets learned at the age of 16 from the *Mid-West's* Erotic Clubs like *"Spanky's,"* in Missouri, qualifying teenagers *"Erotic Dancing"* as a *"Taxable Income,"* giving the term *"Show-me State"* a whole new meaning.

Ny'sha tried one-night. The thick novice fell flat on her ass trying to twirl on the pole. The hating audience parted like the *"Red Sea"* letting her fall hard like an un-popular **"Rock Star."** Her own *Squad* held their laughter, as they collected their fallen teammate, but the *"opposing"* dance *Crew's* laughter would be silenced, challenged to a

"Dance-off." "DJ play our shit!" cued by the Captain of the *Squad*. *Tupac's "Hit'em Up!"* would serenade the courage of the whole *G-Stone Crew*.

"You copy my style. Five shots couldn't drop me I took it and smile!" "Now Bout to set the record straight, with my A-K. I'm Still the Thug Dancer, you Love to Hate!!!" "Mother-fucker I Hit'em up," their re-mixed anthem galvanized the *Squad* to dust-off defeat.

Synchronized dance routines are battled out on stage, they're called *"Group Dance-offs,"* resembling a *"roll-call"* of gyrating, *"Who got the fattest ass!"* twerking contests. The instigating *MC* would judge the *Squads* by the number of tips thrown on stage, rigging the competition by only tipping their *Squad,* but, the dancers knew who the real winners were. Real props got handed-out in the dressing rooms with a handshake, or a fight.

The ones with lyrical rap skills battled on the mic, *"spitting"* rhymes about their Home Club's *Bosses* and *Crew,* telling stories of the money and the swag they have... and of course how well they *"Bone"* their asses.

Philadelphia Female Rap-Artist, "Eve," honed her skills visiting the *Grindstone.* She was *"destined for greatness*," rapping on the mics of various *"Go-Go"* Clubs about pain, domestic violence and other women's rights. The *Crew* remembers the Grammy-award winning, *'Ruff Ryder"* artist. Back then, *"Eve"* begged *Big Country* to bless the mic.

Their fondest memory is of a rap battle between *Jazzy* vs. *"Eve."* They had an epic, heated *"Cypher"* that lasted 30 minutes*. "Eve"* was *"repping"* the *Uptown* part of *Philly*, and *Jazzy* "repped" the *Grindstone.* Witnesses saw two *"Amazons"* battle, verse-for-verse, both representing *Philly* to the fullest.

"Eve" was a rapping exotic dancer that didn't worry about *"tricking"* with dudes, illicit drug use, or being the best dancer on stage. The 18-year-old caramel-complexion, small-breasted, rapping dancer, with a nice ass didn't care for G-strings and small tips. She came for the mic. *"Hip-hop"* is her only *"fetish."*

"Eve Jihan Jeffers" was fresh out of *Martin Luther King" High school* when she started dancing. The *Brothers* around the way was sad to see the *Sister* out of her *"garb,"* but, her plan was clear, she was cultivating her persona and stage presence on a *"Go-Go"* stage. An imaginary line separates *"Showgirls"* from *"A girl giving a show."* The talented battle- "Rap Artist" gave everybody a show, crushing all-comers from *Uptown* to *West Philly,* girls and guys, and *"Go-Go" MC's* who thought they had rap skills, could get it too!

Many of them gracefully bowed out but joined in the *"Rap Cyphers"* at closing-time. *Jazzy* transformed into a *"thug-Rap-artist,"* dressed in street clothes. She couldn't convey her hard rhymes in a G-string and *"Go-Go"* boots. Rapping about *"How Punks step-up to get beat down!"* like, a thugged-out female *"Grand Puba"* from *"Brand Nubian."*

The greatest struggle for all dancers are the *"Stick-up"* dudes. The disgruntled, wanna-be patrons with meager ends; jealous *"Player-haters"* plotting on dancers that are tipped heavily. *Stick-up* dudes would encourage other *"thirsty"* patrons to tip their target, indirectly robbing the whole Club's tips collected in the target's dance bag, becoming targets in the first place by going to *"Go-Go"* Clubs *"solo-dolo."* Being alone in a Club, with a *"submissive"* personality, will *"definitely"* get *"you"* targeted. Walking the dark *"Philadelphia Streets"* is challenging enough as a *"trick,"* when every shadow is your enemy.

"Salty dudes" are guys who couldn't get the *"pussy,"* even if they paid double, gossiping more than the chicks at the beauty salon, exposing dancers to their family, co-workers, and friends. *"How would you know I'm shaking my ass if you're not in there looking for some ass?"* said Kali exposing a religious family member. Maybe, they're jealous of their ex-girlfriend's new hustle, flapping their gums about their ex-lady's business, spreading mostly lies out of spite.

"The Difference between a hoe and a Bitch: "Hoes" fuck everybody, Bitches fuck everybody but you!" sentiments of a wise *"Old-Head,"* explaining the natural order of things.

"Sexual Predators" are always watching. *"One false move will get you killed."* Their targets are under-age dancers with fake IDs, revealing themselves as soon as they open their mouths.

"No! aren't you my Middle-School Gym Teacher?" the *"Kid-dancer"* asks, dissing her secret admirer from recess. No need to sneak in their windows at home, predators can meet and greet them during a lap-dance, a fatal move for a *"little-girl"* trying to wear *"big-girl"* panties, in the wrong Club.

They're *"Young Soldiers"* in their own right, escaping from their *"group homes,"* hiding-out in after-hour Clubs, or living on the streets, dancing just to have something to eat, picking homelessness over incest and rape in the *"homes"* or fighting against *"bottom-bunk"* violence in *"Juvie."* Growing up with *"Pimps,"* instead of *"Crews"* is the most critical decision a young girl can make in this *"Game."*

The **Grindstone** turned some young lives around, offering shelter and the means, looking the other way at their fake IDs, while listening to their horror stories. Sometimes, not saying a word is enough, no judgements between them builds trust, looking after them like play-brothers; guiding them through this thing called *"Go-Go"* seemed just, but waiting for their 18th birthdays, like baking cupcakes in the oven. *"Popping cherries"* wasn't their fault... Step-Daddy did that years ago!

Storm and **Big Gene's** main job on the front door is to *"separate the men from the boys,"* preached by **Q-Deezy,** especially if there's too many on-lookers. *"No Doe No Show!"* loudly shouted in the microphone by the host **Big Country.** This is a no-no for all patrons.

"Ballers to the front, Peons to the rear!" chanted the host, wanting the guys that's tipping to have a front-row seat to the show. The **Crew** wouldn't let broke niggas breathe, pushed to the sidewalk *"real"* quick. *"This Ain't No Free Show!"* said the **MC,** while Security figures them out!

"Ladies please wake these dicks up!" said ... the **Guest MC**, *"I Ain't Lying Leon."* He would expose **Players** vs.

Pretenders, a crowd check would flush them out. ***"Fellas put $500 on this STAGE!" Yawl gonna see some freaky SHIT!"*** The guys would collectively put up ***$1000,*** announcing there's some ***"Ballers"*** in the building. Pretenders saw a different show. ***"Don't Touch that 'Ass' unless you're tipping that 'Ass,' and you better be eating or drinking."***

 "Boss-Lady Barmaid needs tips too! No sleeping during the show, drowsy niggas Go Home!"

 "But if we got some 'Ballers' in HERE!!! Lock the Door!" screamed ***"I Ain't Lying Leon."*** No other patrons are allowed in. Excited ***"Ballers"*** are allowed to have sex anywhere in the club ***(paying of course),*** under dimmed lights at Clubs like ***"Nite on Broadway"*** with **MC Butter.**

 "Lock-Door" freak-fest events are an ***"eerie"*** surprise to a new-fangled patron or dancer***. "If you didn't know, you know now!"*** screamed the **MC.** Everybody and their wallets are hostage for the ***"Lock-Door" freak-fest*** going down! ***Nobody in, Nobody out.***

 "Mud-duck" hoes shine during ***"Lock-Door"*** events. They don't need spot-lights. The sneaker wearing ***"raggedy hoes"*** offer ***$1 "dick-nibbles"*** or ***"dry-humps,"*** allowing guys to ejaculate in their ***"Ass Crack."*** The nasty ***"cesspool"*** resembled ***"Sodom & Gomorrah"*** behind locked doors.

 "Total turn-off!" said **Q-Deezy** *"We don't do* ***"Mud-ducks." Grindstone*** traded ***"One" "Locked-Door"*** event for ***"Player Balls"*** without hesitation.

"Player's Balls" at the *Grindstone* are legendary in the *Hood*. *"Black Tail Magazine"* sponsored events with its talent search for new exotic models, which included celebrity guest lists and a dress-code that's highly enforced. Only players dressed in *"Crocodile"* shoes and *"Fedora"* hats ...driving fancy cars are allowed in.

"Let it be known! Grindstone is your second home!" said the new host of *Grindstone, Q-Deezy*. They're performing water shows, two-girl shows and specialty shows of all kinds. The *Ladies of the Night* are always ready to entertain and please their older, obedient crowd, that's appreciating their efforts by hefty tips of $1000 a night.

Another threat would be the *"Hack-Pimps,"* providing rides to *"New Jersey"* Clubs, for $30.00 each way, later realizing they're being *"Pimped"* for a tank of gas. Those who came up short suffered being stranded, or raped on the way back, taking the *"long"* way home, making quick stops at various *"tracks"* and *"speak-easies"* throughout *New Jersey*, *"Pimped"* as a hostage just to get home. Dancers had to be fearless to travel out of town; traveling up and down *95 South,* some were *"Cool"* others were just plain ... *"Foul."*

"Not our Squad!" said the concerned *Boss*, forbidding many of them to ride with these fraudulent Niggas, *"Pimping" hoes* on the interstate highways. Dumping good *"Freak Bitches"* in the trash!

CHAPTER SIX
"A Bitch Gotta Eat…"

The **Crew's** basking in their new-found success in business, street cred and the fact that every dancer in the City wants to get down. The block is filled with luxury cars. The **"Ballers"** are coming though the Club from all over. The **Grindstone's** contributions to the City Government officials proved its worth with every penny, funded by a heist in **New York.** They're big-time players now, popping bottles is a regular occurrence on the weekends. They love to celebrate any observance, it didn't matter the reason. The City is theirs' for the taking in the after-hour erotic dancing **"Game."**

Other Clubs started banning any **G-Stone Crew** members from taking all their top performers. The local police appreciated the Club because they kept late night **"Hustlers"** occupied. Most **West Philly "Hustlers,"** during 12am.-6am., weren't starting trouble, searching for their rivals, or warring with known enemies. They're all chilling at the **Grindstone.**

The surrounding businesses open during these violent hours, enjoying the extra income from the massive crowds. Their patrons are going to the **Grindstone, Cherokee** and the **Reggae Spot.** The Chinese restaurants, gas stations, and Deli's in a two blocks radius would testify that the Clubs at **52nd & Master Sts.** drew huge revenues to the neighborhood.

Some people hated their flash, prestige and the fact that they're black, making money. **"Being in business for yourself is freedom!"** often said by **Q-Deezy** every time a hater would hate. Some people loved to spread rumors about the dancers, staff and of course,

"The Black Hugh Heffner!"

The **Crew** didn't pay any attention to the rumors, all they ever gave a flying fuck about is the cash. The money is flowing; dancers are making $1,500 a night. Mothers, wives and daughters' fell victim to this so-called dirty money. The men in their lives despised them for it, but

"A Bitch Gotta Eat!" was often expressed by an older, married dancer named **Ginger "Gigi" Howard!**

Ginger is a 30-something, mature, seasoned, veteran dancer with an hour-glass shape and a nice pair of caramel D-cup breasts. Her very seductive eyes can mesmerize the strongest man, possessing the sweetest voice that plays in the minds of *"ALL"* her *"Clients."*

She's old-school, requesting **Aretha Franklin's** *"Rock Steady,"* hitching the audience to a *"70's" "Go-Go" "Odyssey"* with her *"Afro-Puffs,"* or rolling on the floor to *"Proud Mary"* with a **Tina Turner** wig, inviting the *"Big Wheels"* at work to come over the *"Ben Franklin Bridge"* for some *"Motivation."*

"Oh, I wanna dance with Somebody" articulated by the last song of her set, a **Whitney's Houston** hit. **Ginger** is available, *"Fellas"* for steamy $20 lap-dances in the VIP couches upstairs, teasing *"Caucasian Colleagues"* from the after-work parties, hosted by *"Gigi's little Secret"* another **Grindstone** production in the **Hood.**

"The Dookie-Shoot don't even STINK!" said the invited co-worker with his mind-blown, talking by the water cooler, spreading the word about the traveling *"pretty-nurse"* with a very freaky surprise.

The caramel vixen's financial prowess is unmatched by her new dancing **Squad.** She's living in the suburbs with her *"Nuclear Family,"* complete with two kids and a husband. She used to be a faithful wife, working as a *"CNA"* by day, now an entertaining *"Exotic Show-Girl"* by night. Her husband, **George "El-Train" Howard** couldn't complain about **Ginger's** night job, needing the money ever since he got hurt *"off"* the job. Their lavish lifestyle includes a huge house payment with all the amenities, two gigantic whopping car notes, plus a diva-like wardrobe matching *"Good Coochie"* with *"Real Gucci."*

Their dire situation spawned by **George's** bar fight with his *"Gold-digging"* mistress, *"Nikki,"* whose jealous boyfriend, *"Phillip,"* caught the two of them on a date, after he hunted them down to a *"Friday's" Restaurant.*

Big Phil interrupted the romantic date, wanting to finish a heated conversation about him being married to the Mother of his five kids. **Nikki's** caught lying about the *"handsome replacement"* introduced as her *"Amtrak"* co-worker, **George,** who's hiding his wedding ring in his *"Volvo's"* ashtray outside.

The *"Train Engineer"* suffered a broke back from a barstool, several stitches from punches, was stomped into shit-bag material and got a dislocated arm. The ex-boxer *"lined his ass up"* right and pick-pocketed his paycheck from the railroad; snuck from behind for having drinks with another woman.

"Gut-Checked Ginger" was devastated, but *"sucked-it-up"* and decided to stay and care for her husband. After-all, he is the Father of her children. The hospital bills began to swell and so did her anger. *Ginger* decided to dance to finance their lifestyle, long before she ever stepped a foot in the *Grindstone.*

"A Bitch Can Eat Good in The Hood" said the converted exotic dancer, wanting to sell her *"Tail"* on the *"Deuce."*

Ginger's presence alone inspired other top exotic performers to check out the popular night spot. The *"Prissy Performers"* got challenged under the Spotlight to give the *Hood* a little love, but they thought wrong, *"If We didn't wanna a Taste!"* said the well-dressed sophisticated host for tonight, *Mr. Q-Deezy*.

"Can you GET with this record right HERE?" inquired the *"Master of Ceremony"* of this party, knowing *"Just what song you need!"* He played the perfect song for a true dancer, wondering if she's safe being in a late-night *52nd Street* speak-easy, eating a *"Mrs. B's Chicken-Shack"* biscuit platter, cool *"Old-heads"* that knows exactly *"WHO"* you are, a *"Chocolate Star"* given *"Good & Plenty"* tips while *"Juicy Fruit"* plays in the background.

"Respect this Party Now!" says the *MC Q-Deezy*, putting the needle to *Cameo's* classic wax, while the regulars mistakenly look for *"Candie's Water Show."*

"Gigi's" teasing the clientele with her aroma. The scented lotions she uses is just a prelude to her pleasure, whispering seductive, naughty suggestions in their ears and every fantasy has a price tag.

"How bad do you want me Big Daddy?" Ginger asks her high paying groupies. Hundreds if not, thousands are offered to experience every sultry detail. Some paying customers struggle with the fact that she's married. *"My pussy is only for my husband!"* **Ginger** confessed. It's her only rule, preferring to swallow their dicks with feverish blow jobs, or offering anal sex for fantasies that calls for sexual intercourse.

The erotic clubs she's worked at prior to the *Grindstone* didn't have accommodations for such behavior. *They're "Primetime"* Clubs like *"Delilah's Den"* in *South Philly* and *"Tiffany's"* in *Northeast Philly. Ginger* accumulated a legion of admirers from there too and brought them all to the *Grindstone.*

Ginger dabbles as a *Sex Therapist,* inviting couples to meet at the *Grindstone* for threesomes, never making the women feel *"less-than"* during their *"hands-on"* encounters, teaching them how to concentrate on each other.

"Please your man Girl!" she whispers, teaching prudish wives how to *"Deep Throat"* their husband's pricks. She's proud of that the most, saving their boring sex lives with new *"tricks,"* adding spice to any relationship, wanting your *"money not, your man."*

"Who you gonna trust with your man girl?" said *Ginger,* referring to the fact that she's a professional.

Even though, she's saving complete strangers' relationships, or thoroughly fulfilling the needs of a new bachelor's last night of freedom, troubles were brewing at home. *Ginger's* husband, *George,* isn't happy with these *"new"* working hours and he's being neglected on a regular basis.

"Mr. and Mrs. Howard's" bedroom *"pillow talk"* was once filled with *"unfruitful"* stories of lonely men's fantasies, but now, they're motives for his suspicion. He's worried that his wife's exotic shows are turning into reality. *"Curious George"* is convinced that the money she's making aren't *"just"* tips from *"table-dancing."* The *Grindstone* has turned his wife to a full-fledge prostitute, averaging $5000 a night.

Things are different now. *Ginger's* arriving home after 9am, four nights a week, having just enough time to take a nap then wake up to get ready for her demanding shift at the Nursing Home. He used to pick her up from work before the *"Go-Go"* days. Things were so much easier back then, when he was the primary bread-winner of the home.

"Georgie Porgie" knew very well how to hide his cheating ways with a convenient work schedule. Now, he's victim to her late nights, accompanied with the same old lame excuses: flat-tires on the highway, a dead battery, no answering her phone because the speakers are too loud, can't lap-dance and answer calls.

"The Fucking Grindstone," cried *George,* describing his disgust for his wife's secret playground. He knew about *"karma"* and this situation is payback of the

highest form. He's still nursing his injuries from the bar fight. *"You can't hit it from the back with a broken back!"* said *Ginger* heatedly during an argument. His loving faithful wife was kidnapped by a sassy mouth vixen with deep pockets.

"Is this why you're cheating on me?" the feelings of the frustrated *George,* after a heated screaming match. He knows their love-life is on life-support. His back injury made it impossible to make love to his wife, who's getting bored of sucking his limp, one-size, soft "noodle" Long gone were the days of *"bridal bliss"* with a fully engorged, 10-inch tool, now a 3-inch *"noodle"* that's barely getting clean.

"Dick-less Cheating Mother-Fucker!" is his new nickname used every time he tried to feel his wife's warm touch. His cheating ways, nor the injuries suffered from his vicious beat-down caused this, in his mind. It's the *Grindstone* with the *"Double-Dipping Dookie"* bandits inside.

"Nobody's giving your Pussy away!" confessed *Ginger* during her husband's random late-night vaginal exams; fingers couldn't discover his wife's awful truth. If his examinations included a rectal exam, her lies would've been discovered a while ago.

Ginger's juicy tight *"snatch"* didn't tell her secrets. Her only *"rule"* for *"tricks"* proved deceptive. *George's* mind was spinning with guilt, jealousy and uncertainties, accusing every *Crew* member, patron and dancer at the Club of having sex with his wife, envisioning wild orgies and other graphic infidelities. The effects of his pain meds heighten the visions late at night. He's feeling like a helpless by-stander watching his beloved wife ruin her life.

"I'm not going through this again!" declared the grieving **George,** who found her drug stash, he's been down this road before.

"You're Relapsing?" After a 60-day *"Black-out"* in the *"Outley's Rehab,"* court guidelines even required spouses to piss in a cup. Thank God **George** & **Ginger** could maneuver around **DHS's** questions, or their two little sweetie-pies could've been lost to the system. *"What do I tell these kids?"*

"Mimba' that Shit?" reminded the judgmental *"Cajun Swamp-Runner"* arguing with the sneaky-ass *"Viper Snake Bitch!"* He's the one that was there! *"You're in the "Peruvian" marching powder band again?"*

Ginger's marital problems triggered an *"old demon-habit."* Stress-levels from heated arguments keep the *"recovering coke whore"* on the edge, murdering the timeline of getting some good fucking sleep. So, the long hours required more than a caffeine fix...for a booked *"Exotic Show Girl,"* giving a hyper-active sexy show, then dragging across town to a *"double-bubble,"* working for the *"Man"* at the nursing home.

The familiar habit was re-introduced by **Junior**, supplying her with the highest quality of the *"nose candy."* **Junior** became a major *"blip"* on **George's** radar after finding his text-messages. **George's** favorite early morning pastime is deleting new phone numbers in her cellphone, cracking her easy passwords while she sleeps, suffering a small death reading her electronic betrayals.

"I want that good shit," she could text **Junior**, this referring to a drug deal, and her husband assumes it's arrangements being made to have sex. **Ginger** loves twisting the revengeful knife. *"Mrs. Howard"* hates explaining herself to the paranoid, cheating spouse. Every text with *"Ghetto"* names gets the boot. In his mind, it's an invitation to quench his wife's sexual thirst, not realizing that her monthly … *"Medical Sugar Daddies"* pay extra for a *"bubble-bath,"* getting scrub-down by *"Nurse Ginger"* with dem' *"Big Ass Titties,"* letting *"Mr. Henry"* have a **"Tea-Bag"** every 1st and 15th of the month with dem' *"Old Ass Balls."* *"Cat Daddy"* wants a *"blow job"* for his "one-size soft," **Ginger's** lips sparked a huge *"Life Saver"* thrusting in a *"bobble-head"* gripped-up by the back of her hair!

  George is way off worrying about the cellphone contact, *"Tyree,"* with *"North Jersey"* *"Piff"* … *(scrolling though the phone on the "creep" in the bathroom.)*

  "Relax!" She's loathes the intrusion of her privacy as sabotage to making money, switching the light-weight argument to a *"WHERE'S MY PHONE?!"* conversation. She alone pays the bills *"around this BITCH,"* tired of his snooping for the truth…but" … *"This Bitch Gotta Eat!"*

  Ginger's motto was born when this *"Nigga!"* deleted every horny, African-American in her phone, justifying having men numbers locked in her mobile memory, losing all respect for her handicapped spouse who no longer provides. The clientele knows about her marital status too well, explained to them by her only *"rule."*

The *"Cookie Box"* is off-limits to everybody except, her husband. This was the last thing not compromised in her wedding vows. This includes women that wanted to insert her *"sweet pussy"* with toys. *Ginger* craves a little *"Coochie"* sometimes … not *"Amazons"* with a *"bionic strap-on*."

Having *"threesomes"* was a mutual decision for the married couple, using her suggested talented skills on her own marriage.

"George's #1 Rule," No, fun without *"him."*

The lucky husband didn't mind her bi-sexual tendencies, only if he benefited. The steamy-hot sexy co-workers came in all flavors …the butt-licking chop-stick *"Asian-Twins,"* the toe-sucking lily-white *"Euro-Trash"* chick or the *"tail-less Filipinos"* who weren't being invited anymore because of his impotence.

"Girl, he cute and all, but his dick doesn't work!" is recurring theme of the snickering sexual partners. He's regulated to be just a handicap spectator after several failed attempts of a threesome. *George* was quite the lover before his injuries. That long stroke *"sealed the deal"* for their union ten years ago.

"Amtrak" Conductor *"George Howard"* used to be her confident *"Love Train."* These days, her *"super lover"* is not himself. The bar fight caused his plight for the colonoscopy bag and the pinched nerve in his back made walking impossible for months. The head injuries left him with extreme migraines that will probably last for a lifetime, developing into his own nasty pain-killer addiction.

One lonely night, *George* couldn't take it anymore and decided to stalk his cheating wife. He's determined to find out what's going on behind his back, needing to know if *"she's settling the score"* of being a *"whore."* In a jealous rage, spawned by another one of his visions of a cheating wife, the partially-handicap husband mustered up the *"strength and will"* to leave their king-size bed, feeling like a freed captive, searching for his keys to the getaway car. He's on his feet, contrary to the doctor's diagnosis. The triumphant husband has been secretly training himself since the fateful night when his mistress' boyfriend ended his ability to walk.

Ginger wasn't the only married woman with husband issues. *Ny'sha* can relate to *Ginger's* plight. She has her own struggles with an abusive *"Jack-ass"* named *Big Phil.* His name rang a bell as *"Gigi"* quickly pull it all together, speculating her husband's attacker is this poor child's husband.

Ny'sha Rose Smith-Matthews, is a sexy, brown-skinned, thick, perky-breasted, **"Trinidadian,"** with a size-able booty, and blessed with *Pam Grier's* classic looks. The single mother of 5 kids is forced into single parenthood, trying to make ends meet, while her abusive, crack-head husband is serving time for whooping her ass. *Phillip Biggie Matthews Sr.'s* recent stint in *Graterford Prison* will soon end because of lack of testimony from his *"Wife."* She's juggling school, and raising five kids, while married to an abusive, college-educated, fool with a serious *"Pookie-sized"* crack habit. The *"Big Pain in the Ass"* has terrorized his faithful wife since Pastor Muhammad said:

"You may take your property!" translated in the English for normal people with some fucking sense.

"You may kiss your Bride." **Ny'sha** has regretted those words. She's been trapped in this grim situation, chasing happiness like *"Fool's Gold,"* thinking its origin comes from her **"Gangster Bi-Polar Bully"** on a vicious power trip over the *"demons"* that haunts him at night.

When the other dancers get buzzed though the doors, *Ginger* galvanized *Ny'sha's* courage outside the Club, with her motto, *"A Bitch Gotta Eat."* She, too, is all alone, feeding kids and paying the bills. *Ny'sha* was getting use to her freedom though. No longer did she have to deal with his crack-head tantrums. She couldn't fathom being forced to have sex with her husband again. It's like *"eating off a garbage can lid"* because he's a certified *"fuck- boy,"* constantly accused of being somebody else's baby-father.

Ny'sha was *"forced"* to be a submissive wife, because of her allegiance to their *"Ghetto Mafia"* family. They forbade her to divorce, leave, snitch, or do anything whatsoever that's deemed disrespectful in his eyes. Their black-mafia-bonded marriage was doomed from the start. Two years into their nuptials, the *"Gangster Couple"* find out they're first *"Cousins."* Knowing your pregnant by a blood relative proved too much for the young marriage to bear, not to mention her husband likes to *"trick"* with ugly fat chicks with "deep pockets."

It's been 18-months since **Ny'sha** seen her husband. Locked-up for an aggravated assault, his ultimate arrest happened during the domestic abuse case of his battered wife. She refused to press charges back then, but in this moment of reflection, *"It might not have been a bad idea,"* she thought, smoking a cigarette outside the Club, after getting an earful from *"Nurse Ginger."*

Ny'sha's in deep thought, wondering about her options, as her husband, *Big Phil's,* prison release date is just days away. *"Roger,"* is a married, male exotic dancer she's going out with and she is contemplating exploring the City's *"Go-Go"* Clubs, with his sister *"Felisha,"* a skinny crispy-black, *"coke whore,"* who became another *"hater"* after she got passed on her audition by *Q-Deezy*, denying her a chance to dance at the *G-Stone." "Hate-pulling"* a *Squad* member away from the Club is always frowned upon.

"Now, "Flea-lisha" is banned!" joked *Country,* passing by outside the Club after hearing she's the reason it's been a minute *Ny'sha,* the 24-year-old thick, sexy, coffee-complexion sister with '70's classic looks, who's relieved to be in her Home-Club, enjoying her freedom until lasts, wanting a chance to explore some *"bucket-list"* desires, ... and just like that, as if on cue... the *Boss* of the *Grindstone* asks her for a light. *"What you doing outside the Club?"* he asked, knowing *Ny'sha* has been around long enough to know the rules. There's no hanging outside the Club, especially the dancers.

"Just catching a quick smoke Boss" she answered with a devilish grin, her thoughts are written on her forehead, her interests are very apparent with her *"Foxy Brown"* eye contact. *Ny'sha,* without a word, fucked him with her mind, but time is ticking fast before her *"fantasy land"* gets permanently shut down. *Big Phil* is coming home, so she only has days to conquer her newest desire, *Jazzy's* beloved *"Poppy."*

Ny'sha didn't notice the **Boss** at first. *Jazzy's* embellished stories of constant love making, shopping sprees and future-plans of a relationship did that. They were discussing the truth during a smoke break. *"Don't break my girl's heart!"* she said referring to *Jazzy's* tall stories.

"Stick around later. We'll talk all about your girl, if you want?" he chuckled about testing some of the embellished lies on the new fan entering the Club.

Back at Ginger's residence…

George is searching though his wife's drawers for clues and finds a color flyer for *"Ginger's Little Secret,"* performing live at the *Grindstone.* He always knew the name, but not the address, criticizing his wife's choice to dance on the *Strip.* The *"Five-Deuce"* has bodied legends; he's cringing that his wife just might need his saving.

"Oh Hell Naw!" shouted the determined husband, who didn't know she is *"Jiggling in the Hood."*

He finally found his keys to the black Volvo station wagon, parked in the garage of their Jenkintown home, barely starting with a dying battery, thankful *"Jehovah's on his side,"* who's trying to save a lost soul again. Propped up by a back brace that's relieving a lot of his pain, *George* threw his crutches in the backseat and proceeded to drive to *52nd & Master St.*

Meanwhile inside the Club...

The vibe is festive, and the dancers are having a good night. Money is flowing heavy because it's the first of the month. The disc jockey is playing ghetto anthems back-to-back. The *"Ballers"* are in full e-f-f-e-c-t, as the rap music plays in the background like a fixed soundtrack. The cover charge is $50 tonight. VIP members only had to pay $25 for entry. The door is set to *"weed out the men from the boys."*

Tonight's cover charge weeded out the silliest drama, deterring a lot of spying boyfriends and husbands.

George paid the cover, thanks to *Ginger's* stash at home. She thought, *"if"* her husband's nurse needed anything, she could use the petty cash of $1000 to handle any emergency. The only crisis tonight is catching a *"cheating wife." George* couldn't wait to see his wife's face. He wanted to catch her red-handedly cheating on him. He's used to her working Clubs where men couldn't touch the erotic performers, reading the sign by the *"Go-Go"* stage that read,

"Don't Touch That Ass, Unless You Tipping That Ass!"

The *"creeping husband"* grabbed a chair in the darkest corner of the Club. He wanted to watch his wife slither around the room, asking guys for a dance, rubbing on their *"packages,"* whispering freaky shit in their ears, while licking the earlobes of strangers.

"How much for a lap dance sugar?" one man asked his wife. Her husband secretly watched and listened to their conversation, just two feet away. She laughed and flirted with the older man. The patron showered *Ginger* with $20 bills, *"groping and sucking on her beautiful tits!"* as he lightly smacked her ass.

George watched in horror as his wife gets fingered in her butt. The patron ravished the mother of his children like a farmer eating a peach with no teeth. *"You taste good Peaches!"* he said with a southern accent, licking his probing fingers clean!

Ginger collected her tips and went to the upstairs' dressing room to freshen up. *George* is still downstairs witnessing the older patron and his buddies brag about which dancer will *"screw"* for cash; teasing their freakish *"home-boy,"* by not shaking his hand.

"These girls fucking in here?" *George* asked the patrons, like a rookie undercover-cop trying to fit in, breaking the mood between the clowning patrons, looking nervous asking obvious questions with the ass-fingering dude.

"Are you a member?" asked the hesitant exclusively connected guys, waiting for the secret response. The answer known by every member of the secret clique is,

"Members already know."

The patrons faded from the intruder. *George* is recognized by *Ginger's* friend *Crystal.* She remembered him from a failed threesome attempt. He grabbed her and sat her down for an imaginary lap dance.

"Don't tell Ginger I'm here" whispered *George,* filling her G-string with a $50 bill.

"Your secret's safe with me baby" said *Crystal,* caressing *Ginger's* sneaky husband's ear, who's buried under her heated lap dance.

Christina Crystal Jefferson, is an 18-year old, thin build, attractive, 34C breasted vixen. Her *"Barbie doll"* legs are her best feature by far. As she wrapped them over his shoulders, the flawless smooth legs sparked some tension in his loins by becoming fully erect watching his wife's return.

Ginger changed outfits and reunited with the older patron and his boys. They brought her drinks via bottle-service. Laughing at their jokes, the gracious *"old-schooled"* dancer has a tendency of making customers feel special on a personal level. She's engaging and dutifully pouring drinks with a southern hospitality attitude, while the *Commodores* sing about a *"Brick house."*

George watched his beautiful wife lead the patron by the hand to an empty seat for another lap dance. *Ginger* flips in his lap like a sex-crazed acrobat, her small frame is easy to handle with a juicy *"Muffin"* in his face. The older gentleman enjoyed every sultry *"trick,"* feeling like *"the man of the hour"* at a bachelor party, trying to taste her forbidden center cause she's letting it all hang out. *George,* watching his woman being tossed around like freaked-out gymnast, kept his manhood hard.

"She makes an old man wish for younger days!" screams the older patron enjoying the lap-dance.

The 10in. prick is a pleasant surprise for *Crystal,* who's grinding on *George.* She didn't remember this much *"tube steak"* at their last encounter. *"Got two hundred dollars?"* asked *Crystal,* as she straddled his legs. He handed her the money and let her ...do all the work.

Crystal secretly pulled his penis out. He noticed she applied a *"Magnum"* condom with the wrapper still clenched in her teeth, pleased he deserved such an "honor." His limp dick had been ridiculed for months. Threesomes wasn't the cure, but apparently watching strange men grind on his beautiful wife is. He's fully erect and slowly getting *"lap-fucked,"* while *Ginger's* lap-dancing just a few feet away.

He's watching *Ginger's* every move but feeling every inch of *Crystal's* deep tight center. She's stifling her moans, climaxing all over his *"resurrected"* penis that's so hard it popped the condom. *George's* raw stroke felt too good to stop. His wife was faking a wild-sexual frenzy, while her husband busts the biggest load of his life inside *Crystal's* vagina.

Suddenly security catches the two having sexual intercourse during a lap-dance. His moans gave away their secret transgressions. Flashlights revealed his identity, while he was stumbling to fix his pants. *Ginger* noticed her *"husband"* and her so-called *"friend"* snatched off his hard-raw dick. He came there to bust her in the act of cheating but got caught fucking a stripper during a lap dance.

Ginger is *"shocked!"* He couldn't even get out of bed this morning. The betrayed wife didn't believe her eyes at first. *"Crystal, of all bitches!!!"* said *Ginger* angrily, as she scowled at her new nemesis. *"You fucked my man Bitch? Right in my face?"* She proceeded to leap onto *Crystal's* thin, model-like frame. *Ginger* beat her ass like she stole something. Security let the punishment fit the crime and broke it up after *Ginger* got a few good hits atop her nasty, trifling ass.

"Really George?" Ginger sobbed and ran upstairs, crushed from the embarrassment.

George was helped to his feet as the bright flashlights exposed his adult diaper. Security started laughing. The whole club joined in, *Big Country* announced his humiliation over the mic.

"Take your side bitch to the motel next time diaper boy!" joked the *MC*

Q orders security to throw the *"Stupidest man alive"* out the Club. Security did just what they were told to do and bounced that *"fool"* to the curb... tossed his cripple ass out on his neck!

Outside the Club...

George pulled himself together. He's upset the whole Club made him out to be a ridiculous joke. His pride is on the line now, waiting outside for his wife to rush to be by his side, while growing even more upset watching other *"tricks"* and their *"dates"* roll off to the moonlight together.

The embarrassment weighed heavy on *Ginger's* mind. She couldn't claim her *"distraught"* husband, who's waiting outside in the rain. Not after this betrayal. His miracle to walk, drive and eventually fuck her co-worker didn't move *Ginger.* She's done with his cheating-ass, even though she cheats for a living, putting stranger's *"fingers"* in her *"butt."*

George was obsessed to turn his wife back to the loving woman she used to be. *Ginger's* the enemy now, siding with evil forces at that *"Ghetto-Ass Club."* His *"fine-ass wife"* was snatched-up by the *"devil himself,"* leaving him outside in the cold-ass rain, while entertaining the rowdy crowd inside, letting the *"Old-head"* pop her *"cherry"* for vaginal sex with a *"John."*

Suddenly, *Crystal* busted-out the front door with the help of *Jazzy's* strong pushes, *(the Club's security when they need a female Soldier)* slamming the door on the *"Harlot,"* robbed her of her date money and tips, cussed out by every dancer in the dressing room feeling *Ginger's* pain.

Crystal broke the *"Golden Rule," "never fuck another dancer's man,"* but she's got her own pressing obligations. *George* paid her $250 altogether for the dirty deed. *"They stole my money bag!" Crystal* screamed, banging on the locked Club's front-door. The weather worsened while she waited for an answer.

Storm opened the door to diffuse the situation. *"Clear the front!"* he ordered with a look that spoke for itself. *"I just want my money bag Storm!"* she pleaded, feeling the force of the slammed metal door in her face. The ejected dancer realized, at that moment, she's not going to benefit from breaking the Club's rules. Her pleas, once again, fell on deaf ears. *Crystal* has crossed the line, feeling double-crossed by a freak with the broken condom. Thankfully, the wet rain hid *Crystal's* stained jeans from his *"ooze,"* but in her mind... *"A Bitch Gotta Eat!..."*

CHAPTER SEVEN

"Everybody Ain't Your Friend"

Crystal's stranded in the drenching rain. *George* stood there sobbing with tears being camouflaged by the heavy downpour. He's been standing outside the *Grindstone* for thirty minutes waiting for *Ginger "to come the fuck on!"* said the pissed-off *"Diaper-Boy."*

"I wanna go outside in the rain," by *The Dramatics,* played though the Club's speakers. *George* thinks the disc jockey is playing that song at his own expense. *Big Country* tends to slow down the music towards the end of the night. Either way, the soundtrack played on, while the bright lightning cracked though the pitch-black evening, exposing some real truths in its flash!

"Y'all don't have to go home, but y'all got to get the fuck out of here!" Big Country yelled effectively. The host wanted to end the show early, and he received his achy feet' wish when the *Boss* ordered the closing of the Club with a nod. The last song of the night, *"End of the Road,"* played by *Boys to Men,* and it's dedicated to *"Mr. Huggies standing outside!" Big Country's* naturally clowning this man standing in the rain.

"Although we've come to the end of the road ... still I can't let go, it's unnatural, you belong to me, I belong to you!" The soulful lyrics cascaded all over the room. Various

dancers are still grinding on patrons, whispering in their ears, the digits to their phone numbers. Some are finalizing the details of having sex for a fee, while others are snickering about the *"diaper-boy"* and the *"lap-fucker's"* betrayal of the poor-little *"tricking Ginger."*

Meanwhile in George's Volvo Station wagon...

Crystal accepts George's free ride home. She feels bad about his situation, but quickly remembers pressing concerns of her own. Broke and starving, she asks for a couple of dollars from the busted, cheating husband.

Meanwhile out on the main floor...

George is scared to go home. He didn't want to face the music; his wife's jealousy has visual confirmation. "It wasn't me!" won't be the convenient excuse for this blunder! **"Hell-raiser"** is Ginger's nick-name when gets mad, now stewing in her own emotions waiting for his dumbass to come home.

He needed more time for her temper to cool. Too many raw feelings to sleep safe in their martial bed. "12:01 am." is always the next day, but it's now 4:00 am and George knows better than to "**stir the pot**" by not beating Ginger home. It's his second mistake tonight. He's at another "Go-Go" after-hour waiting for Crystal to finish thinking, "his situation is some bull-shit, compared to Jimmy's plight."

George's wife's "**freaky lap-dance**" vs. Jimmy's girl's sex-capade" made the paranoid-husband realize things can always be worst. He imagined a slow death if his wife fucked 10 dudes, enduring broken condoms filled with the next man's seed. On the other side of the coin, Crystal would die for Jimmy! Screwing for bail money is easy; she's feeling like that's her duty. The "Ride or Die Chick" proved that tonight.

The dimly lit **"date-room"** smelled musty from old leaky water pipes. One 40-watt light-bulb couldn't reveal "what's" waiting for the thin sexpot. Her "date" sat on the twin-size bed with no sheets stroking his **14inch cock!**

Crystal could barely see; she didn't like watching herself in the mirror anyway. She assumed the position and went to her knees. Her seductive oral-sex tease has been working all night. **"Shit got deep,"** when she grabbed his **"meat**."

The massive **"date's"** erection seemed longer than her arm, twice as thick too. The thin-build whore is in serious trouble now, as she couldn't' even stretch her lips around his rock-hard snake. Fear consumed her body when the "**Wiffle-Bat"** rubbed against her clit.

He quickly gagged her mouth with his bandana and tied her up with his du-rag. The creepy **Big-dude** planned this assault. That's why he went last. Like a "Lion" pouncing on a "Gazelle" after being bothered by some "Hyenas," Crystal found herself "Pig-tied" and unable to scream. The "Predator" slowly penetrated his "Prey!"

The last "date" of the evening turned into an evil joke. The punch-line is nowhere near funny. He paid for extra time, "45 minutes," instead of 15 for sex, with his obvious hunger. He wanted to feel each tight inch of the *"nookie,"* while stretching her tightness to its limits.

The vaginal tearing wasn't the horror of the attack. *Crystal* could feel every vein on his *"unprotected shaft!"* her biggest *"pet-peeve,"* shattered with every stroke. The second raw dick tonight, discovering the first mistake and changing out of the milky panties earlier before the first *"date."* Even *Jimmy* straps-up for his precious *"Cookie."*

The raping *"date"* talked dirty to the trapped *"whore."* *Crystal* can't holler rape because she sold the *"Punany."* She can't say she didn't like it, because her *"Punany's"* betrayal started when she got wet, a natural lube to lessen the pain, *"telling signs"* that she needed this *"Dick-Down!"*

The muffled screams were mistaken for *"good-sex"* outside the *"date-room"* door. Everyone in an ear-shot of the *"sexual carnage"* entertained their own lust. *"They getting it in!"* said *Page,* listening to her prissy friend getting demolished by a *"Big-Ole"* Country boy.

The set-up worked perfectly. The scheming *"date"* got the idea from an unknown Columbian dancer. He was told by the sneaky *Nite on Broadway* dancer that *Crystal* likes it rough. *Page* told the naïve *G-stone* dancer to hide her cash. It made sense to have the *"informative"* co-worker hold the large sum of money; the perfect amount for someone who's flying to *Miami Beach* for good in the morning.

Page hatched the diversion during a *"lap-dance"* with the big-dicked bandit; a willing distraction to tie her up and have his way with the bonded *"Freak."*

"Not my style, but Crystal likes that!" said the conniving **"so-called"** friend.

Crystal just closed her eyes and waited for the **"date-room"** buzzer to sound. This would've been music to her ears 10 seconds ago, but she forgot the **"Cocky"** lover bought extra time. The tied-up victim moaned in defeat. The **"duped" "whore"** must endure 30 **"more"** minutes of the vicious pounding. Every unprotected inch slid **"in and out"** of her like an **"oil-drilling pump."**

The rape fantasy wasn't getting a standing ovation. She begged for the punishment to stop with sorrowful eyes and tears of agony. He wanted to ejaculate his seed off inside her. She just wanted the buzzer to alert **N.O.B.'s** security to clear the room.

Page gathered her things in the dressing room. She looked back at the **"date-room"** door and calmly walked outside with **Crystal's "date-money"** and fancy dance outfits, relieved the muffled moans occupied her **"Mark."** Her plan worked. The Colombian vixen robbed her of everything, while **Crystal** was getting pancaked by a huge rapist with the giant **"Dick!"**

The buzzer rang like the bell at a **"Championship Fight."** The urge to finish was triggered by the first knock at the door. **"10 seconds!"** announced the **"date-room"** doorman. **Crystal** feared the worst when his dick got even harder, indicating an explosion was about to come. She tried to make eye contact with the foolish **"John,"** Who likes to fuck **"Raw!"** He doesn't notice the despair on her face, his eyes are closed shut. Nine, Eight, Seven, Six, Five, four, Three, Two,

One…the biggest *"cream-pie"* filled her vaginal cavity, setting off an alarm in her brain.

Crystal passed-out from the fear. Security discovered the mayhem too late. This hasn't been the first time a *"trick"* took off a condom. That's why 15-minute security checks were introduced as Club policy. They dropped the ball on this one, thinking she didn't want to be disturbed. After all, she was the only one *"tricking"* that night with ten customers lined up at the *"date-room"* door. They too heard Jimmy got locked up. Security was letting her do her thing.

A state of *"panic"* set-off in the minds of everybody involved. Nite on Broadway has enough problems. The owner, *"Fishman,"* prayed for the life-less body to regain consciousness. The guilty culprit of the condom-less rape stormed out the room. The trusted *"thief"* has already left for an early flight. They're both left her for dead, thinking of their own selfish needs.

Crystal's awakened by a bucket of ice-water. The shock of a stranger's semen entering her body was too much to take, waking up to a room full of people *"thanking God,"* she's alive. They helped the terrorized *"whore"* to her feet. She thanked them for their late concern. Like a *"strong trooper,"* she looked around the room for her reward. *"Where's Page?"* she asked, when an eerie feeling crept up her spine…robbed by a *"Bitch Who's Really Gotta to Eat!"*

Nite on Broadway decided to close early. The events of the night wore out everybody's patience. They were lucky to end the night without police questions and hospital stays. The buzz in the dressing room was another *"slip-up,"* caused by insufficient security. The whispers of *Page* moving down *"South Beach"* hits closer to home.

Crystal* never saw this coming. *Page* was *"considered a true friend … "Squad even!"* Not knowing *"Karma"* snaps back so quickly, she cried on the shoulders of *Trudy,* the barmaid; the nice-looking, dark-skinned, *"Old-Head"* with "*Submarine-sized"* tits. She's a mother-like-type when things get bad, preaching sobering words of wisdom to fallen *hoes* at the *N.O.B.*

Trudy"* could relate to most betrayals. Being the *"side-jawn"* of the *Fishman* has its own guest-list to a gigantic-sized pity-party. *"These Bitches Ain't Your Friend!"* said *Trudy,* searching in the lost & found box for the naked, naïve *Crystal* some clothes. Common sense rattled the *"illusion of true friendship."* The truth bit her in the ass as she faced the sad reality she's still no closer to her goal.

Crystal* thanked *Trudy* for the mustard-yellow party dress found in the bin. It was probably left after one of their police raids. She would've been *"barefoot and pregnant,"* if *Page* had her wish. The betrayal stung like a bumble-bee sting to the *"clit."* If getting robbed, for the second time tonight, by two so-called friends wasn't the biggest diss, then the semen oozing out her *"snatch,"* from two different men, *"must BE!"*

She's shocked her *"friend," George* decided to stick around when he heard the news. *"Shit like this!"* is why his wife needs a different profession. He couldn't leave until *Crystal* came out of that dressing room. Finally, she emerged safe and sound. *George's* thinking his job is finally done.

George hugged her good-bye and proceeded to go home to face the music. *Ginger* been called, wanting to talk at the house. He promised to be on his way an hour ago, taking the call in the quieter bathroom, lying already about being with another woman.

Crystal needs another ride. Desperate times call for desperate measures. She needs to hit the *"Track."* The *"Hoe-stroll"* is a great *"ATM"* for $40 *"tricks,"* but it's fiercely protected by *"Pimps"* and the *"Po-Po."* One false move can catch you a *"case"* like the *"clap."* Undercover Vice Cops are always looking for *"whores"* that's slipping.

"Jimmy D. Travis" still needs bail money. He's pacing in his cell at *"CFCF,"* tossing and turning on the lower bunk, waiting for his trial in two more days, hoping and praying *Crystal* comes though with the money. Making *"Salat"* not knowing the words, he wishes *"Allah"* sees his heart, despite asking for huge *"Go-Go"* tips for his fornicating girlfriend.

Meanwhile, the *"Tracks"* begin to heat up. It's the perfect time for late-night treats. *George* and *Crystal* headed to the *"Old York Road Strip."* They rode in the black *"Volvo,"* quiet and reserved. *Crystal* broke the awkward silence by revealing her plan. She needs a *"Pimp"* for a day.

She asked *George* to role-play as her *"Procurer"* for *"dates,"* as protection from ejection from the *"Tracks,"* or from being snatched as a *"Pimp's"* selection. All he had to do is look tough, when *"cued,"* and don't give away the fact that he's handicapped. He's barely walking, but he'll have to do. Time is of the essence as *Jimmy's* scheduled to go to court soon. *"It's always better to fight a case as a free man, than a "shackled" prisoner wearing blues,"* taught by *"OG's"* everywhere.

      Crystal had to suck it up. Another $1000 needed to be raised. *"Please George?"* she asked rubbing his genitals while he drives. This sounds more fun than hearing *Ginger* bitch all morning, feels better too, while she's licking his sticky pole with her juices still on it; swerving in and out of driving lanes, she's begging him to *"bust another load."*

      "Don't stop baby" he said, pushing her head down, making her swallow the entire shaft, caressing the tip to the base, moaning and feeling guilty all at once, watching the time on the dashboard, he's falling into his character with every slurp.

      George agreed to play the part and turned his baseball cap backwards, trying to fit in *"again,"* while sticking out like a *"sore-thumb." "Maybe they'll think you're a cop and just leave us alone,"* joked *Crystal* wishing for *"this"* to work, jerking his seed to explode all over the steering wheel.

      This is her last attempt to raise *"Jimmy's bail-money"* tonight. *"It has to work!"* said the desperate *"whore"* itching from dirty, unprotected *"Rape-Sex."* Her inner walls screamed for relief. Vaginal tearing is perceived as a worn-down *"snatch."* Exposure to a dirty *"one-eyed monster"* must wait for clinical determination later.

      Crystal heard the *"Track"* is very different than the Clubs. The *North Philly "Pimps"* are notorious for snatching young girls off the streets, making them *"trick"* for $50 bucks; a hundred for *"Bareback."*

Little did *George* know, they snatched guys too. Any *"fool"* who even thinks they can invade their *"territory"* could get snatched. Imposters got it the worst, dressed up in *"Drag"* like a cheap *"Trick;"* held hostage by gunpoint to fuck. Their fateful mistake was to even try.

The Dynamic Duo pulled up to the block. Luckily for them, the vehicle's headlights didn't draw attention to them; the *"one"* thing they did do right. Station wagons don't turn heads. They sat in the car and watched the slowed-down traffic survey the *"Human Wares"* of the *"Track."*

The *"Street-Walkers"* looked like working bees, buzzing by each passing car, talking nasty, and quoting prices. The sun isn't quite up yet, but when the black night-sky starts to turn blue, the *"tweaking"* hour begins. This is the time when the *"Freaks of the Night"* finish their business. They can't be caught by prying eyes during the morning rush hour traffic. Seizing the moment right before the sun comes up, *Crystal's* plan is working so far.

She wants to *"blend-in"* with the busy *"whores"* on the *Strip,* but forgot, her mustard-yellow outfit glows like the dreaded rising sun. She was instantly noticed talking to *"Johns"* like a *"Bull's Eye"* target at the *"Fair."* The real *"Hookers"* resented the bright yellow *"Imposter,"* and starts whistling their secret code. No one thinks, she's a Cop! They alerted their *"Pimp"* that there's a *"fraud"* in their mist!

The biggest *"Snitch"* for an *"Imposter"* is always a *"Hooker." "Did you think you could come here and make your own money, while we slave every day for our Pimp?"* said the whistling *"trick"* ready to beat this *"Bitch's"* ass.

Crystal played her part, screaming she's authorized to be here. *"By who?"* the *"Hooker"* asked.

The *"Jacked-up"* imposter pointed to her fake *"Pimp,"* waiting in the Black *"Volvo."* Cued to look tough, *George* nervously nodded his head. The unbelievable *"Tough Guy"* got snatched out the car by a real *"Pimp"* named *Serrano;* the same *"Pimp"* that used to terrorize *Mamasita,* before *Q* and *"Charm's"* take-over.

He quickly recognized the *"Canary"* trying to work on his *"Track." Crystal* instantly poured on the charm of an appreciative *"Hooker,"* who just got saved by a real *"Pimp."* He laughed at the irony of the situation, licking his lips at the *"Bargaining Chip"* to get *Mamasita* back!

Serrano and his cronies kidnapped both imposters. They drove up the *"Blvd."* with the tied-up, frantic actors in the trunk, just in time for the sun to come up. *George* and *Crystal* were snatched-up by the *"Game;"* helpless to their clutches, trapped for the bumpy ride over pot holes to the *"Bad Lands."*

They arrived at *Serrano's "Chop-Shop;"* an old garage used to *"plate-up"* stolen cars. His other business made him a *"Mercedes-Benz"* driving *"Baller, Pimping" new whips"* every week giving the impression that *"Pimping is easy."* The fancy car's interior fooled many eager *"Gold-digging hoes"* into his kidnapping grasps.

He must protect his *"Track." "My girls slave out here though rain, sleet or snow!"* said *Serrano* proudly, of his grinding *"Hooker-Squad,"* rarely fleeing... always bringing daddy's *"bread"* home.

The imposters are strung up on the engine crane, handcuffed and chained, pleading for their lives. The *"Fake-Pimp"* quickly downgraded himself as an unpaid *"Hack."* The *"fake-Streetwalker"* is still sticking to her story from earlier, wandering on the wrong side of the *"Track."*

Crystal continued to flip on the helpful *"friend,"* playing the victim of a *"fake-Pimp."* She promised to thank *Serrano* for saving her life with *"oral & anal"* treats. *"Just please let me go!"* cried the *"Canary-Yellow whore."* She's told that her "Grindstone *Boss*" would have to collect his *Squad* member. An even trade for *Mamasita* will be... *"her only path to freedom!"*

George's fate would be more treacherous. *"fake-Pimps"* catch it worse than wandering *hoes.* The *"Diaper-Boy"* is exposed again when the *"Pimp's"* cronies stripped him for punishment. His spoiled diaper happened in the trunk. He's scared shitless, to say the least.

George, for the first time, welcomed his incontinence as a great deterrent from *"Gay Rape!"* He alone embraced his condition, while the *"bi-sexual"* cronies beat him with baseball bats that resulted in another set of broken ribs. *"Bad luck"* with another *"Bitch on the Side."*

"Closed mouths don't get fed! Prove your worth!" hollered *Serrano* trying to jog the memories of the forgetful hostages dangling from the engine crane.

George screamed in agony, begging for the *"Sammy Sosa"* body blows to stop. He shouted his wife's cell number. She's only person that can buy his freedom. He wonders if she'll be as committed as *Crystal* is, to getting her

Jimmy out of jail. Boy, did he wish his wife cared half as much.

       Ginger didn't even answer the phone at first. *George* begged his captors, for hours, to try again. She couldn't believe he had the nerve to even call this late after cheating at the Club. Her annoyed demeanor changed when her husband's phone-call had a different voice on the line. *Serrano* was very believable. No fake *"Gangsta"* here. The *"Real-Deal Gangsta"* needed ransom. *Ginger* needed $5000 for his freedom. Whether it's the nursing paycheck, or the *"Go-Go"* stash. *"You decide!"* threatens the real *"Gangsta"* on the fucking phone, knowing about household secrets inside their home. *"If you call the Cops, we'll kill him!"* promises the intimidating voice, calling the shots, while her husband wails in the background.

       Crystal's forced to watch *George's* beat-down. She trembled in fear, witnessing blood and feces dripping down his naked legs. Her turn is next. Luckily, *Serrano* doesn't want to damage his new *"Bitch,"* But, she needs to be *"Broken-In,"* with a *"Gangbang."*

       "Serrano's" cronies cheered, stripping the *"Canary-Yellow"* dress off with their greasy-mechanic hands, a tasty treat for his arriving *"Chop-Shop"* workers. The *"diabolical-minded Pimp"* thought of a great punishment, offering *"Viagra"* to his willing crew of rapists. Drinking coffee to wash them down was extra motivation for the horny *"savages"* with *"morning wood."*

       Crystal's violently thrown over some used tires, and *"ran-through"* by eight hungry, undocumented, Spanish freaks. She's made to take on *"four"* at a time; jerking *"Dicks"* with both hands and *"Double-Penetration,"* with motor-oil for *"lube."* There's a revolving marathon of group sex, with partners slapping hands to switch positions. None of them cared to *"strap-up."*

The dirty-dick bastards ejaculated their seed in all her holes. They haven't had this much fun since *Mamasita's* gang-banging for coming up short. The Spanish run-away could relate to *Crystal's* pain, but her plight fell on deaf ears when *Crystal* called *Jazzy* for *Q's* number.

The hungry rapists, hyped-up on *"Blue pills"* and coffee, wanted more. They decided to anal-rape the disabled *George,* while the *"Diaper Boy"* screamed in complete Horror. First, the idea was to wash away his stench. It was breaking the mood. The power washer made him soft and clean as newborn baby's ass.

The *"Gay-Rape"* is also lubed-up by motor oil. His attackers didn't think they were *"Gay,"* they were just robbing a *"Grown-Ass"* man of his manhood. Teaching the fallen *"Fake Pimp"* a very important lesson.

"You still want to be a 'Pimp' now nigga?" teased *Serrano,* watching the savages sodomize him on a stack of old tires. The handicapped hostage, too weak to close his mouth, suffered the greatest humiliation ...A *"cum-shot"* to gargle with for trying to be *"slick"* on the *"Track."*

George is cleaned-up by the water hose again and forced to dress up in woman's clothing. The raping kidnappers smeared ridiculous make-up on his face and forced him to walk the *"Track;"* strolling and limping up and down the *"Blvd.,"* until he passed out from the internal bleeding.

Ginger frantically called her husband's phone back, after cashing the paycheck and hitting the *"Go-Go"* stash to pay his ransom. Unfortunately, the pay-off was too late... His Charge Nurse answered his cellphone.

"I'm Sorry to inform you, that your husband is in the I.C.U." said the nurse on the line, informing the worried wife of his critical injuries on his personal cell phone. Brought to the *Einstein Hospital's* emergency room, *George* now clings to life, from the beating and rape from *Serrano's* boys.

Meanwhile back at the "Chop-Shop"...

Crystal's chained to the wall naked. Four-point restraints held the sex-slave for $5 walk-up *"pumps;"* another one of *Serrano's* sadistic ideas he came up with to torture the skinny *"Trick."* They blindfolded the kidnapped *"whore,"* and recorded voice messages to send to *Q* and the rest of the *Crew,* while any dude that wanted to *"bust a Nut,"* ran a never-ending *"Train"* on her.

Serrano and his cronies want *Mamasita* back. *"Maybe not such an even trade"* joked the crazed *"Pimp"* on the phone, while, *Crystal* screams in the background. He's got *Q's* attention Now! "The *Grindstone Boss* had both dancers' lives in his hands. One is being raped by hordes of Spanish rapists deep in the *"Bad lands,"* while the *"other"* hides out at *"Junior*'s" house.

Mamasita's fate lies in the balance. She needs to sway her own captors, who's ordered to watch her every move just in case, they must trade her for *Crystal.* The situation is intense for the Spanish runaway, needing the **G-stone Crew** to choose her over the trapped hostage, already being raped. **Mamasita** sparked their sexual interest weeks ago. **Junior** and his roommates been fucking the impressionable ex-hooker for over a week now. They shared the Spanish concubine; passing her around like a *"blunt."*

Another *"orgy"* involved **Junior** and his two roommates, **Anwar** and **Boo,** who, despite **Mamasita's** shady past, ate her *"Punany"* like a *"Krimpet,"* and started falling in love with their in-house *"whore."*

Anwar used to be the **Grindstone's** bartender, until **Charmaine** showed up. His high school *"crush"* was supposed to leave **Munchie** for his *"back-stabbing ass."* Instead, she chose the **Boss** over the wimpy *"bartender"* with the *"Hook-up."* He got himself fired over spreading *"vicious"* lies about the *"Old-Head Pimp"* at the **G-Stone,** who's learning quickly, *"Everybody Ain't Your Friend,"* hearing about **Anwar's** jealousy and envy going on behind his back. Out of respect for **Charmaine, Anwar** was spared from a vicious *"Beat-down,"* slightly keeping them in the *"Game,"* by housing this Spanish run-away.

Boo is another *"hater"* talking *"shit;"* unable to keep his *"baby-feelings"* out the workplace. He's just another *"flunky"* for **Charmaine;** angry that his lies got his ass fired, and jealous of **Junior's** still being in the good-graces of the new *"Power couple,"* but forced to move in with **June Bug** because of his recent unemployment.

Charmaine's flunkies were all over the place mentally. One-minute they're plotting against her employer, the next minute they're helping the *"Power couple"* hide a run-away prostitute. *Mamasita* is a money-maker on the *"Track."*

       "The Bitch got two left feet at the Club!" said *Charmaine,* trying understand why this *"Puerto Potty"* doesn't have more rhythm. Bottom-line is, she was a *"New-Jack,"* earning pennies at the Club. It wasn't even worth taking fifty percent. As a woman, *Charmaine* didn't have the stomach for trading *"Tricks,"* but knowing *Crystal* is *Squad,* she's hoping both these chicks get it together.

       The *"Trio of Flunkies"* washed their faces with her *"Spanish-snatch"* every day, all week; *Mamasita's* trigger for having sex with the naïve, teen-aged flunkies. They're having a ball with the *"live-in hoe."* Fighting and arguing to snuggle up with her in the spoon position, strained their friendships.

       Mamasita was *"their"* girlfriend by the end of the week, sleeping with each friend every night, together and separately. She slowly influenced their minds, thinking her plan was working in her favor, every time they fought. She's living her *"Nympho-Fantasy"* with three guys, secretly *"burning"* every *"one"* of them with *"Gonorrhea;"* a parting "gift" from the Spanish guys at the *"Chop-Shop."*

       The foolish flunkies turned on their girlfriend real quick, when their symptoms kicked in with swollen glands. They could barely swallow with their enflamed throats, while *Junior* strained, pissing *"razor-blades!"* Screaming at the sight of his own blood in the toilet bowl.

The diseased *"trick"* got the last laugh, walking out the house that imprisoned her, while the flunkies graveled from pain on the floor. *Mamasita* walked over her ailing, so-called boyfriends like a *"Praying Mantis."* The fleeing *"whore"* looked at her fever-ridden counter-parts like they suffered from the *"Plague."* The foolish young boys wished they gave *Serrano* his *"Bitch"* back! instead of hiding her out for *"Charmazinn."* Duped by both, they wallowed in the searing pain of *Mamasita's* outbreak. Fooled by *Charmaine,* to hide the *"Dirty-Trick"* from *Serrano's* grasp.

The *"Domino-Effect"* caused problems at the *Grindstone.* Word of the *"venereal disease"* impacted some of the VIP clients from the Club. Affected *"High-Rollers"* blamed the Club, instead of their stupidity for eating her out. The *"Blow-back"* from the rotten *"snatch"* hurt the Club's reputation; not to mention its revenues. *"Ballers"* screamed for justice with hospital bandages wrapped around their throats, blaming *Q* for not having cleaner *hoes,* shamed by the infectious *"coochie"* of *Mamasita.* Now, he's ready to trade the flunkies' *"whore"* for the dancing *Squad* Member.

Anwar suffered the most. He's a babysitter in the day-time for a family living on his block. They trusted the young man to watch their 8-year-old son while they worked 9 to 5 on the grind. Secretly, *Anwar'"* been *priming* the kid, watching pornos with the pre-adolescent, spinning his mind away from cartoons, and washing him up with hour-long *"shared"* baths, using his bare molesting hands as the rag.

He's been rubbing his genitals against the baby skin for years. When he contracted *"Gonorrhea"* from *Mamasita, Anwar* passed it to the young boy that he baby-sits

5 days a week. Now, the child has a serious infection on his rear end.

The parents called the police after the pediatrician told them their 8-year-old son has a *"sexually-transmitted"* disease, and that the *"culprit"* didn't penetrate the kid. The lack of DNA evidence on his young body made everybody a suspect. All the pieces came together when the police found *Anwar* rolling on the floor with his *"Wrecking Crew"* at their bachelor crib. They're a welcome sight when *"Philly's Finest"* appeared at the front-door of the duplex, thinking the neighbors called them hearing their screams of agony, but they were breaking in to serve a warrant on the screaming recipient, ... and arrested *"Mr. Anwar Simmons"* on the spot. Ultimately, he received 10 years in prison, lying every day, about touching the boy.

Back at the Serrano's "Chop-Shop"...

Crystal's plight continued to go on. It's been a week since the kidnapping took place. She wondered if the *Grindstone Crew* even cared. The bonded *"whore* envisioned laughter at her expense. Getting caught by security at the Club should've *Squad.*

Serrano's only feeding his hostages bread and water. A wicked reminder for *"hookers"* stopping by the *"Chop-Shop"* to pay their $1000 daily quota. The hardened sex-slaves felt sorry for *Crystal's* plight and even the snitching *"hooker"* from the *"Track"* had to question her *"Pimp's"* methods.

"Crystal's crucifixion," on display for everybody to see, resembled the same *"Biblical"* affliction of *"Jesus"* dying for **Mamasita's** sins, reminding *"Serrano's"* *"hookers"* of what can happen, if you wrong the mighty *"Pimp."*

The **G-Stone Crew** would've traded the *"burning hooker"* for **Crystal,** but **Mamasita** was gone! She wasn't feeling the deal. The Spanish *"whore"* was now on the run, while the *"slick-dancer"* gets her asshole ripped out of place.

Quintin and **Storm** visited **George** in the hospital. They needed him to remember where they had held him. Any clue that he can come up with could help. **Ginger** held his weakened hand as he tries to think of any landmarks to describe.

George remembered one thing. The sign above the garage that read: *"Pimp Out Rides."*

The recollections manifested his uncontrolled seizures. **George's** nightmare consumed his mind, he stroked-out from pure fear. **Ginger** screamed for the medical staff to save his life, but he died in the arms of his *"forgiving wife,"* begging for **Quintin** and **Storm** to right this wrong. They vowed to find the culprits that did this, and to find **Crystal.**

The hospital staff cleared the room, so they can transport the body to the morgue's cooler downstairs. The nurses admired the fine specimen of a man, taken from this earth too soon. Most of the single staff could feel his wife's pain, losing a pretty-boy like that with a rock-hard *"schlong."*

Ginger had forgotten how handsome her husband was, arguing all the time, instead of flattering the hunk with the curly waves. She had forgotten how accomplished he was, greeting his co-workers from the railroad. Storming the hospital with grief and concern, she, being the widowed wife to countless family and familiar friends, is listening to whispers of his male cousins joking about *George's "Mistress"* in the waiting room.

Quintin and **Storm** had to switch to security detail, breaking up **the "girl-fight,"** while escorting **Ginger** to her car. Police arrested the **"Mistress,"** who's waiting for information about the whereabouts of her boyfriend. The aggravated assault from 2 years ago, just upgraded to homicide in an instant, because of lies from the **"grieving wife's"** accusations who knows the **"real"** truth.

Ginger knows **Serrano** killed her husband, but pointed the finger in the wrong direction, out of spite, blaming the **"Mistress"** arguing in the waiting room who announced she's 5-months pregnant with **George's** baby.

The drama continues to roll in, watching the paramedics bring in the dying **Crystal,** who was released from captivity by the **"whistling-whore"** from the **"Track." "Hershey Kisses"** risked life in itself to save the **"imposter."** It's just a matter of time until they figure out who saved her. Now she needs protection, clinging to **Quintin's** sleeve, begging for help from the **Grindstone Crew** against **Serrano.**

Tonya **"Hershey Kisses" Douglas,** is a darkly-packed, bodacious, rump-shaker, half-way cute **"hooker"** who may have saved **Crystal's** life. Visions of this sad thing strung up on the wall, crucified as **Serrano's** sadistic joke, shook the very essence of her soul, thinking **Crystal's** death would leave blood on her hands as well. Haunting dreams awakened *Hershey Kisses"* commanding her to save that woman's life!

She stole *Serrano's* key-ring during his daily *"tune-up."* He loves to bury *Hershey's* head in his lap, choking his property with his heavy seed. She's skilled in *"chroming domes,"* waiting for the *"Colombian Green Giant"* to fall asleep, escaping with the padlock key to the back door.

She returned this Sunday morning to *Serrano's* *"Chop-Shop,"* possessed with saving the impaled hostage from the *"Pimp's"* grasps, capitalizing on *Serrano's* his weekly ritual of taking his 90-year-old abuela to the *"Roman Catholic Church"* on *25th & Allegheny,* sitting in *"Mass"* wearing his late-father's *"crucifix,"* without any shame that *Crystal's* impaled on his garage's wall.

Crystal's affliction is being guarded by two *"rottweilers" called "Two the Hard way."* They've smelled her before, thanks to the daily visits to the shop, slightly growling when she unlocked the back door. She smartly brought two *"Quarter-pounders"* from *"McDonald's"* to draw off their attack. Limping out the back door, they both escaped while secretly being video-taped by *Serrano's* security cameras.

The *G-stone* duo eventually hid her in one of *Q's* family rooming houses.

At the hospital...

Ginger felt no sympathy for the arrested pregnant *"Mistress,"* or the dying betraying *"friend"* in the Trauma Room. They're two *"Bitches,"* in her eyes, who tried to take her man away and got caught-up in a *"that's what a bitch gets"* situation, and she's not giving two fucks!...driving away in the moonlight in her luxury sedan.

Crystal's in critical condition. *Storm* and *Quintin* stayed by her side until her family arrived. Only her sister knew who they were. She remembered them from the few nights she danced at the *Grindstone,* trying to get some money for an abortion. She thanked them for calling the family. They'd been looking for their loved one for weeks. Now, they're praying that she makes it though her insidious ordeal alive.

She seemed to hold on for her one-true love, *Jimmy."* The judge dropped his bail because the victim didn't show. He rushed to her side when he got the call, knowing she was in those streets for him, trying to raise his bail money, blown away hearing she's been brutally raped.

The police is very interested in the both cases, remembering *George's* beat-down 2 years ago at *Genesis,* a Jamaican Reggae spot *"Uptown." George* identified his attacker of being his *"Mistress's"* baby-father, *Big Phil, Ny'sha's* husband, who's secretly been out of jail for a week.

Later at the Grindstone...

Q and *Ny'sha* watched the clock, anticipating a time to finish their conversation, observing all the remaining patrons and dancers leave, one by one. She's thankful *Jazzy* took off with a *"date,"* promising to meet up with her new roommate in the morning. *Jazzy* and *Felisha* have recently moved into **Ny'sha's** apartment, free-loading on her giving-nature for these so-called **hoes.**

"If your girl only knew," by **Aaliyah,** played in the upstairs' CD player at the Club. The random tracks provided their own personal soundtrack to their conversation. The pair laughed at **Jazzy's** embellished stories, but, **Jazzy's** the furthest thing on his mind inside the empty after-hour.

Watching his new chattering *"friend"* gossip about his reputation, **Ny'sha** confessed every lie that she was told to dissuade her from wanting him. She gleamed with appreciation for his attention. He's seriously checking her out, lost in each other's eyes, **Q-Deezy's** complimenting every curve on her body, knowing flattery is a very effective tool.

"Your thicker than a snicker!" he said licking his lips, kissing the talkative little spy with passion. He wanted her to know how sexy she is. The horny dancing vixen hasn't been touched romantically in years. **Ny'sha** welcomed **Q-Deezy's** advances. This wasn't like the few *"dates"* she's had trying to feed her hungry babies. This was personal.

She almost forgot how it felt to be wanted. Sleeping in the same bed with her children prevented this kind of affection. **Ny'sha's** free to explore her sexual desires for once. Being touched all over sent her into a relaxed, euphoric state, when she abruptly stopped.

"How's Charmaine?" she asked, pushing away from her horny **Boss**. He didn't know she knew about his *"main girl."* They were on a break. *"She quit!"* he lied thinking, his girlfriend's days were numbered. **Charmaine's** immaturity

was straining their relationship. He needed a grown ass woman; Tonight.

"She is your girl, right?" she asked trying to sabotage her own selfish desires. *Ny'sha* doesn't like drama. She has enough of that in her life already. Her thoughts battled with inner sexual inhibitions, free at this moment, if only for days, her better judgement didn't prevail. *"Nice & Slow"* by **Usher** played, while *Q-Deezy's* rubbing his engorged penis against her body.

"I'll freak you right...I will," **Usher's** lyrics echoed in her ears, wanting to do something freaky. She's receptive to his demands. *"Turn your ass around and stick it out,"* he instructed his willing lover. *Ny'sha* didn't care if this is a one-night stand. The opportunity presented itself and they will not be denied.

Ny'sha's ass has plenty of *"cake,"* wonderfully stacked, ready for that *"doggie-style,"* looking like a music video vixen, still wearing a *"Go-Go"* outfit, backing that *"thang"* up like it's her **Boss's** birthday. Her tight, juicy pussy needed that thick long dick like an *"addict"* hooked on the very first *"fix."*

The pretty young thing *"Rocked his World"* as *Michael Jackson's* song played in the background. They pumped each other on beat, starting a sexual contest. They both wanted to *"whip"* the other, sweat glistening all over, pounding their bodies like the sea crashing against rocks on the shore. *"Give me more,"* she whispers, never wanting this moment to end, then the unspeakable happens... *"Boom,"*

Ny'sha didn't think she could have orgasm. In the past, she would come close, but no cigar. This sexual episode included several. Not comprehending these new sensations, fear consumed her mind trying to figure out why she's busting nut after nut. Orgasmic shock-waves were being felt, tunneling his manhood in her sweet spot.

Big Phil was once her sexual *"plight."* He thought *"he"* alone satisfied the enlightened sexpot. His memory dissipated with every long glorious stroke, amazed by her body's betrayal. The sex-deprived *Ny'sha* played it tough, but deep inside she's way out of her league.

She was used to *"eating off the garbage can top"* in terms of love-making, finding herself cringing from exposure to her husband's infidelities just 18 months ago, shielding her life with a condom. Holy matrimony with her husband was a distant memory.

Ny'sha didn't like doing sexual chores intended for her husband, the *"male whore."* She's loving the luxury of having an opportunity to *"even the score,"* by having sneaky sex with her *Boss.* Payback would cut like a knife if *Big Phil* ever found out that her *Boss* is smacking that bodacious ass right now, making her wail in ecstasy from every orgasm. She stopped counting them after 10.

"You sure 'Charm' is leaving a stroke like that?" she said, laying in the bed, out of breath, trying to catch her second wind during the marathon of unbridled bliss. Her legs shook uncontrollably with a tear running down her face, wishing to do this again before the first tastes were even over. Doubting her drama would never be evicted from her life, *Ny'sha* savored the moment, holding back the biggest orgasm of them all.

Suddenly, they heard footsteps running up the steps. *Big Country* and another *Squad* dancer named *Emotions* snuck back to the Club, planning to use the same *"date-room,"* not knowing it's already being occupied.

Emotions is a neighborhood *hoe* turned into a ghetto *"Go-Go"* dancer. She's a brown-skinned, slightly out-of-shape *"Mud-duck,"* best known for her exotic show smoking cigarettes with her vagina. She's a very loud, ignorant woman, becoming *Squad* long ago, spreading word about the Club, when it first opened.

Tonight, she's *Big Country's* late-night pick. The other dancers had more lucrative *"dates"* with real *"Ballers."* *Emotions* found herself passed over, like most nights, because she's always drunk. Now, the *"Mud-duck"* is staggering in the room, crashing *Q* and *Ny'sha's* private party.

They had their own sneaky plans. Neither intruder expected to witness *Ny'sha* riding the *Boss'* dick. Screams from the back bedroom should've been a clue. *Emotions* was too busy making sure *Big Country* had the money they agreed upon, but he was only willing to pay for a bag of *Junior's* coke.

Big Country thought it was his homeboy, *Junior,* occupying the back bedroom, eager to join his punkish friend's private party. Instead, he interrupted right before *Q* busted his nut.

"My bad dawg!" *Big Country* said expressing his deepest apologies. The first apology was for interrupting him, and the second, was allowing a blood relative of *Charmaine's* to witness the cheating carnage.

"You're cheating on my Cousin?" she asked, while her crack infested mind pondered how to turn this information into cash, because *"This Bitch Gotta Eat Too!.."*

CHAPTER EIGHT
"Get-Ready, Don't Beat Ready"

Emotions' discovery was only fate in *Ny'sha's* mind. Karma was invented for times like this. *Ny'sha* felt no different than the *"whores"* that used to fuck her husband, while she worked.

Big Phil was notorious for bringing his mistresses back to their home. She felt no better than the *"home wreckers"* that she fought for disrespecting her. "*Who fucks a married man in his wife's bed?"* she thought, every time she tried to understand the stupidity of the women her husband chose.

Ny'sha's on the other side of the coin this time around. She's the distraction stealing another woman's joy. He's caught red-handed, cheating on *Emotions'* beautiful cousin."

"Charm isn't going to like this homeboy!" confessed *Emotions,* adding up all his secrets; looking *Ny'sha* up and down, as she jumps off *Q* and runs to the bathroom to hide.

Emotions knew about *Jazzy* too. She's tallying the score, wanting to strike a *"deal"* for her silence. Her dislike for her own cousin multiplied, because of her own desires for the *Boss*. She never told her cousin, *Charmaine,* about *Jazzy* because her evidence was only a rumor. *Emotions* wasn't into *"he-said, she-said,"* but this time, she witnessed the betrayal with her own eyes.

She figured, her cousin's man just couldn't help himself. He's always around an unlimited supply of naked ass for sale. All she wants is her *"cut."* Secrets about his fetish for prostitutes would be kept secret…for a price.

"I don't want your money!" confessed *Emotions,* wanting to sell her man's drugs in the *Grindstone. "We don't sell crack!"* he said, with a nervous laugh. *"We sell the crack of women's asses!" Big Country* humorously snapped back.

Q didn't want to add drug dealing to his criminal record. This was the reason he was in the *"Go-Go"* business in the first place. He didn't like the clientele. He traded crackheads for dancing tricks years ago.

Emotions pleaded, her drug dealing boyfriend's case. His name is *Bugg,* a 6 ft. tall, big, fat, black, 25-year-old hustler from the neighborhood. People said he resembled the Brooklyn rap artist," *Biggie Smalls.*

The famous *"rapper's"* verse describes *Gregory Bugg Williams* to a tee.

"Heart-throb never… black and ugly as ever, however, I stay Gucci down, the socks, rings and watch filled with rocks"

Bugg asked, a year ago, if he could set-up shop at the *Grindstone.* Back then, the *Crew* was sharing one-dollar hoagies from the *"Poppy Store,"* but they still didn't take his offer; now, they were making *"G's"* and their answer would still be *"No!"*

"Well why you let Junior sell packs then?" snitched *Emotions.* She was blowing the whistle on *Junior's* apparent drug empire. He's only *"bumping"* off an *"eight-ball,"* at best. His meager weight wasn't turning any heads. *Junior* received the *Boss'* blessing months ago. He was a highlight to a heated party. *Bugg's* would be a hostile takeover.

Bugg and his brother *Black* ran the dope around the neighborhood. They're regular customers at the Club, with deep pockets, making their rivals buy their weight from them. When *"Street-Hustlers"* come up missing, the people of the neighborhood usually blamed those two. Their mysterious trips to the *"Asbestos Fields,"* took away too many mourning families the honor of burying their own dead.

Q knew better than to return to the dope *"Game."* He felt it wasn't for him; his current situation was enough. *"I'm good,"* he said thinking.

"Why Emotions?" She's beneath the drug dealer's taste for women. Even his baby-mama looked better than this *"Mud-duck."*

"What's the end game?" thought *Q,* wondering if she was sent to infiltrate his *Crew;* she was directed to spy on their weaknesses. She had him *"by the balls,"* with this secretive intel. The smell of black-mail was in the air if he didn't, at least, *"reconsider"* *Bugg's* offer. He was feeling trapped to decide right there on the spot, while she played like a queen on a chess board for her *"Big-Black King."*

Ny'sha came back out to grab her clothes, then awkwardly excused herself, wondering if *Emotions* is going to tell *"Jazzy*." She didn't need a love triangle, while making all the money she could, before *Big Phil's* return.

"Can we do some business?" asked the *Mud-duck,* looking like a Pitbull ready to pounce, wanting to deliver a favorable agreement between the *Grindstone,* and her murderous boyfriend.

"We all got secrets" warned the naked *Boss*. He stood up with his half-hard dick. *Emotions* is detracted by his manhood, that dangled exposed. *Big Country* went downstairs to lock the door behind *Ny'sha.* Little did she know *Big Phil* was standing outside the *Grindstone,* waiting for her.

Back upstairs...

Emotions tried to touch his erect tool. *"No touching baby,"* said *Q.* He knew to prolong the illusion. She was reduced to an unwanted sex-hound, begging for a *"feel."*

"Thought you had a man?" he asked, slowly getting dressed, teasing the *Mud-duck,* accusing *Emotions* of cheating with *Big Country,* as a late-night treat.

"I'm just one of Bugg's Bitches!" she answered, knowing a girl has needs. *Bugg* didn't touched her much. They had a verbal agreement, *"repping"* their relationship for *"Street Cred,"* to sell his drugs in exotic Clubs across the city, *"tricking"* with whomever she wanted, as long she brings his money *"back"* like a *"Running back."*

Q felt like one of his dancers selling a fantasy to an unwanted *"trick."* *Emotions* had to admit, she was a little jealous seeing him with the Trinidadian vixen *Ny'sha,* who's now being ruffed up and dragged by her husband, *Big Phil.* She was contemplating a more personal trade for her *"hushed words."* Seeing *Q-Deezy* stroking the orgasmic thick dancer stirred something inside *Emotions.*

The horny *"Mud-duck"* wanted that work she observed him doing to *Ny'sha.* This was inspired by his peep-show; now, she wanted to suck that big-cock. She didn't care that he just fucked his secret lover. They couldn't have finished their fun; there wasn't any semen in the condom wrapped around his exposed shaft.

He didn't want to play this game, moving around the bedroom like a matador, dodging the bull-shit, from an acne-riddled *"Hood-rat."*

Meanwhile, *Ny'sha* arrives home and has to face the music for not having any panties on, and just like *Q-Deezy,* she has to play matador to the bull-shit. *Big Phil* is home now, purposely trying to impregnate his wife with prison balls. He's thinking, impregnating her for the fifth time would shut this new freedom down, not knowing she's already pregnant by the male erotic dancer on the side.

Back at the Club…

Emotions needed satisfaction quickly before the window of opportunity closes. *Big Country* stayed downstairs to allow, them time to negotiate their deal. He drank a shot of *"Henny"* to ease his mind, staying out their conversation, having nothing to do with this ambush, thinking unemployment was eminent for cornering his **Boss** with **Bugg's** messenger.

The aggressive, groping hands were rough from burning her finger-tips off with hot **"straights,"** *(nobody knew about her secret habit)...* **Q-Deezy** needed security, not a blow-job.

"Why you tricking anyway?" she asked in disgust, admiring his sexiness. **Charmaine** didn't share stories with her groping cousin. **Emotions** could only imagine how good his stoke is.

"Fuck me or I'm telling my cousin!" threatened the aggressive **"Mud-duck."** Her desperate cries seemed like a foreign language to her. Men don't turn-down her **"monster"** sucking skills. She makes good money pleasing her **"tricks."**

"Why you don't want me?" whined the neighborhood **hoe. Emotions** played herself, exposing her hand like a **"novice"** playing poker, **"bluffing"** to tell, got eclipsed by her own actions.

"I won't tell, if you don't tell," he said, knowing **"Charm"** wouldn't believe her over him. She vowed to tell her drug-dealing boyfriend the bad news though... **"No Deal"** on any level.

That **"threat"** was very real! Fueled by her vindictiveness. The scolding looks on her face told it all, the hairs on the back of his neck did the same, knowing the **"truth"** would be twisted... and wars have been fought in the **Hood** for less!

The next day...

  Bugg's relaxing in his criminal head-quarters, which is a converted 10-unit apartment building and the nucleus of an elaborate cocaine distribution operation called the ***"Factory."*** It houses armed Soldiers to protect his profits, and a crack-lab filled with the best ***"cookers"*** in the ***"Game,"*** punching time-clocks, on all 3 shifts, supplying the ***Strip*** with any drug.

  Emotions couldn't wait to report the bad news. ***Bugg*** and his dancing ***"whore"*** cooked-up this scheme months ago. They devised to take-over all the black ***"Go-Go"*** spots in the city. Inside these Clubs are safer than the street corners.

  The ***Grindstone*** is on the ***Strip,*** at a prime location, to compete with ***Cherokee's*** dope-sales numbers, double-crossing their clientele by supplying rivals in their face across the street.

  Bugg was being nice when he asked the first time, giving the ***G-stone*** a pass. His admiration for the ex-radio personality is wearing thin, compounded with the fact that the club had a new partner, ***Quintin***.

  He knows how the ***Brotherhood*** gets down. Devoted Soldiers are equivalent to suicide bombers. The Club's drug take-over would need a slicker approach. ***"BBO"*** is unwanted ***"Beef"*** in any weather.

  The anxious crack dealer sat down his spying ***"Mud-duck,"*** eager to hear about agreements made, or settling for a weakness to exploit. The frazzled freak sat silent, waiting for an offered shot of ***Bacardi 151 Rum.*** He even politely lit her ***Newport***.

Bugg's baby-mama is sitting in the dining room counting drug-money. *Emotions* nodded her head to the *Queen* of the fortress. Showing respect was a must or feel the wrath of a crazy *Bitch!*

Queen's a caramel-complexion, big-breasted woman, with a small waist. She has an hour-glass shape with a fat ass. As the *First-lady* of his empire, *Raina "Queen" Smith* never cared about his indiscretions on the side. At a moment's notice, she'll fuck whomever *Bugg* chooses, for pleasure to profits. He knows *"Everybody has a price, and a vice too."*

Emotions drank her drink; the brown liquor scorched her throat. *Queen* rolled her eyes when *Bugg* leaped to fetch *Emotions* some water. He never jumps like that for her, enthusiasm wasn't sexual in nature. Information to infiltrate the *Grindstone* took his attention, not the *"Mud-duck."* Either way, *Queen* doesn't like his so-called home-girl.

The *"Bottom-Bitch"* could care-less about *Queen's* insecurity right now. She has one mission and that's to egg her man's ambition to conquer the *Grindstone.* She started sharing stories of *Junior's* meager *"8-ball,"* to the *Boss'* awkward situation of being caught red-handedly, cheating on her cousin; then flipping the story on the *"sexual assault,"* playing the victim, blaming the *G-stone Boss* for having disrespectful hands...

Her lies went on and on. She told twisted stories of how he disrespected him as a man, teasing his *"mediocre"* operation. This touched his *"baby feelings,"* getting clowned by a man he once admired. *"Rep"* means everything in this *"Game."*

Queen burst out laughing. The Bahamian girl-friend was listening from the dining room table. She knew best, after 8 years, that *Bugg* never asks, he just takes. Busting shots to earn his position. *"Mediocre Never!"* His operation was making *"50-Grand"* a week. You couldn't tell him shit about this *"Paper!"*

Emotions stirred the pot of deceit with the biggest lie of all, saying that the *"Go-Go"* Club owner raped her for being his messenger, and she was robbed of her *"date"* money and tips. She kept it going, saying the big bad wolf of the *Grindstone* made her cry fake tears, and she now needs cash for her hungry babies at home. *Bugg* handed her $300 for her troubles, a small price to pay for enduring anal rape. The humbled liar hobbled to the door, thanking *Bugg* for the funds.

Perceptions got clouded by *Queen's* laughter and *Emotions'* tears. The lies rang in his ears like a shot-gun blast. It was on! His baby-mama reminded him to rule his *Strip,* pumping his heart-up calling him the *"Don of the Deuce,"* jingling her fat ass, only for a "*BOSS*."

"If you want it... then take it!" said the orchestrating *Queen.* She loved when *Bugg* got *"Gangsta!"* Caution wasn't being sought by his *"Crew of the Operation"* neither. They didn't give a fuck about the *Brotherhood,* or the *Grindstone.*

The young, ruthless *"crew"* was getting tired of the peaceful approach. They felt *Emotions'* pain, acknowledging she was paid the lowest *"Diss,"* being *"raped in the ass"* as a messenger, and told to run back to the *"crew"* that sent you. Bleeding out the *"butt"* have snatched the pride of many on the **Strip.**

Bugg's **"Street-Cred"** suffered a devastating blow. Playing back **Emotions'** story in his head, he'd smoked and partied with the **G-Stone Crew** many nights, and never felt any animosity. There was nothing but love and respect. He sat, wondering how to handle his new projected enemy.

The **"Round-table,"** with the young brothers at the **Operation,** included discussions of a fearless war with the **Brotherhood,** not knowing their clout and their **"Rep."** Grindstone's a new-jack to *"their"* murderous pass, joining forces when **Quintin** became a partner. Props on the **Strip** are always paid in blood.

Bugg's brother, **Black,** sat quietly as the **"Youngins"** of the **Operation** spoke. They cocked their 9mm pistols to make a point. Anybody can bleed. **Black's** a quiet assassin to whomever opposes him. He's a 5ft. 9in., slender, dark-skinned **"Gangsta."** This hot-head doesn't need muscles to shoot his **"Tec-9!"** With 32 bullets in the clip held steadily in his hand, he doesn't need accuracy for his over-killing rampages!

Jerome "Black" Williams is the Enforcer for the **Operation.** He's the Collector of his family's business debts; the Equalizer of all their **"Beefs."** The fearless assassin fooled many, with his quiet demeanor, but his victims understood the **"Operation's"** threats are deadly and real, spraying rivals' **"Trap-houses"** like target practice; secretly a **"mixologist"** of **"fire-bombing"** cocktails served straight up to the front door!

"Killers respect Killers, Soft "Niggas" respect "Fear." Burning babies keep things in the right perspective. *"Don't Fuck Wit' The Operation!"*

"If you ain't about that life! Stay out that 'Game!'" was chanted by brothers who've sold their souls to the *"devil,"* banging on the round-table, thirsty for another taste of blood, breathing in the fumes from the factory's cooking lab, where the *"Peruvian-Cooks"* manufacture the *Operation's* dope, the second-hand vapors were from cocaine turning into crack. The toxic gases from the embalming fluid for the *"Sherm-Sticks"* stunk the most.

Black allowed his Soldiers to smoke the *"PCP"* dipped cigarettes, sending the crazed, enraged bunch over the edge like wild dogs, snapping at anybody against the *Operation,* carefully restrained by *Black* on a very short leash, while *Bugg* leaves the serpents in his clique alone to slither amongst themselves, closing his private door on the *"basket of snakes."*

Queen's waiting in the living room, wearing only boy shorts, that looks like thongs, because her ass swallowed them whole. She's sitting on the suede, two-seat sofa sipping on *"Taylor's Port."* The late 30-something *Queen's* been patiently waiting for *"Buggy"* to tear her *"Ass"* up; wanting to suck the *"Fat Man's'"* manhood with her bubble-lips.

"Not Right Now Raina!!!" shouted the frustrated *Bugg,* stressing over the wild ass *"Sherm-Heads"* in the garage, leaving the *"Coco-Puff Queen"* stewing in her own juices. Once again, the younger *Bugg* doesn't want to have sex with his *Queen.*

Later that night at the *Grindstone*…

Bugg arrived to the *"Go-Go"* spot in his *Lexus GS 400.* He put the *"all-out"* war on pause. Deep down, he didn't believe *Q* raped *Emotions*. *Black* backed his brother's decision. *Bugg* had to find out if the *Grindstone* declared war.

The over-weight drug dealer approached the Club's front door. *Bugg's* one of the first *"Ballers"* to support the *"Go-Go"* spot. *Storm* and *Big Gene* were posted at the entrance, ready to search everyone who enters. Security is tightened, mandated by *Quintin.* Word on the street, rumors are going around that *Emotions'* been disrespected by *"somebody"* at the *Grindstone.*

Back at his Fortress, *Queen* is his lady. On the *"Go-Go"* scene, *Emotions* is his *"Bottom-Bitch!"*

"Houston, we have a problem!" said *Bugg,* wondering why *Big Gene* wanted to frisk him. He used to have the privilege to carry a fire-arm in the Club. Those days are over since *Quintin's* arrival.

"Storm get your man!" said the disrespected dope dealer. *"I can hold it for you,"* suggested the tired *"H.N.I.C"* of the front door. New Rules are for *"All"* patrons, no exceptions. *Bugg* put his 45 Caliber *"Ruger"* inside the trunk of his *Lexus.* His *"side-kick"* did the same, right next to an *"Ak-47,"* also in the car, with a 100-round clip attached.

Bugg's "Enyce" velour sweat suit hid his *32 Cal.* pistol well. *Big Gene* missed it during the second search. *Bugg* clowned him on the spot, pulling it out and then handing it to

Storm to hold, exposing the amateur's searching skills, wondering what all the fuss was about. *"You Can't Search!"* snapped *Bugg,* talking tough to the *"dude"* who has the primitive searching skills.

Big Gene felt like his face got egged on Halloween, during the awkward stare-down between them, fueling more disturbing thoughts by the *"Big Bad Bugg,"* assuming maybe the new *"Beef"* is just good old fashion *"Set-Tripping,"* when dumb-ass *"Nigga's"* forget their place.

The visiting drug dealer joined *Q* at a VIP table upstairs. He wasn't glad to see him, thinking he already knew what the *"Gangsta"* wanted. His facial expression told it all. *Emotions' "Spin-Cycle"* was in full-effect. Once again, the truth got swept away with the most vicious lies.

"What's up Dawg" said *Q* with a fake smile.

Bugg's bad mood is blamed on *Big Gene's* weak body search. Rumors about *Emotions* didn't even enter their conversation. He wanted to analyze his movements. *Bugg* knew *Emotions* is a *"puzzle."* The worst part is... *"all the pieces ain't even in the box."*

The elephant in the room sat reserved. Deep down, there's kindred spirits with the whole *Crew. Bugg* went to high school with *Q* and *Storm.* They never noticed, with so many school days compromised. The drug dealer would rather *"slang"* than *"sang"* at their musical alma mater. He was a fixture around the playgrounds. Simply put... everybody knew *Bugg.*

He never *"welshed"* on a tab or a bet at the *Grindstone.* He gained 100 lbs. on *Mrs. B.* soul food platters alone. He's a generous tipper to the *Ladies of the Night,* but never used the *"date-rooms,"* a virgin to *"Grindstone Finest,"* choosing *Emotions* for his *"Bottom-Bitch."*

"Did Emotions come by here last night?" he asked.

Bugg needed to confirm his *"Crazy-Bitch's"* timeline. Accusations have gotten good bullets wasted on the *"Best of Friends."* He demanded the facts, not fiction. His *"side-kick"* played his part well, standing at attention, while *Bugg* speaks with *"Gangsta"* tone.

"Was she here!?" he asked again, slamming his glass drink on the table, not understanding the delay on the information, thinking he's hiding the facts about the rape.

The *Grindstone Boss* was thinking the hyped-up dope-man was mad about not doing business with the *Operation.* The answer would still be *"No!"* Everybody in the room knows this...

"Get-Ready, Don't Beat Ready"

Q's "side-kick" was *Super D.,* the VIP Soldier, trained on how to read lips talking *"Gangsta"* shit. He radioed the front door. His only question, *"Are they rolling heavy?"*

Storm was holding *Bugg's* gun at the front door. He also searched the *"side-kick"* personally. His answer was confident. *"They're very light,"* announced *Storm,* while *Super-D* sizes up the situation, waiting for *Q's* cue to handle his business. The secret fight code was *"Doctor."* Choose your words wisely or hear ambulance sirens in the *G-stone.*

"She came by," answered **Q,** ready and willing to turn-down his proposal. The two **Bosses** had their signals crossed. **Bugg** had another matter on his mind, introducing his non-animated friend.

Bugg's "side-kick" is **Emotions'** dumb-founded brother named **Webb.** Her lies had gotten family members involved. **Bugg,** being the closest thing to a boy-friend for her, made this an **Operation** issue.

"What's the problem?" asked **Q,** not understanding any new *"Beef."*

Webb was fooled by **Q's** slick suit and fancy shoes. He thought wrong. The un-talkative family hero of **Emotions** tried to sucker-punch the **Boss. Super D** stepped in front of the lazy right-cross, absorbing the punishment like a secret-service agent. Presidential protection for the only Club owner that gave him a second chance, he wasn't allowing some punk to punch his **Boss** in the fucking face; not on his watch!

"You raped my sister bitch!" hollered **Webb,** ambushing Mother-Fuckers with **Emotions'** lie. The dumb-founded brother jumped the gun in handling this situation. His sweet sister deserved better. **Bugg** wanted answers first. **Webb** wants blood!

Webb got himself tossed down the stairs. **Super D** scooped his legs and dragged him though the crowd and delivered him to the heavy-weights at the front-door. Blood leaked from his head, while his pride swayed in the balance. The **Operation's** low-man on the totem pole won't be running to the trunk. He was bounced to the curb under watchful eyes.

Bugg didn't want this to get out-of-hand, needing this to go over smooth as Brandy. *Emotions'* brother, *Webb,* put a serious wedge between them all. *REPERCUSSIONS WILL COME*. The cool, calm and collected *Bugg* won't be able to stop it

The Captain of the *Operation* wanted to do business, not protect a lying *"trick's"* honor. He knew deep in his soul she lied. Right or wrong it was a real *"Beef"* now. *"He'll be back!"* said *Bugg,* knowing that to be fact, once he tells the rest of the cronies at the *Operation.* Gun-shots have rip though *"Trap-houses"* for less.

"I didn't rape his sister!" explained *Q,* with a dumb-founded look on his face. He knew *Emotions* was lying out her rotten teeth. His truth fell on deaf ears. *Bugg* warned him of the thin line of control over personal feuds. This horrendous event can be washed away by joining forces with the *Operation.*

Quintin enters the room, arriving late, watching *DK* throw the punk out the Club, thinking the rowdy patron got tossed for breaking the new rules.

Quintin didn't bother with petty *"Beefs"* between dancers. He wasn't concerned with violators of house rules. His security handles that in a heart-beat. However, when the *"real"* danger comes a calling, death can claim his enemies easily, with one phone call. Being connected to the *Brotherhood* has its perks. They're capable of squashing all *"Beefs."*

The new partner's *"swagger"* complimented the polished movements of the new reign at the *Grindstone. "If*

you fuck with Q? You're fucking with the Brotherhood
announced **Quintin**. Their allegiance to one another had a
useful by-product. Well-trained Soldiers fighting for a *"Made-
Man,"* trumping the drug dealer's entourage on any given
night.

       Quintin's demeanor changed in an instant. This
wasn't the *"Go-lucky"* tenant of **Q's** family apartment building.
This was a *"Lieutenant"* of an enforcing *"Circle"* of **Brothers,**
bound by blood and the love of *"Allah."* Indeed, his threats
were also deadly real; only if his *"Call to Arms"* is righteous.
He knew better to take this *"Beef"* to the *"Captain."*

       The higher-ranking Soldiers of the **Brotherhood**
would frown on a *"Go-Go"* alliance. *"Sisters"* have better uses
than tricking for dollars. To build a new enlightened *"Nation,"*
it needs clear-minded women. Any *"entity"* that doesn't
support that is the *"devil."* That includes places like the
Grindstone.

       Quintin was walking a thin line with the
religious-minded faction. Dissention of the basic ideas and
principles can result in expulsion from the *"Clique."* That's why
Quintin's always kept a low-key at the *"Go-Go"* Club. Making
matters worse, he knows secretly in the past, that the
Operation has been robbed by the **Brotherhood** all for the
benefit of the *"Nation."*

       Bugg knew the *"splinter group"* does the dirty
work for the *"Nation."* He grew up watching the *"bow-tie"*
Brothers talk religion by day but, wear black masks at night,
ready to stick-up any *"set,"* especially an outfit like the
Operation. He chose his words wisely. *"No problem from me,"*

said **Bugg,** knowing better than to start a war. The **"Big Bad Bugg"** came in peace, thinking that this was shown by giving up his pistol at the front door.

Storm's on full-alert, since **Emotions'** brother got tossed out on his head, preventing **Webb** from grabbing the **AK-47** hiding in the trunk. He's watching every slow-moving vehicle, bracing for a drive-by; ducking head-lights like gamma-rays. Stress is at an all-time high, and they're chain-smoking their lives away. It's **"Code-red"** for the whole **Crew.**

Bugg played the concerned friend of the Club. He explained it was out of his hands. The **"Beef"** was personal. The violent expulsion of **Webb** earlier, wouldn't sit well.

"I guaranteed you he'll be back!" said **Bugg,** promising **Emotions'** brother isn't wrapped too tight. The **"jail-bird"** doesn't know **Emotions** is a lying **hoe.** His memory of his beloved sister restricted to their child-hood years. **"Big Sis"** took care of him when their mother died, and she was the only person that held him down during his incarcerations.

At the Operation's headquarters...

Webb informed **Black** about lies of his beat-down. His brother **Bugg's** kidnapping compounded with confirmation to **Emotions'** rape-telling falsehoods; an apparent family trait. **"Doubts"** got upgraded to **"fact,"** all thanks to **Webb's** lies. He needs some serious **"heat"** to even the score!

The **Operation** would die for their **"Niggas."** Blunts filled with **"Wet"** clouded their common sense. The weed drenched with embalming-fluid is a catalyst for disaster!

They loaded their cars with an arsenal of weapons to save the *"Captain"* of the **Operation, Bugg**.

"It's on NOW!" shouted **Black,** cocking his **AK-47,** while Bone Crusher's *"Never Scared"* serenades the **Ford-150** pick-up truck, filled with hyped up killers with guns!

Back at the Grindstone…

Bugg agreed to calm his misinformed *"Clique"* down. No need for bloodshed. Hot shells from an **Ak-47** wasn't warranted until **Webb's** feelings got hurt. An agreement must be made. Being a part of the **Operation** would give them a pass. After long consideration, the two partners agreed to **Bugg's** proposal.

It was just in the nick of time. As they walked **Bugg** to the front door, the **Operation** showed up with their weapons of mass-destruction; ready to kill everybody in sight! The **Crew** wasn't ready for the slaughter coming their way. They opened the door to 10 crazed disciples of the **Operation,** with **Storm** and **Big Gene** pinned against the wall outside, ready to spray them and the entire Club with automatic weapons.

Thank God, **Bugg** left out the door first. **Black** immediately told everybody *"Hold your fire!"* "The **G-Stone Crew** was spared with a wave of his hand, and the **Grindstone** was now a part of the **Operation.**

Webb is livid they didn't kill these rapists. He thought, they should *"ride or die"* for him. His prison incarcerations were the results of *"slanging,"* on behalf the

Operation. He was locked up for years without a snitching word. All he ever asked for was this *"one"* favor, turned-off by *"Street-Politics."* He wanted blood anyway, but his main target was standing too close to *Bugg.*

Q noticed the menacing stare from *Webb.* Their *"Beef"* had to be settled another night. On the cold streets of *Philly,* payback can lie dormant for years, then cash your ass in when you least expect it.

"I'll see you again Mother-fucker!" hollered *Webb,* knowing their paths will cross each other's again. The *Strip* ain't that big.

The *Boss* of the *Grindstone* was glad for this moment but knew *Webb's* promise was not an idle threat. *Webb's* beloved sister's rape must be avenged. Even if it was a lie!

The next night...

The *Crew* at the *Grindstone* had a meeting. *Quintin* and *Q* decided to revamp their security. They decided to hire *"Bro. Lt. Melvin X,"* from the *"Nation."* He's a 5ft.9in., martial-artist, with impeccable searching skills. His skills are badly needed after the mishap of *Big Gene's* last night. Missing that *32Cal*. was a breach of security.

The new addition to the front door is a calculated move for the *Grindstone.* They're planning to renege on the agreement with the *Operation. Bro. Lt. Melvin X's "Crescent-kicks"* are legendary in the body-guarding circles. He's a fearless member of the *"Nation."* They would never condone him working at a *"Go-Go"* Club, but $120 a night, 7 days a week, he secretly took the job.

The first night, he worked beautifully. Patrons heard the rumors of the **Operation** pulling up to spray the Club, but their doubts faded away when they saw the new door man. The **Militant Soldier** wore a black beret, boots and *"BDU"* pants. He stood defiant to anybody that had an issue with the Club.

He's a shining example of what the *"Nation"* can do for you. Rehab and jail couldn't rehabilitate the former crackhead. *"Smokey"* is his nick-name around the neighborhood, because of his addiction. He was known as the most vicious crack-addicted, *"ragamuffin"* the **Hood** has ever seen.

Q-Deezy didn't recognize him at first. Many years ago, they had *"Beef."* Crackheads clean-up nice after gaining some *"jail-weight."* He's in total transformation, because of the Minister's teachings. A Black Man held the front-door down, but his *"Inner demons"* started gossiping with the old Nigga's *"soul."*

Boss-man can I have a beer?" asked the star employee. **Bro. Lt. Melvin X** is given an open tab at the bar. **Charmaine** reported that 2 to 3 beers, turned into a full case in a week. Erratic behavior started, fueled by the sauce. He was nightly banging away *"Buds"* while searching patrons.

Emotions profiled the *"Karate-man from the "Nation,"* while dancing in the Club. The **Operation** decided to add *"insult to injury"* by posting her there. She would be the one *"dealing"* in the Club; agreed by both sides, for a 20% cut. They didn't even have to get their hands dirty.

The dancing-drug *"Mule"* conveniently had an instant attraction for the *"Crescent-kicking"* action-figure. They knew each other from **Girard Ave**. She watched crazy *"Smokey"* rob a few dope-boys. Now, he's back looking good enough to eat.

Emotions was forced to deal drugs at the **Grindstone.** The lying heifer didn't wanna bear the dirty looks from the **Crew** and **Squad,** but she feared the backlash from the **Operation** more. It was a strategic move for the criminal enterprise, placing her at the Club to *"woo"* the heart of a very old friend.

She quickly caught **Bro. Melvin's** attention with a few flirts. She charmed him, by squeezing his muscles. *"Smokey"* was skin and bones back in the day. He's now turned into **Bro. Melvin,** all beefed-up, doing a thousand push-ups a day. **Emotions** was ordered to corrupt him and turn a muscle-bound asset into a coked-out weakness.

Like *"Adam"* and *"Eve,"* both **Melvin** and **Emotions** knew better. The *"forbidden fruit"* for *"them"* is cocaine. Some brothers can't handle being around naked women every night. The un-married hired *"Muscle"* fell for the *"Mud-duck"* with the fat ass.

Emotions lured the liberated Soldier to the *"date-room"* on his third week working. His tense body was the result of 4 years of prison, without sex. The devoted believer took a vow abstinence, and just like *"Adam,"* he got duped by the *"serpent."* **Emotions** cracked his will for lust and drugs with snort-lines placed on her titties.

Her guilty conscience kicked in when the target took the first sniff; she triggered the return of *"Smokey"* in a whirlwind of drugs and sloppy sex. The sexually deprived ex-con tore into her *"snatch"* like a caged animal. **Emotions** is pleasantly pleased by his ferocious appetite. The *"Apple of his eye"* rooted him with the *"Tainted-Cocaine."*

The newly freed felon came home to lonely sheets. **Bro. Melvin's** welcome-home party was 4 years in the making, but his wife left with the kids the day the guilty verdict dropped on the troubled brother's head. New religious values forbade masturbation; it's been years since he's released himself. He's been drug-free for just as long. **Emotions** gave the gullible, recovering addict a *"blow-fly."* Bad habits comeback like good dope, with freedom from sexual restraint behind *"date-room"* doors, that hide a whole lot of dirty little secrets.

Bro. Melvin tapped that ass like a freed slave. Sparks flew from the jail-house friction. He used to day-dream about this in the showers up-state; penetrating the sweet flesh of a female. Drunk off the *"serpent's"* lies, he took a taste of her clit and started sucking it til it swelled twice its size. He was digging in **Emotions'** pussy *"raw-dog,"* like a husband fresh from the war. His exploding orgasm released a pool of semen all over her body.

Emotions laid there, drenched in sweat. *"Round 2"* was just seconds away. His manhood was getting hard again. She liked his vigor. **Bugg** or her *"tricks"* couldn't matched his hunger. She went with the fantasy. The secret technique to make her climax, is un-protected sex. A little *"booger-sugar,"* applied to the tip of his dick, didn't hurt either.

The *"tainted"* dope focused his *"love"* for his estranged ex-wife, *"onto"* *"Emotions."* The potion worked on the **Militant Soldier** from the *"Nation."* He was under the **Operations'** control. An unknowing *"inside man"* was molded over-night.

The potion was concocted by the chemists at the **Factory.** They crushed exotic, intoxicating flowers into powder, and used it as *"cut,"* to imprison a starved lover. The *"Tainted"* drug was designed to be a *"Love Potion."* Some call it a *"Root."*

Emotions administered this concoction in his *"coke"* and in his *"Tanqueray."* A double-cross fit for a Big-Bad Soldier of the *"Nation."* *"Believe in a lie long enough, Lies become Truths."* The wronged *"Mud-duck"* planted her seeds of deceit, while, playing with his chest hairs; snuggled up like springtime lovers.

The potion begins to take effect. The Spanish *"cook"* told the sneaky *"wrench,"* to use it in *"one or the other,"* but **Emotions** thought he needed a double-dose, so she opted to poison him by drink and blow. *"Smokey"* snorted several lines and took a *"blow-fly."* The ex-alcoholic drank the spiked *"Tanqueray"* like a *"Boss."* His tab steadily grew with every round of drinks. After closing hours, usually staff is entertained by late-night treats. **Junior** runs the over-time activities at the Club. His main job is to keep account of all party-favors. *"This shit ain't free." Junior* had the only key to the liquor-case. He's delegated to run things, when the boys have their fun.

Bro. Melvin and *Sis. Emotions* consummated their un-holy union in a twisted circumstance, spawned by *"Voodoo."* They opened a *"Pandora's Box"* of crazed, jealous lovers. His mental-status, mixed with a *"root,"* created a powder keg, ready to explode!

"Smokey" needed more lines. *"Set me up Baby!"* he said wanting the *"Mud-duck"* to apply more dope on her cleavage. The real *"set-up"* is laced in every *"sniff."*

"Round 5" is just seconds away. The sexual roller-coaster ride didn't stop. *Emotions* was glad she's on the pill. He's dumping his seed heavily, making her climax 20 times is *"his root;"* possessed to knock a *"bone"* out her *"ass."* Breaking the *"Harlot"* down to tears, once again, she went with the flow. The man made his point. After one night of marathon sex he whispers, *"We go together."*

Junior was the first *"victim"* of the boyfriend's jealous rage. He knocked on the *"date-room"* door to clear the building. The *"tab"* is colossal. The rooms are complimentary for employees, but the drinks service is another matter. They drank a whole half-gallon of *"Tanqueray." Emotions* only owned 20% of a $1000 pack.

"Fuck a bill!" the *"rooted"* Soldier screamed though the *"date-room"* door. The unruly guest wasn't finished with his *"rooting"* hostage yet. Sadly, she brought it on herself. His psychotic nature didn't intermingle well with

the *"root."* The *"coked-out"* recovering addict over-stayed his welcome. It was time to go.

He knocked again after an hour had passed.

Junior interrupted an endless *"carnival"* ride inside the smaller *"date-room."* It wasn't safe to disturb the sexual *"Carnage."* The beast in the room was feeding on his sultry meal. She almost couldn't get wet anymore. The multiple orgasms had taken its toll. Raw friction made an imprint on her hurting vagina.

The bothered after-hour guest swung open the door. In an instant, he smacked the young man in charge. Then he choked-out the over-time bill collector. *Junior's* clinging to life, gasping for air; assaulted for his insolence, while *"Don't disturb this groove,"* by **The System,** played on the CD player, like a singing reminder.

"Baby let him go!" cried **Emotions,** saving the life of her **Girard Avenue** neighbor.

Junior clambered to the pay-phone by the bar. He called **Charmaine** to pass on the word. There's a *"Brody-Artist"* in the Club. The **First-lady** of the **Grindstone** woke up their **Boss** from his day-time nap. The out-of-control door-man turned to a serious breach of security. *Junior* snitched on the marathon sex-act, colossal tab and the undeserved *"Pimp-smack!"*

"Say no more. I'm on my way." Replied the half-woke Club owner.

Back at the Club...

Emotions had bigger problems. *"Check-in"* for over-night *"Hustlers"* at the *Operation* is a tight noon. Late-comers usually are punished by a beat-down. *Black* and the *"Goons"* loved tap-dancing on *"Hustlers that don't Hustle right."* *Bugg* checked his list of *"Street Hustlers,"* his morning ritual in his make-shifted-out Penthouse suite above the *Factory.* Most 3rd shift *"dope-boys"* turned-in by 6am. They didn't want any problems. Accused of stealing was the worst scenario. Beat-downs for over-sleeping was just plain stupid.

It dawned on the devious drug dealer, that *Emotions* must be still busy *"wooing" the Inside Man."* This task is a surprise gift, in terms of danger; conquering their weaknesses from the inside out. He wondered if the *Squad* tossed her on her *"dance-bag."* The dressing rooms are forever dangerous for *"haters,"* especially the ones spreading vicious lies about *Q-Deezy*.

Jazzy and the rest were told *"Don't touch her!"* *Emotions* is representing the *Operation* now. They incredibly followed their orders for the lying *"Blasphemes."* The *"Mud-duck's"* lying to herself. Nobody at the *Grindstone* believed her.

"Rape?" questioned *Jazzy,* huddled-up in the dressing room. The comparisons were hilarious.

That's like *Sean "Puffy Combs"* raping *"Chewbacca."* The shit just didn't add up! The *Squad* didn't touch her or speak, just pissed in her bag, and she never even noticed. The *"Bitch"* didn't change the entire night!

Now it's 11am. in the morning...

Emotions is trapped in the *"date-room,"* hand-cuffed to the cast-iron radiator. *"Round 11"* is just seconds away. She tried to kiss the *"Beast;"* trying her best to *"tame it,"* by sucking away his never-ending *"Mojo"* juice using deep-down strong stokes for his "Power-tool." She embodied his prison dreams to a tee, a submissive victim devouring his built-up passion.

"Get Ready Don't Beat Ready!"

The exhausted *"Freak"* did what she was told in the room and the scheme. The *"root"* executed beautifully, but the effects didn't resemble *"Love."* The potion turned to a relentless aphrodisiac. *"Smokey"* snorted the entire $1000 pack, sprinkled across her tits.

The *Militant* lover still had some *"faith."* Luckily for *Emotions*, *"sodomy"* is *"forbidden."* *"Round 12"* was the breaking point for the sex-slave. With the fever-pitched passion, spawned by the mixture, fear began to set in for the weak fluid-deprived concubine. She was trapped in a psychotic, sadistic love triangle of *"voodoo"* vs. *"psychosis,"* sparked by a drug-binge.

"King Kong" is back on the *"coke."* His nervous infatuation barely allowed the *"Damsel in distress"* to pee. *Emotions* wanted a boyfriend out of this. The diabolical plan was side-tracked by her selfish wish. She could play all the instruments in her own pity-party parade, struggling all alone to keep a roof over her head, always choosing the wrong

father for her 4 children lost to D.H.S. Ms. Desperate herself is caught-up in a whirlwind of a *"sex-maniac!"*

"No more than Veinte' grams Mami," instructed the Spanish cook. A 20-gram sack was all that's needed. Anything more would have him *"love-sick"* for years. That's the moment she thought to fix his dosage, which was her worn-down *"coochie's"* first mistake.

In the bathroom...

She's urinating blood from the cervical pounding. The *"coochie"* has a black-eye, for sure. *Emotions* looked at her reflected image of a sexually battered woman, wondering, if he even *"likes pussy."* The sting from her urination spelled *"hate"* in any curse.

"Emotions come here!" shouted the hungry new boyfriend. *"Round 13"* can't happen. The scared captive hid in the bathroom with her *"pussy"* pounded shut. She didn't have this many problems when she lost her virginity!

The anxious new boyfriend searched her wallet and stole her ID. He ransacked her purse looking for more dope. Only a twenty-dollar bag was allotted for the *"Sidious"* plan. The spiked coke triggered his incredible greed. The love potion triggered the giant-sized lust and he's beckoning his concubine back to the *"date-room"*... *"Right Now!"*

Meanwhile...

The street stop-lights can't turn fast enough for *"Q Dog."* He's speeding down *"63rd Street"* to rescue the Club, and apparently, everybody in it. They needed a *"fairy-tale"* escape. *Emotions* is terrorized and hiding in the bathroom's *"Tower"* like a ghetto *"Rapunzel."*

"Smokey the Dragon" wanted to hump again. While the *Jackson 5's "Can you feel it?"* played on the box, the naked monster roamed the hallway looking for his nervous bride. *Emotions* couldn't believe his sexual appetite was this large. *"Daddy want some more!"* he said scratching at the bathroom door. His ex-wife suffered the same fate.

"Be careful what you wish for," *"Melvin's"* wife would tell his beaten-down girlfriends, after they begged her to take him back. She's the luckiest person, now in a secret location… thanks to *"Melvin"* getting locked up.

Emotions witnessed a crazed addict banging on the bathroom door. *"I love You!"* screamed the *"rooted"* lover. She's longed for those words by *"somebody,"* now they're words of a sincere *"psychotic's"* rage. The domino effect collapsed in her crotch, and she is *"done!"*

The bathroom door's hinges strained to hold off the demented power of his *"Crescent-kicks."* The running tab includes damages too. His debt is slowly rising to higher proportions. He finally kicked the door down and snatched his reluctant bride, who's screaming and kicking, trying to get away.

Suddenly, *Bro. Lt. Melvin* paused with some restraint. The rejected lover switched to an obedient gentleman. Her tears triggered the *"trance." Emotions* is slowly beginning to learn how to control *"The Ghetto Frankenstein."*

"Play-time is over!" said the relieved captive. Her plight elevated from *"Prisoner"* to *"Princess"* in a matter of minutes. The reigns are in her hands. She quickly commanded they get dressed. Like *"royalty,"* she summoned the brute to accompany her to explain the missing dope, back at the factory.

The **Grindstone Boss** arrived to a deserted Club. The *"date-room"* is a wreck. It looked like two rhinos had a fine time. They filled their bellies with expensive gin. The blood-stained, torn sheets mimicked a crime scene, and empty bottles and dirty straws littered the floor. The CD player was skipping on a scratched track.

Nas' *"Hate Me Now,"* featuring **Puff Daddy,** serenaded the situation.

The smashed bathroom's door resembled a wild beast being thrown though there by a tornado. Trash is everywhere from the coked-out *"Bruce Leroy"* dumping the cans of bar trash over the knocked-out **Junior's** head. He's slowly coming too after **Q-Deezy** smacked his face.

"Yo! Clean this SHIT UP!" hollered "**Q-Deezy**," taking out his frustration on the only person still there.

At the Factory…

"Here they come!" alerted the *"look-out."* **Emotions** knew better not to arrive without back- up. Her new

bodyguard didn't think being late should be a problem. The **$1000 "short"** is a guaranteed ***"Beat-down!"*** She would like to ***"see these fools Try!"*** **Emotions** stood defiant with a menacing look. Her ***"one-night stand"*** husband wasn't having ***"none of that!"***

The **Operation** has a rule to enter the circle located in the garage. The electronic gate opened for the couple. **Bugg** had slightly jealous thoughts, seeing these two hugged up, which showed on his face. Video surveillance provided a detailed look of the new lovers, but they had more pressing concerns when the ***"DRAMA"*** broke out!

Bro. Lt. Melvin went to work with a ***"Leg-sweep"*** for the first line of defense, then ***"Judo-Elbow-Strikes"*** for the unprepared body-searchers, stripped of their weapons. Now, the late-arriving employee's friend is ***"carrying real heavy!"*** packing two ***"9mm Berettas."*** Shots-fired in the direction of the inexperience gun-man high off ***"Wake-n-Bake."***

The Islamic marksmen found his targets running for cover; even **Black** had to duck his bullets. **Bugg** searched for his target though the gun-smoke with a ***"357 Magnum"*** in his hand, wishing he didn't wake up the ***"Beast,"*** that's popping off shots, in his place of business.

Emotions broke the ice during the seize fire. ***"I thought ya'll wanted to talk to him?"*** she asked, clowning the punkish Soldiers at the **Operation,** smiling at her ***"savior"*** shooting a few more shots, missing his targets by mere inches.

"Listen, you Devils! You best be leaving my 'Queen' alone!" stated **Bro. Melvin,** referring to **Emotions"** **Bugg's** baby-mama, **Queen,** is hiding under the desk. She could only wish for a *"Big-Bad Nigga"* to come though and rescue her.

The **Militant Soldier** knew to save his ammo. A few gunmen got clipped, but nothing serious. He wasn't playing any games… better leave his *"girl"* alone!

The escaping *"Bonnie and Clyde"* galloped out the emergency fire-exit door, into the day-time traffic. Nobody had the balls to follow them. Regrouping and crawling on broken glass, the front-door security team was still feeling the effects of **Bro. Melvin's** rampage.

He showed *"them." Emotions* hid him out at her newly acquired room. She fed her *"man"* grits, eggs and fried whiting fish; a meal fit for a King. The freed *"Mud-duck"* has been under the **Operation's** thumb for three years. Now, *her "love-sick"* refugee earned *"Round 13,"* but there's a change of plans this time. He can only lick her swollen *"cookie-box." "Kiss it. You… Greedy Monster!"* she said. Once again, *Emotions* went with the flow.

Back at the "Factory…"

Black is livid. His team looked like amateurs out there! There's *"not a real Killer"* in the bunch! Just scared *"Pussies"* in the paint. "**When the "Shit" goes down, you throw your guns down? Really?**" asked the disappointed *"Enforcer."* Things are different when your targets shoot back. Quiet *"row-homes"* burning down, followed by *"pop-shots,"* during drive-byes, couldn't compare to a skilled marksman clipping limbs for fun. They were out-matched in a gun-fight with their own weapons.

"You were ducking too" mumbled a "young recruit." **Black** quickly pistol-whipped the smart-mouth recruit.

"No hesitation!" preached the disrespected *"Enforcer,"* while beating his recruit to death!

Everybody in the **Factory** took notes. This was a lesson learned, as they carried the life-less body out to the trunk. Extra work for the humbled pall-bearers of the mumbling *"Smart-ass."* A long ride to the *"Asbestos Fields"* at the *"City Dump,"* replaced many *"funerals"* in their line of work.

Another mourning family won't get the chance to bury their young because the **Operation** sentenced them to shallow graves. *"Get Ready Don't Beat Ready!"* when you open your motherfucking mouth!

CHAPTER NINE
"The Judas Effect"

The first order of business, every **Sunday** morning for the **Militant Soldier,** is to rally the **"Brothers of Arms"** at the **Temple. Bro. Lt. Melvin** was absent from his mandatory 5k run with his loyal fellow Soldiers. The required ritual was picked by him. After the rejuvenating run, sidewalk cleaning duties are done at the **Temple.**

As a **"Lieutenant"** with the **"F.O.I.,"** the standards are clear for a **"Black Man."** They are expected to be bright-eyed, and wide-awoke, to hear the **"Minister's"** teachings. Whispers of concern begin to circulate among the flock about the **"Fallen Brother."** The **"Ushers"** stood silent about the **"nasty"** accusations. They rather revere the **"Man"** they know.

The **"Poster Child"** of the rehabilitating powers of the **"Message"** was missing for the second week in a row. He agitated matters worse, by not reporting-in to his worried **"Fruit."** Many of them, **Bro. Lt. Melvin** help grow **"Sensei"** of the whole team's treacherous fighting style. The mixed-bag of **Military** take-downs and **"Ninjutsu"** stealth tactics served well on several covert missions. Missing **Brothers** don't go un-noticed.

Bro. Antonio was delegated to find the missing **"Lieutenant."** He's a long-time friend of the beloved **Brother.** The search started when **Bro. Lt. Melvin** blew-off **"F.O.I"** classes. He never misses a Monday. The two-week head start on his assignment proved useful. *Bro. Antonio* followed-up on rumors of his friend's *"new"* night job at the *"Erotic Night-Club,"* called *"The Grindstone."* He now has permission to investigate under every stone.

The 6ft.5in., athletic-built *Brother* arrived at the Club's front door. *Bro. Antonio* looked like a well-dressed preacher. His bow tie was replaced by a neck tie to ward off the prying eyes. He didn't need criticizing testimonies and jumping to conclusions as folk drove-by. *"Another Brother" caught Back-sliding on the Strip," won't* be in his reputation.

Bro. Antonio paid his $25 cover charge to get a closer peek. He came for information about his *"fallen cohort."* They came-up the line together; Both subordinates for the *"cause."* Collections needed to be made. Quotas needed to be met. The whole *Strip* was looking for the charismatic *"Bean Pie"* selling *Brother.*

Bro. Lt. Melvin appeared on the Club's front steps, reporting for duty after his *"rhino-sized"* tab. The audacity of this *"Gorilla"* from the other night. He wants to explain the blatant disrespect, but the *"Boss-man"* wasn't there yet.

His replacement instructed him to *"Please put your arms up and take a search."* *Bro. Lt. Melvin* felt Instantly jealous. The inside man is now an outsider, and *The New Guy* wants to pat him down.

Debo, the 6ft.3in., husky-built, *baby-brother* of the leader of the *BBO.,* is his replacement. He's the youngest of the pack in this body-guarding *"Juggernaut."* The young Soldier was fresh off tour with *"Naughty by Nature"* when he took the job.

Quintin made the call for *Bro. Lt. Melvin's* replacement. *Big Wayne,* the massive 6ft.5in., 400 lb. leader of *BBO,* suggested his baby-brother. Their daddy must've been a dinosaur, because the whole clan of eight brothers are big men."

The disgruntled, former door-man pushed passed the baby-brother. He didn't notice his fellow *"Fruit,"* sitting on the leather couch receiving a lap-dance. *Debo* jumped to action to bounce the non-complying intruder out the Club. *"Wrist-locks"* applied to the over-zealous bouncer, shut-down his aggression.

The first day on the job had *Debo* crumbling in agony from a *"pressure-point"* strike. The foreign sensation impacted his body like an *"ice-pick"* to the nervous system. The *"Sensei"* of the *"Temple"* needed to get paid! His last pay is being held for his wild night with *Emotions.*

Bro. Antonio watched in horror. His former cellmate dominated the larger bouncer. The opening Club isn't packed yet, but everybody there witnessed the *"timber-falling"* event at the front-door. The disgruntled ex-employee looked scattered. The spit-shined *Brother* is ruffled, glassy-eyed and broke!

Bro. Lt. Melvin snatched the cash register from the bar, while *Charmaine* is trying to break a twenty; grabbing the Club's change of a would-be-busy night, when the regular bars closed. He didn't care who's watching... "Smokey Needs his PAPER!"

Bro. Antonio hasn't seen *"Smokey"* since lock-up. In prison, they shared their deepest secrets. He's the one that showed the lost **Brother** to the light. Now, **Bro. Lt. Melvin** is a *"Judas"* of the *"Way of Life."*

      "Smokey" is back! Lost again in the depths of addiction. **Bro. Antonio** tried to sway his long-lost **Brother**-in-Arms, with the universal greeting of peace; *"As-Salamu-Alaikum my Brother Fruit!"* The *"call"* to smoke crack weighed heavier than the *"Call to Prayer."* Back-sliding, on so many levels, he ignored his own **Brother** from the *"Nation."*

      The arriving "**Storm**," got a **9mm** *"***Beretta** stuck in his face. The fleeing crackhead went postal and scared everybody inside. The *"Fruit"* robbed the bar's change to break big bills; trashing Mama's register that held it. **Charmaine,** the *"Star-maid,"* questioned her safety, as she watched the **Crew** get chumped by a real *"Nigga,"* with a gun.

      The late arriving **Quintin** knows **Brother Lt.'s** handy-work. **Debo** is living proof of that. The bodyguard-in-training felt embarrassed and discombobulated from the lasting effects of the *"Ninjutsu."*

      They trained at the **Red Dragon Dojo** together, and broke bread with one-another. He also worked several concerts at the *"Spectrum"* with the **Brother,** protecting **Tupac** and **Biggie,** like **Martin** and **Malcolm,** spitting lyrics and philosophy on the back-stages. He knows the disciplines and the antidotes of the same Ancient Arts.

      The pain-relieving, counter-measures were greatly appreciated by **Debo. Quintin** owned the room when he re-manipulated his muscles like a Kung-Fu Master in the movies, while the young bouncer took a seat, trying to figure out why size doesn't mean a damn thing!

The consoling leader snapped **Storm** out of his depression. Close calls are God's signs to **"atone"** for one's sins. Even though the **Brother** didn't pull the trigger, the cold steel of a barrel can change anybody's mind about their profession.

Storm's anger kicked in again. Talking loud about revenge after-the-fact. That's when **Bro. Antonio** introduced himself. The soft-spoken Soldier from the **"Nation"** warned against revenge. His tall, opposing presence represented just a fraction of what could come their way.

"If You harm our Brother, the weight of the 'Nation' will fall on your head!" He warned, not as a threat, but as a promise. The **Brothers** at the **"Temple"** didn't know **"Smokey,"** but they would die for **Bro. Lt. Melvin,** elbow-to-elbow, in the thick of war.

Q and **Mrs. B** entered the Club. The **"Mother and Son"** duo had other business to handle. Their Real Estate racquets had pressing matters, before the full report could catch up with the truth.

"We need guns!" demanded the provoked **Storm**, feeling punked by a scary **"Nigga"** with a **"Nine."** The irritated **Head of Security** wanted blood. He wanted revenge for having to watch his life flash before his eyes.

Mrs. B watched the **Crew** help the ailing **New Guy** to his feet. She laughed at the **"big fella,"** bested by the sexy **Brother** from the **"Nation."** Mama is an apparent fan of the **"Spit-shine Brother"** too. **Melvin** reminded her of the early days of the **"First Resurrection."**

She met Aquil's father at the *"Temple."* He too was a *"Spit-shined Brother,"* spreading the *"Message."* Q's father used to be a devoted member of the *"Nation"* of Islam. He went by the of name of **Jeremiah 9X,** dropping his supposed *"slave name,"* not knowing his Great-grandfather did that for him, in the 1870's, by dropping the **Mc** on **McTerrence,** naming their legacy just **Terrence,** clearing the way for new beginnings. He's a special **Brother**, with a unique skill as the fabricator of The **Honorable Elijah Muhammad's** Dentures; his highest honor to date.

Jeremiah R. Terrence aka **Dr. Abdul M. Bashir** learned how to make dentures in prison, during a 10 year *"bid"* in California. Bank Robbery was the charge for the biggest heist in the "State's" history. A revolutionary freedom-fighter for *"The Cause,"* the young impressionable follower stole $180,000 to buy *"Weapons for the Revolution!"* It was Illegally withdrawn from his Naval Base's bank.

Three things went wrong back in 1963… "Blood is Thicker" excerpt:

The first thing that went terribly wrong, is that his partner in crime left identification at the scene. No need guessing who the masked men were, the perpetrators dropped a duffle bag with a name on it.

The second thing that happened is the Splinter Cell of the *"Black Panthers"* wanted the stolen money for fancy houses and fantastic mink coats...Not *"Freedom and Justice for All."* They tried to kill the young Naval Officers, to keep the money for themselves.

Third, but not least, they picked the wrong day to rob a bank. They did it on November 22, 1963; the same day **JFK** got shot. Getting out the Country was impossible. Aquil's father got locked up by the Federales at the border after a cat and mouse chase by the government spanning over 12 states. The **"Nation"** quickly recruited the fearless young **Brother** in the papers, as soon as the revolutionary Soldier arrived at **San Quintin**.

Yeah, Mama knows about the **"Fruit."** She couldn't even laugh long at **Debo. "Them some Bad Boys!" Mrs. B** confirmed, shaking her head at **The New Guy**.

"I know you ain't paying these worthless Negroes! Are you?" Mrs. B said, referring to **The New Guy** and **"Fruit."** The replacement and former employee wasn't worth a dime, she thought. His fall from grace was just too sudden, too easy. **"They don't make Brothers like they used to."**

Meanwhile at Emotions' hide-out...

Emotions waited hours for her **"Muslim-man"** to bring home the bacon. The bride of the **"Ghetto Frankenstein"** fears the worst. The **Operation** is still gunning for them. Unemployment, evidently, will be the case at the **Grindstone.** To make matters even worse, the extremely fertile **"Mud-duck's"** period is late.

The couple needed money bad. Their crack habit have exhausted all forgiveness from their enablers they used to know. She couldn't call home. The family was too scared to get involved. *Emotions* knew better than to roam the streets with her face exposed, so she looked for her *"rooted"* boyfriend in *"Muslim garb."*

The *"Hijab"* served well as a mask. She passed by life-long friends on the avenue and was invisible to her nosey haters and so-called friends. As she looked for her only *"ticket"* out of danger and her only *"savior"* against all foes, her anxieties triggered an age-old fear of abandonment, already caused by her four baby-fathers before him, leaving her to take care of their seeds by herself.

Emotions has been a sucker for so-called love too many times. Her lovers sure had fun letting loose those *"mega-nuts"* in her soft sweet *"ass."* Granted, they probably woke up, looked at her... and ...wanted to change their entire life, but leaving *Emotions* with four kids is just plain wrong.

"Shit gets real when the babies come!"... said the voice of her late Ghetto-grandmother, having thirteen herself, teaching *Emotions* don't listen to a man when his dick is hard. He'll say anything to bust a nut. One second of weakness can cause a lifetime of pain.

That's why all *Emotions'* kids are in the system; spread all over the city with different families. She's doesn't want the side-effects of sexual intercourse. Every guy she's ever loved has gotten the privilege of busting a load inside her. Wanting a one-night stand to stay longer than 15 minutes, thinking it's their lack of commitment

Emotions just gotta look in her kitchen at all her roaches, to find out why... NOBODY... spends the night!

Meanwhile...

"Smokey's" coming up short. He's job-less and tempted to resort to his **old ways** He's wandering the streets looking for a target. The brisk night air reminded him of the homelessness and despair. It's the life he vowed never to return. Plotting on a **mark** to rob for dope money sparked his old anxieties of despair, but his addiction to cocaine is completely out of control.

Passing by old ladies gripping their purses out of fear of the black menace that knows better than to harm the elderly **Brothers and Sisters** of their pennies, but his inner demons, talking shit in his head, could care less ...They needed that dope!

Melvin? asked the elderly lady, recognizing her favorite pie-selling **Brother** from the corner of **52nd St. and Lancaster Ave.,** stopping the hoodie-wearing would-be thief in his tracks, bringing him back to form, shook out his trance, leaving the cross-wearing grandmother alone.

In a flash, *"Mel, the stick-up Kid from Hell,"* notices some Jamaican *"rude boys"* sitting in their **Beemer,** flossing gold chains and *"grillz,"* distracted by the chocolate snow bunnies running in the Chinese store. They're blasting their Reggae on the colossal **Alpine** speakers, oblivious to the **stick-up artist** creeping up on their chromed-out vehicle.

The dreaded *"rude-boys"* were puffing on the *"Ganja,"* when **Melvin** snuck up on the driver's side window, sticking his **9mm** under the startled Caribbean's nappy ass chin.

       "Stuck like Chuck! Give that Shit Up!" yelled the recognizable **Brother** from the Avenue.

       "Blood Cloth it's the Brother!" yelled the passenger from Spanish Town. *"Why yuh a deal wid mi so star?"* asked the driver from Montego Bay, wanting to know what the hell is his problem! Just last month, they had a heated discussion about religion, questioning **Melvin's** message of betterment, knowing his crazy past. Now, proving his point, once again, he's getting robbed by the **Street Messenger** on a *"2-week crack binge."* Once again, **Melvin** is stopped in his tracks.

       "You Brothers want to buy two nines?" asked **Melvin,** spinning the entire situation into the deal of a lifetime, haggling prices for the fire-arms in the middle of the street on a bended knee, rushing the spooked *"Rastas"* in the flashed-out **BMW** to get-up his asking price.

       "How much Mon?" asked the nervous driver. Not knowing whether to grab his wallet or his tucked **4-Pound** neatly stashed by his side.

       "Whatever's in your pocket Nigga!" said the fallen **"Soap-Box Minister,"** falling apart at the seams, forgetting that you can't go back to stupid once you know the truth, selling the *"hammers"* for a hundred dollars, instead of robbing the Caribbean brothers speaking knowledge.

       Meanwhile on 52nd Street…

The garbed-up impersonator walked straight to the **Grindstone.** She gave **The New Guy** the "Greetings." The disguised **"Mud-duck"** wanted to know if **Bro. Lt. Melvin** was working tonight, introducing herself as his **"attendant."**

Debo sucked his teeth when she asked. Just the name of the man that bested him, turned his stomach. **Emotions** quickly got his name out her mouth, stripping quickly in the vestibule. **Moose** got a peek-show by the cash window.

"You're his girl huh?" said **Debo,** admiring **Melvin's** Fiancé's curves as she transformed into a dancing freak. **Debo** stopped **Emotions** from going in, to inspect her more closely. He grabbed two handfuls of ass, then began sliding his finger around her waist to probe her sweaty **Puss,"** rubbing her **"Goodies,"** checking for weapons. She returned the favor and grabbed his **"Trunk."**

Emotions was back baby! Her regulars were thirsty for her **"lap-fucks."** She needed **Old Grand-dad** whiskey to fix her present plight. Having a baby wasn't in the insidious plan. She didn't need a hexed baby by a crazed lunatic, turning on her **"Savior,"** as soon as she swallowed the first shot.

She played the drinking victim, swallowing free shots bought by her regulars. The whiskey loosened the words for more lies. She confided in **Charmaine,** painting a picture of a battered woman on the brink. The cousins treated each other more like co-workers than relatives. There's only fake concern by the **"Star-maid"** at the bar.

Charmaine knew her cousin was up to something. Their men now have **"Beef."** Their blood-relationship isn't precious enough to wave the white flag, from either side. *Emotions* swore on a thousand *"Qurans"* and million *"Bibles,"* she didn't know what was wrong with her new boy-friend. *"He's Crazy Cuz!,"* she sang like a canary, telling the so-called facts of the *"woman that screamed rape*!" For the second time in a row, *Charmaine* wanted to attack the elephant at the bar.

　　　　　"You accused my man of raping you! Bitch!" declared the pissed cousin. She's been wanting to clear the air between them since she heard *"THAT BULL-SHIT!"*

　　　　　The *First Lady of the Grindstone* snatched the lying blood-relative by the collar, against the Club's orders, and, dragged her upstairs to the dreaded dressing room, where all the *"Beefs"* are settled.

　　　　　Charmaine tossed her trouble-making cousin to the floor, as *Jazzy* watched the dressing room door. Nobody's gonna jump in this. "The *First lady"* and the *Bottom-Bitch"* get to check this *Fake Bitch.* No *"Vaseline"* needed for this box. *Emotions* never could fight. The cousins rumbled several times in the school yard. They haven't boxed since *pop-rocks"* and *hop-scotch,* for the same-old reason. *Emotions* likes the same *"toy"* that *"Charmazinn"* has.

　　　　　The *"Mud-duck's"* man-stealing ways started in *Sayre Junior High School.* She was an ugly duckling back then too, and jealous of *Charmaine,* the *"Pretty Thang"* legion of fans. The prettiest girl in school stole all the boy's hearts, but she wasn't putting out. Young *Emotions* fucked every potential boy-friend of *Charmaine's* while they caught blue-balls, waiting for sex from her stuck-up little cousin.

This is a grown-woman kicking her in the stomach now. She knows not to strike her in the face. Family get-togethers for the holidays are just around the corner. Auntie would never forgive a black eye. *Emotions* would never forgive getting tossed like a bowling ball in the dance-bags.

Jazzy stood guard at the dressing room door. She watched the pretty *"Star-maid"* handle her business. *Charmaine* is earning her respect, beating up her own cousin, fighting for *"Poppy's"* honor. *Jazzy* was never that committed. Fighting blood over a dude was never her *"forte."*

Jazzy is impressed that the pretty-girl could fight, though. She held her hands well. *Charmaine* was taught how to box a *Bitch* by *Big Sis.* Her upper-cuts to the guts of *Emotions'* were vicious. The blows dug deep into the mid-section. The brawling pretty *Bitch* executed her strikes well off the pivot foot, dropping her weight in every punch. *"Nice!"*
"Charmaine beat that Bitch outta of her shoes!" reported *Jazzy* when security stopped the fight. *Emotions* got saved by the bell. Spitting-up blood stopped the fight all together. The *First Lady* retains her crown. She beat that *Bitch* down, and didn't even have to kick-off her Stiletto shoes either!

"That's a Bad Bitch! Right There!" said the onlooking crowd in the hallway. Even, *Jazzy* winked her eye at the brawling beauty from *South-West Philly,* parting the crowd, making the *hounds* step back with respect.

"The Bar is Back Open!" said the *"Star-Maid."* She won't be needing a security detail for bathroom breaks tonight. Even *Q-Deezy* looked at her different, but happy *Emotions* got what she deserved. *"Writing Checks with her*

mouth her Ass can't cash!" thought the Club owner, as he watched his security carry her punk-ass out!

The secretly pregnant *"Mud-duck"* welcomed the kicks like a cheap abortion. The *demon-seed* of the *Voodoo* tainted conception has eerie side-effects. A direct connection to the *father,* can cause it to grow at an accelerated rate, and finally after it's born, the baby that can morph into 2 or more creatures!

Meanwhile in the cold streets of West Philly….

"Smokey's" stalking for some corner-boys to stick-up, when the pain hits. Visions manifests of a psychic connection with his unborn child under attack. He fell to his knees, thinking the pain was food poisoning from the Chinese store's chicken wings. The sharp throbbing discomfort's origin is realized quickly as visions of a beat-down of his newly pregnant *"Queen."* He has demonic images of his *demon-seed* under duress, and all roads to rescue his family lead to the *Grindstone.*

The debunked, former employee arrived after a 5k sprint to the Club. His legs burned from the familiar exercise. His body-conditioning used to be a daily chore. The athletic Soldier from the *"Nation"* materialized at the *"Go-Go Club's"* front-door. *The New Guy* got his chance for Round 2 with the *"Sensei,"* while *Big Country* played *Public Enemy's* *"Welcome to the Terror Dome;"* a fitting song for the make-shift *"SW- 1"* standing at the front door.

He came back for his woman carrying his **seed.** **Debo** radioed **Storm** immediately. The **Apache** look-alike hurried his piss break. **The New Guy** knows he needs back-up for the **"Sensei."** He's no rematch for **Bro. Lt. Melvin,** walking in unsearched.

He joined the **Boss** of the **Grindstone** upstairs in the **VIP.** The tense meeting is over-whelming, especially for **Storm**. The cracked-out Soldier is suspected of carrying extremely **heavy.** Even though, he could probably kill everybody in the room. The stolen **9mm Berettas** was sold for crack. The bulge in his waistline is just a mask.

Nobody moved while they're sizing up the trained killer. **Storm** had a hand on his borrowed **38 Cal.** pistol. **Super-D** drew both his knife and the ice-pick, ready to cut his throat and poke him in the heart. **Big Gene's** stun-gun is ready to shock the smile off his face.

Mrs. B joined the meeting. She became another liability, if the fired disgruntle ex-employee snaps. She didn't care about the threat of danger. Mama walked right up to the **"Brother,"** and slapped him in the face for stealing the cash register. The humbled killer cowered by the motherly slap. She'd reminded him of the stern hand of his own mother.

"Didn't my son give you a job?" asked **Mrs. B** like a respected elder. The **Crew's** amazed how she handles the trained Gorilla on coke, apologizing for starting trouble in the first place, standing there like a disciplined child rubbing his face, trapped in a trance spawned by mom's scolding, and unable to be the beast everybody in the room fears.

She questioned his behavior, feeling sorry for him, picking-up old bad habits, because of this environment.

"All them beautiful Sisters at the Temple" she said, wondering why in the hell he picked **Emotions.** She knew he needed a righteous **Sister** to help keep him on the righteous path; like the **MGT Sisters,** that wear white, sitting up front every Sunday, during the **Minister's** teachings.

Mrs. B knew he needed to hear the holy words of the *"Al Fatiha,"* knowing that would rid whatever possessed the mind of this talented Soldier. She's reciting the *"only"* words of truth that can bring him back. Something evil has got'em; more evil than lust and more deliberate than revenge. He's been touched by a *"curse."* Now all the roads to redemption led to **Emotions,** twisting the *"Sura's"* meaningful words and following the blood drops towards their hide-out.

Later that night…

Charmaine's breaking the bar down. **Quintin's** happy to help the **New** brawler at the **G-stone**. They laughed on how she wiped the floor with her cousin. The laughter broke the ice between them. She often thought **Quintin** didn't like her, but that's far from the truth.

He found himself attracted to the young, chocolate beauty, frustrated she's spoken for by his friend and business partner. You can trust him with anything, except a beautiful woman. His greedy appetite for females is legendary. That's why she shied away from him in the first place.

Charmaine has a condescending attitude with men in general. They always want some *"Ass."* She goes out her way not to make eye contact with them. Looking in guys eyes have started all kinds of trouble; from inappropriate behavior from her boyfriends' fathers, to her girlfriend's so-called significant others' googling eye-balls.

"What if he did rape her?" **Quintin** asked, out of nowhere, turning her thoughts from defending girlfriend, to scorned side-chick that got cheated on.

"You know Q's married … right?" said the snitching business partner, bringing up sensitive subjects while they worked, revealing his secrets inside casual conversation.

Quintin stroked her ego by complementing her beauty, brawling skills and intelligence. His seeds of doubt stirred in her mind, like a detective on a case. Beautiful women make the worst scorned lovers. They're always trying to figure out why the *"lucky"* gamble with *"perfection."* There's always an instigator lurking around the corner, painting an ugly picture in the minds of the fragile lovers. She's already on edge. The **Ladies of the Night** love flirting with the **Boss,** and not just with batting eyes either. They lust for him, either for position, or attraction. Every *"Bitch"* was a suspect.

Charmaine couldn't fathom the idea that her man would want **Emotions,** instead of her. Those cocky attitudes were the same with **Munchie.** That's why she's the last to know. Her new relationship is now in doubt … thanks to **Quintin's** greedy ass.

The new partner promised to betray a friend, if she likes. He offered to be her *"Inside-man"* for his cheating; a witness for the *"Young Spring-Water,"* his nick-name for the **First Lady.** She shook her head in agreement for the secret *surveillance. **Charm*** knew he'll want something in return. They all do.

Meanwhile out in the cold streets of "West Philly…"

   Bro. Lt. Melvin sprinted though the neighborhood, straight back to their hidden love nest. ***Emotions*** is balled up, like an infant, on the couch-bed. The crooked ***Hijab*** indicated submission to a new ***"Way of Life."*** The G-String suggested the ***"old way's"*** resistance!

   He's starting to remember his ***"teachings."*** If there's a ***"God"*** there's must be a ***"devil."*** Stranger things have happened in this world. The unholy union spawned the conception of a ***demon-child,*** that's directly attached, spiritually, to its father.

   Emotions, beaten and scared, is starting to have a miscarriage with profound pain manifested by the signs of life clinging to this world. It also revealed the true intentions of a very silly girl that's in way over her head.

   The ***curse's*** control is getting weaker and weaker. ***Bro. Lt. Melvin*** stood vigil as his unborn child bleeds out the mother. Making matters worse, is the faint acknowledgement that the pregnancy contained twins. Two lives lost just flashed in his mind.

   The visions kept developing a telling argument that ***Emotions*** hasn't been completely honest about her intentions. She didn't want the offspring in the first place. There's images of hatred in her heart. The two cursed entities snitched the *Harlot* out. Their distaste for her willingness to harm them felt depressing, like the gloomy overcast outside.

Emotions had an abortion before, but nothing like this. She could feel the babies' pain, ripping from her womb, jolted from their souls, unable to thrive in a hostile environment, but still trying to cling to life.

Bro. Lt. Melvin instinctively started praying. *"His-slam"* is being practiced in this situation. He felt **"wronged"** as the visions continued to report, to its *loving father,* full of deception and deceit, turning the love potion effects from infatuation, to hatred.

The intense loathing feeling got stronger and stronger. Lighting struck as if on cue. The abominations couldn't live to term because of the sneaky mother's ways. Cast back to which they came. There's nothing *God-like* about this. *Emotions* is blamed for their demise. The drinking and fighting are contributing factors. *In his mind,* wearing a *"Muslim Garb"* to a *"Go-Go"* spot is the most damning betrayal of all... While his rage grew with every sultry vision, the *"devil-himself"* wished for a better outcome. He's the true father of these *demon-seeds.* The one and only true puppet master's spell is broken, thanks to the miscarriage, but the whispers weren't going anywhere.

The *"voices"* snitched out another *"culprit"* that's kicking *Emotions* in the stomach. Now, he's criticizing his over-night bride for not protecting the child against *Charmaine's* blows. By blatantly not blocking the damaging strikes, she allowed her cousin to harm the unborn seeds. They've been snuffed-out by their own family tree.

"Kill her now!" they said.

Emotions looked so peaceful laying in his arms, but all bets are off since she killed his babies. Snugged-up in his grasps, he squeezed harder and harder. The awakening sleeping girl-friend is slapping at his arms, trying to tell her lover his grasp is too tight. She begins choking and gasping for air. The wronged boy-friend just squeezed harder as she kicks and twitches until finally,... her neck snapped! The *"whore's"* no more.

Once again, all roads lead back to the *Grindstone.* It's *"Star-Maid"* has a brand-new enemy, and his name is *Bro. Lt. Melvin*. He must revenge the *demonic-twins'* death. He vowed to kill the familiar *"pretty-girl"* from the neighborhood. *Charmaine* is now his new target.

She's just a kid in his eyes at 19 years old. He didn't know *Emotions* was only two months older than her beautiful cousin, who he sees strutting down the *Deuce* by *Papp's Pizza* buying slices, giggling with the *"Wrecking Crew,"* after visiting their brother from the clique, *Junior*, the delivery guy and back-up cook in the daytime. *"Trust,"* *Charmaine* will be easy to find.

CHAPTER TEN
"Philly's Homegrown Porn Star!"

The next night...

The ***Grindstone*** is buzzing with excitement. ***Champagne,*** the ***Porn Star,*** formally a ***"Blue Velvet"*** erotic dancer from ***Philly,*** is in the Building. She's promoting a show with ***Janet Jackme*** and ***Ménage A Trios***, that's taking place across town at ***"Second Cousins"*** in ***North Philly*** on **5ᵗʰ and Diamond St.**

Champagne's considered a living legend by every dancer in the building. She's accompanied by a ***Brotherhood*** security detail. The ***Porn Star*** fell in love with the Club's ambiance. She vowed to put them on the map for celebrity guests.

The legendary ***Porn Star*** grooved to every record ***DJ Irv*** played. The reggae and hip-hop selections inspired the tipsy ***Porn Star*** to bless the stage. Patrons couldn't believe that their exotic crush was live on stage. Many of them use to jerk their ***"pricks"*** as high school kids watching her movies. She hasn't danced in the ***Hood*** in years. Nobody in the ghetto could book the high-priced ***Porn Star*** anyway. She's pulling down a hefty $10,000 booking fee these days.

Many dancers have tried her path to success but failed. The porn business is a tough living. She's one of the lucky ones. Others have been duped by ***"wanna-be"*** movie producers, or worst; even she's been raped and unable to press charges, because she signed a contract of consent. You wouldn't know it tonight. She's reliving her dancing days, by performing to **Michael Jackson's** song *"Pretty Young Thing."*

Everybody in the room watched her "set" in awe. Dancers wanted to be the legend, not knowing her long-hard struggle to the top. They wanted her money and fame regardless of the price she's paid. They didn't know about her early days, when she had to fuck whoever to get a part. In the beginning, she was paid pennies just to get her name in lights. Now, after over a hundred films, she's a star now.

Champagne's true to her word. She called her newest protégé, **Ménage A Trois.** She's an erotic dancer from **Texas,** in town for their upcoming show. She's in the beginning of her porn career, long before she became a music video vixen in the music video featuring **Beanie Sigel's "In the Club."** The young protégé is jealous of her mentor's legendary status.

Ménage A Trois, is a 22-year-old, **Texas** native, with small, perky breast and nice rump. She's known for her freakish blow jobs in her movies. She's only three years younger than the Legendary **Champagne.** She answered her call to meet the Headliner at the **Grindstone,** but she doesn't like last minute instructions.

Champagne's diva-like persona clashed with **Ménage's** personality, but she bit the bullet and met with the porn legend to help with the promotion. Even with a sizeable cute butt, **Ménage's** biggest attribute is her freakishly long tongue. In her films, her greatest attraction would eventually become her calling card.

"Ménage" arrived at the after-hour club thinking, they're far away from the mansion parties in *Miami, Florida* ...*52nd & Master St.* will never be *"South Beach."*

This is *Champagne's* hometown. She's the *Erotic Queen*, calling all *"Ballers"* to spend some money at her upcoming show. *The North Philly* Native approached the task of getting the word out by bringing the show to the streets.

The mean streets of Philly are unforgiving to the phony. The legend knew she'd have to connect with the *"Hustlers," "Dealers," "Ballers"* and the *"Gangstas."* Then, she'd have to fill up the rest of the seats in the huge banquet hall with straight working Joes. She'd sprinkle one or two celebrities to the recipe via the guest list. She also must recruit 100 dancers to shake their asses. The finishing touch for this masterpiece would be the Headliners, including *herself, Janet Jackme* and *Ménage Trios;* the *"dream team of black porn."*

Quintin noticed the reluctant *Ménage* wandering on the corner, debating if she should come in or not. He recognized her immediately. The newly acquired partner was the one who invited *Champagne* to the Club. He isn't surprised when he saw *Ménage* outside trying to conjure up the nerve to party in the *Hood.* He introduced himself to the up-and-coming erotic headliner. *Ménage* is impressed by his approach and his quick wit. He quickly gained a rapport with the nervous Diva, who appreciated the friendly face of her escort.

He gave *Ménage* the star treatment. She could bypass the usual security search and cover charge. He then escorted her to *Champagne's* table. He's in full *Boss* mode, offering free drinks to the valued guests. *"Sex on the Beach"* is the drink requested by the **Porn Star** with the freakish tongue.

She's admiring his tall, chocolate stature. He favors **R. Kelly,** complete with the bald head and everything. **Quintin's** dating the famous comedian, **Sommore,** so this gave him some experience in dealing with B-list celebrities. Star-struck eyes for the XXX **Porn Stars** wouldn't be an issue for him. **Champagne** sat at their table, glad **Ménage** has blessed them with her presence.

"You made it! I didn't think you'd come," said the legend, wondering if she could handle the Ghetto.

The drinks changed **Ménage's** mood. The alcoholic beverages helped her remember the **Hood** back in **Houston, Texas** called the 5th ward. She's from the projects, but her reluctant behavior was because it wasn't *"her"* Ghetto, **Ménage** explains, as they joked about her scared looks from earlier, with the envious *"Dope Boys"* on the corner.

Champagne feels like *"Moses"* trying to get her people paid. She's recruiting dancers that reminds her of her younger days. She's reminiscing about shaking her ass, for what seemed like days, for a dollar bill.

The legend is feeling proud she's putting on the biggest erotic show in Philadelphia, ever, telling the girls there will not be a cover charge for dancers. *"Bitches dance for free?"* asked the dumb-founded recruit named **Poundcake.** *"Yes!"* The **Porn Star** hates it when dancers have to pay to perform. They're the unpaid labor at the show, hoping for tips. **Champagne** went on for hours, like a union rep for **hoes.**

The liberated **Ménage** is working the crowd, mesmerizing them with her freakish tongue. They went into a sexual frenzy every time she flicked it out. Every man fantasized about putting her tongue to good use. Every woman too.

Suddenly, **DJ Irv** played **Prince's "Let's go Crazy."** **Champagne's** favorite song spawned another dancing performance. She jumped to her feet and hit the stage. The brass dancing pole felt so familiar in her hands. She used her big beautiful breasts to give the brass-pole a proper squeeze. Every man with a pole between their legs wished they felt that good.

Quintin watched the legendary performance right beside her protégé, **Ménage A Trios "She still got it huh?"** said the protégé, thinking the legend was much older than she is.

Champagne's age difference is exaggerated by years of Hollywood make-up. **Ménage's** perception of her mentor is strained. She thought the legend's reign was coming to an end, wanting to be the Star of the show herself. She didn't think a woman with **"that"** many secrets deserved the spotlight.

Quintin quickly stroked her ego. **"She's alright,"** he said. He's not impressed by her secret rival. They turned their surroundings to a regular Club atmosphere, by slow dancing to **Prince's "Purple Rain,"** by the steps.

He has the young, up-and-coming Star feeling like a prom date. **Ménage's** eating out the palm of his hands, laughing at his jokes, and feeling more and more relaxed. She didn't even bat an eye, when he escorted her to the **VIP** area upstairs.

The mood upstairs is always laidback. **DK** ran the **VIP** room like a '70's speakeasy. The CD player is playing songs from **Teddy Pendergrass' "Greatest Hits,"** while they continued to dance.

Ménage began to feel the **monster** growing in **Quintin's** pants. The **Porn Star** had no idea that her escort's packing like that! Her curiosity consumed her mind. She had to ask...

"Is that a weapon in your pocket, or are you happy to see me?"

"If that's a gun baby, it would have a 12-inch barrel," said **Quintin** pressing against her body even harder.

"12 Inches huh?" said **Ménage,** inspecting his shaft with her very small hands. Her movies were documented proof, that she could handle every inch. **Ménage's** used to her men being well-endowed. She prefers a huge, chocolate penis over the smaller ones her White co-stars were packing. She didn't have to day-dream about having sex with a *"Mandingo"* co-star. She has *"good"* dick right here.

Quintin continued to let the **Porn Star** molest him with her wondering hands. He's used to fulfilling women's dreams with his porno-sized shaft. She would have agreed, with those previous lovers, that he could've been a pleasing co-star in any XXX film.

Ménage and "**Quintin's** conversation turned personal when she asked about his marital status. She knew somebody had to be waiting up at night for his return. His estranged wife wasn't his girl. The famous comedian **Sommore** is claiming **"boy-toys"** all over the country. But, in Philly, **Quintin** is the best.

His guarded answers heightened her woman's intuition. **"Don't lie to me baby. Lie to your girl"** explained the horny **Porn Star**. She didn't care if he has a girlfriend. She just wanted to know if she's got to watch her back, at that moment.

He agreed to having a girlfriend, and she would not be crashing this party tonight. He just didn't tell "**Ménage**" her name. He continues to slow drag with her while **Teddy's** song **"Close the door"** plays in the background.

"Close the door, no need to worry no more," the lyrics are whispering in her ear. The song confirmed she needn't worry about getting caught by his nameless lover.

"Let me make sweet love to you baby!" rang out in the speakers, like a question.

Quintin's karaoke impression sealed the deal. She's his only audience. Everybody else faded downstairs to watch the legendary **Champagne** give a lap dance live on stage.

The lucky pair used this opportunity to escape to the back bedroom. The clean sheets caressed her naked body. The bedroom was set-up by **DK**. He would've gambled his most prized possessions that this wouldn't go down. All he needed was a nod to assemble their accommodations. **"Nothing but the best for a Star,"** thought **DK**, when he equipped the room with aroma candles, champagne and the Club's best linen.

The rose petals on the bed weren't even used in her movies. She's instantly feeling romanced, instead of being rummaged-off like a trick. There won't be a film director yelling *"cut"* tonight. This torrid sex scene will be sexy and passionate, without anybody's direction. *DK* placed a sign on the bedroom door that read: *"Occupied"*

They didn't have much time; not because of the 15-minute time limit allotted during Club hours, they're rushing because the two cohorts are supposed to be on-the-clock. *Quintin* has a Club to run, and *Ménage's* got a show to promote. Neither didn't care.

Quintin laid the XXX *Porn Star* down on the bed. He stood at attention, savoring every moment. She noticed the *Champion Lover's cock,* while the Jamaican reggae artist, *Shabba Ranks,* played though the first floor's sound system. Her long tongue almost choked him. This reminded him to put the freakish tongue to good use. She obliges his fantasies just like the sex scenes on his hidden VHS tapes. He will always be her biggest fan, for good reason.

Ménage A Trios is the best name for her. She sucked his mammoth penis and licked his testicles at the same time. She felt like a one-woman threesome with her long freakish tongue resembling a snake wrapped around a branch. The *Porn Star's* films didn't give her the justice she deserved. *Ménage* slopped and slurped every throbbing inch.

Quintin didn't flinch when she sucked his *manhood* like a vacuum. She likes to bite her sexual partners; another reason why she asked if he has a girlfriend. The violent lover sucks for cum like vampires' suck for blood, ravishing single men, because her sexual prowess leaves incriminating marks, thinking his nameless girlfriend will know he's been unfaithful.

Quintin wasn't about to show weakness. He allowed the *VIP* vixen to have her fill of all the dick she could swallow. He flexed his pecks when she bit his chest. *Ménage* likes the fact her *prey* didn't flinch.

He didn't move a muscle when she put passion marks on his inner thighs. When she licked his whole-body head to toe, he didn't squirm. As a true sexual Soldier, he stood defiant, despite her ticklish torture. He did better than most, by withstanding her *sexual test.*

Ménage has literally scared professional athletes, like *Dallas Cowboys' Emmitt Smith,* to death with the same test. *Quintin* wasn't those prodigious celebrity dudes, she was used to.

Ménage loves to expose lying married men at $1000 a pop. They couldn't pass either. The scratch-marks would usually be a deal- breaker, clawing at their backs.

She wants to administer her final *sexual pop-quiz.* The heated *Porn Star* wanted to switch lanes, seizing her opportunity, when he laid on his stomach. *Ménage's* long tongue, camouflaging as a simple kiss on his ass, hid her true intentions. She wanted to expose any *"Fruit Loop"* tendencies. Her freakish tongue is 7 inches in length, a worthy tool for her lesbian lovers, but a scary tool for all those metrosexual tough guys she's fucked.

The **Champion Lover** is an **"amateur"** to her freakish fetish. She likes to **"toss dudes' salads,"** (the term originated in prisons) by penetrating guys' butt with her mammoth tongue. She's just like the hounds downstairs, that love eating strange **Punany.**

"Oh Hell No!!" snapped **Quintin,** flipping the script in an instant, clamming up like a virgin on a prom date. The fantasy was over. If this was a contest, the home team is losing. Her dominatrix-style love games were going for the gold right up **Quintin's** ass.

He needed a fourth-quarter comeback fast to turn this freak back into the obedient regular **hoe,** he witnessed on film. She needed to be conquered by a real man.

"What's my name?" DMX's rap song played on cue downstairs. He made her assume the **doggy-style** position. **"On your knees! You crazy ass bitch!!"** he said with something to prove.

"What you Niggas WANT!" DMX chimes in his thoughts.

He started to pull on her hair. **Ménage** became more aroused from the pain. She could dish it and take the rough stuff. The **Texas-Native** loves being put in her place. **Quintin's** violently penetrating her **"snatch,"** thinking her vagina would be worn-out from all the huge dicks in her films, but she's surprisingly tight for a **Porn Star.** They looked like unscripted adult film actors **getting it in!**

She didn't have to fake an orgasm. **Ménage** climaxed repeatedly on the 12-inch power rod, squealing like a stuck pig from the serious pounding. The tables turned when his ego kicked in overdrive.

"You really don't know who you Fucking Wit!" he hollered, harmonizing with the *"Ruff Ryder,"* while *Ménage* holds on for dear life, dominated by the *"Dark Soldier."*

"Looking like some brand-new Pussy trying get FUCKED!" **DMX** is still talking all the *"Shit"* she needs to hear.

Meanwhile downstairs…

Champagne finished teasing the crowd. Now, she's snatching some lucky fan out of the audience. Her undercover *"flunky"* knew just what to do. They had the crowd thinking they were complete strangers. *"I need a willing volunteer!"* she said, cueing her willing assistant to raise his hand. She ordered him to lay flat of the stage. The walls seemed to be on fire from the anticipation of what could happen next. Everybody in the room thought she was going to perform a live sex show.

"Do you know what a golden shower is sir?" *Champagne* asked her so-called fan. He played his part well. He shook his head no. The crowd hollered out to warn him, even though his fate is a calculated trick.

"Close your eyes and open wide then! I'm about to show you!" she said.

Champagne ordered two dancers *Jazzy* and *Tasty* to blind-fold him, helping her build the suspense, while they held down the willing *"flunky."*

The legendary **Porn Star** almost started a riot when she tossed her panties into the crowd. All the **"real"** men in the crowd watched in **horror** as she stood over him and **peed** in his mouth. Her aim was impeccable not a drop hit the stage! He drank every drop and the jam-packed Club went wild!

Quintin's famous girlfriend, **Sommore**, arrived to the Club. She's taken aback by all the **"hoop-la."** She quickly understood why. **Champagne's** corrupting some poor soul; Live on stage. She spoke to some of the familiar faces at the door.

Storm radioed **Quintin** on the walkie-talkie. He knew to alert him immediately. Especially, about a surprise visit from his girlfriend. **Storm** paged him again. No answer.

Quintin turned his radio off when he started his slow dance with **Ménage.** He's most definitely busy. **Storm** knew to cover his whereabouts, turning into a gracious host, introducing the comedienne to the XXX legend. Thankfully, they both are fans of each other.

Storm walked **Sommore** by the DJ booth. **Big Country** asked her to say a few words to the crowd, while secretly buying **Quintin** some more time.

"How's everybody feeling tonight?" shouted the sexy comic. **Sommore's** wearing a tight fitting **Fendi** jumpsuit. The mic echoed her voice throughout the Club. She likes trying new material on audiences, and she's having a field day on the **Pee-Pee Boy.**

The shenanigans going on there served her well. No need to re-collect her jokes. She's witnessing real-life humor right there. No other Club in the city offers this kind of entertainment.

"What's this the little 'whore' house of the Hood?" joked the comedienne.

The crowd laughed hysterically. **Sommore** joked about how she's going to tell their *"women at home"* where they're at, snitching on their cheating activities, Only, if they didn't tip her too!

"I need some money too shit!" she said, showing some cleavage of her beautiful chocolate tits. The crowd rains dollar bills on the stage without hesitation, while **Storm** watches her back from aggressive hands tipping the comedic star.

Meanwhile upstairs…

Quintin and **Ménage's** sex battle must abruptly stop. He heard his famous girlfriend's voice on the mic. The shook boyfriend is scrambling to fix his clothes. **Ménage** is disappointed they didn't have an opportunity to perform his *"cum-shot"* finale. She clawed at his back for wanting to leave.

"Don't go!" she begged.

Quintin confessed that his girl was in the building, revealing that his girlfriend was none another than the comedienne **Sommore!**

"I love her…She's funny" said **Ménage,** who's starting to get mad at **Quintin** for promising that they would

"not" have any interruptions. She doesn't like being lied to. *Ménage* had to teach him a lesson.

"If you don't want me to go downstairs and tell her, Assume the fucking position!" said the *Porn Star,* flipping the script again. *Ménage's* back in control of their erotic sex match. She lost the previous battle but was determined to win the war.

The *Porn Star* smacked his ass for bruising her tight pussy. He knew exactly what she wanted... her silence will cost a heavy price. She needed another notch on her belt. *Ménage A Trios* had him by the balls, literally.

"Promise you won't tell?" asked the defeated *Casanova. "Your secrets are my secrets...Lover!"* she said, flicking out her freakish tongue.

DK lightly knocked on the door. He knew *Quintin's* radio is off during his sexual episode with the *Porn Star.* He must alert his new *Boss* that... *Sommore* is waiting downstairs.

Meanwhile on the first floor...

The very funny *Sommore* is roasting the Club's crowd downstairs, while *Quintin's* getting turned out by the adult film star upstairs. *Ménage A Trois's* turning a foreign fetish for him, to a new-found pleasure. He no longer felt violated. The shit feels good. Even though he thought getting his *"Salad"* tossed was gay-like behavior, she is a woman, after all.

The newly learned fetish made him climax. She's pleased that he finally came. The crazy freak is proud of her conquest. He's paid for her silence, in advance, simply by letting her lick out his *"Ass."*

Meanwhile downstairs…

"Where's my Chocolate Man!" said *Sommore,* continuing to hog the mic. The comedienne is starting to feel a little tipsy. *Storm's* complementary drinks are the blame for that. *Sommore* won't be denied. She's there for one reason, *Mr. Quintin L. Shavers.*

Ménage watched her victim get dress. *Quintin*'s nameless girlfriend now has a name… *Sommore.* The tipsy comic is screaming in the mic. *"Chocolate Man!"* shouted the embarrassing, unannounced *"lady friend."* He quickly downgraded her status in his mind.

She's starting to piss him off. *"These bitches are taking over!"* mumbled the irritated *Quintin*. He's referring to his *"ass licker"* and the crazed comic tripping downstairs.

Big Country snatched the mic back. She's having a meltdown, live on stage, but the show must go on. The *Ladies of the Night* are getting restless. Patrons didn't wanna see that shit either. *Champagne* chimed in on the Comic's rampage.

"Quintin, you better get your ass down here!" she said. After looking around the Club for her protégé, she figured out quickly that her fellow *Headliner's* and the *Casanova's* slow drag must've turned into a sexual *"Tango."*

"The legend" stoked the comic's jealous rage, asking her entourage very loudly…*"Where's Ménage?"*

Sommore started a rapid search for her *"Chocolate Man"* hiding with the **Porn Star** with the freakish tongue. She looked in the first-floor restroom, then she started to look behind the bar.

"Slow your roll Miss!" announced the chocolate *"Star-Maid."* *Charmaine* stopped the crazed comic in her tracks. She's wearing a cherry red catsuit, that's clinging to her camel toe like a wrapper on a life-saver, complete with red clogs to match, giving her 4 more inches to her height.

"Damn it's pretty bitches everywhere!" said *Sommore,* trying to push pass the bootylicious bartender.

Charm's red outfit is a stop sign on so many levels. *"First," "Stop" and "Pull it together!"* The 19-year-old bartender always has wise words for **scorned** women. She calmed the hysterical comic down. She knew her drink order is Hennessey. That was it.

The *"Star-Maid"* didn't recognize the stand-up comedienne. She only saw another *"Sister"* desperate over a man; another duped woman crying over a **Crew** member. She didn't have time to console this one. The slightly concerned bartender knew the code

"They pay me for the silence."

Translation: What goes down in the **Grindstone,** Stays in the **Grindstone.**

She had an idea someone was fucking in the *"date-room."* The kitchen is directly under the back-bedroom's floor. The noisy sex game upstairs didn't exactly go unheard. *Charmaine* and *Mrs. B.* heard the muffled contest above their heads, while they prepared food orders. The kitchen is just beyond the bar. *"No freaky bitches back here either!"* announced *"Mom-Dukes"* from the kitchen.

Quintin and *Ménage* weren't hiding among the liquor bottles. They crept out the back bedroom. The guilty couple found a table upstairs to *"pretend"* to have an *"innocent"* conversation.

Sommore went upstairs to finish her search. She's a little bit of a player herself. Her only *"Beef"* is that she doesn't want *"sloppy seconds!"* She didn't have exclusive rights to her *"Chocolate Man,"* but she didn't want to share *"that"* dick tonight either. The horny comedic star's been looking for *Quintin* since he left the Night Club business for *"Go-Go."*

She was jealous back then, about regular Club *hoes,* now, there's famous *Porn Stars* added to the mix. The jealous meltdown was bound to happen. She told herself not to approach them, but did it anyway, when she saw the sneaky couple acting innocent at the *VIP* table.

She asked one question. *"Who this Bitch?"*

Ménage didn't appreciate getting put in this position, having been in this predicament before, ever since puberty. She didn't like drama from these jealous, always-blame-the-woman-types. She pitied them. The freakish *Porn Star* envied the men. Her reasoning for harsh treatment on guys that lie is once again justified. The **Porn Star** felt she shouldn't have to answer any questions.

   "He's your man not mine" said the erotic film star, with a condescending look on her face. **Ménage** didn't believe men could be faithful. *"Too much good pussy out here,"* her brother's words rang in her head. Her *"coochie"* has famous **Porn** status.

   "How could he pass this up?" thought **Ménage** She thought having sex with a **Porn Star** was every man's fantasy.

   Her expression said it all, sitting at the **VIP** table with **Quintin** with a confused look on her face. **Sommore** sized up her *"competition."* Her *"Chocolate Man"* is in the company of this freak. She's out gunned but, not out-matched in wit. The sexy comic looked at the **Porn Star** with a territorial stare.

   "Fuck with me, you stuck with me!" She reminded **Quintin** that he made the fatal mistake of knocking a bone out of her ass. She was *sprung.* He didn't hear her phone calls. He was too busy humping around with the **Porn Star** to check messages. He's her *"Mr. Good Bar"* when she performs in the **Philadelphia** area.

   They met months ago. **Quintin** was working a security detail, while she was on a comedy tour. She didn't mine screwing the **"help."** The problem is, he pleases her too good. She would usually fulfill her needs with her #2 choice, if her **"main"** dude goes missing. Tonight, she's looking for her *"favorite"* lover with a flashlight, because her bones needed shaking.

   She asked again. *"Who's this bitch?"*

Ménage understood why the comic is tripping. She didn't like being disrespected by a *"regular"* bitch. In her mind, she didn't think any female could compete with the fantasy of a *Porn Star,* but she wasn't going to be called to many more *"Bitches."*

"Don't asked questions you don't want the answers to," said the *Porn Star.* She had to put the comic in her place. She stood up from the table; the two rival lovers are in each other's faces. The *Porn Star* clowned the comic by exposing her baby feelings over a man.

The secrets about *"their"* earlier behavior was never told during their argument. Her silence never wavered. Her breath told it all. *"Don't talk shit…with your breath smelling like doo-doo, boo boo!"* said the famous comedienne, like she's just dropped the mic!

CHAPTER ELEVEN
"Welcome to Philadelphia Mr. Number Three"

Later in the week, word about the famous night at the *Grindstone* spread around the City like wildfire, and there was no need for embellished lies. There was the *Porn Star's "Golden shower,"* and the comedy act about a *Porn Star* with a *"shitty"* freakish tongue. Rumors isn't needed to fuel this fire. The truth rang in the ears of hip-hop celebs, influential business moguls, professional athletes and one legendary sports figure, *Allen Iverson.*

Champagne, again, was *"true"* to her (excuse my language) *"Mother Fucking"* word! Everything the *Hood* was saying about the *Grindstone,* was being confirmed by her. She put the popular hot spot on the map, causing a chain reaction with powerful social effects. The *Crew* is making connections *Players* only dreamed about. Popping bottles with Celebrities is becoming a weekly habit.

The *Grindstone* gets the honor of welcoming a new Celebrity to the *"City of Brotherly Love."* He's the professional basketball player, *"Allen Ezail Iverson."* The number one draft pick of the NBA chose to celebrate at the popular after-hour *"Go-Go"* Club everybody's talking about.

He wasn't a household name in Philly yet. The 21-year-old ball player and his entourage arrived in 15 matching, rented, black *Lexus* cars, screeching to an abrupt stop. They started jumping out their vehicle and walking up to *Storm*, who was posted at the front door.

"We're Allen Iverson!" said the cronies of his *Crew.* *Storm* replied to the entourage, *"He's Allen Iverson!"* pointing at the young athletic star. *"The rest of y'all gotta to pay!"* *Storm* started counting the heads of his homeboys. The cover charge was negotiated at $15 per person. The group rate was paid solely, by the basketball star. He had a wad of fifties, thanks to his recent signing bonus.

The entourage is very excited to be celebrating with the Star, but the festivities were on his dime. The newly *"Million-Dollar Athlete"* looked like a thug-rap artist, ready to celebrate his colossal *"come-up."* They arrived early. Only one dancer is there. They just opened when the *VIP* party arrived at the Club's door step. The entourage gets properly searched. The Club's reputation had the Star and his friends anxious to see what goes on inside. They didn't even mind hiding their weapons in their rented cars.

Meanwhile…

Q and *Charmaine* are having a lightweight heated argument by the bar about the rumors of his cheating ways. She's been snatching *Bitches* up by their collar all week, accusing all of them of *"plotting on her man."* He can't believe that she wanted to discuss their personal issues while they worked. She could care less that *Allen Iverson* is in the building. He's just another so-called *"star"* she didn't know.

The *Boss* knew how important the *VIP's* surprise visits meant. He needed to make sure his Celebrity guest has a good time. He didn't need an immature meltdown right now. *Charmaine* wants out of this kind of employment and threatened to *"leave the relationship"* if he doesn't want the same. He could feel her pain, but he knew they needed to put their game faces on.

"Come on, let's get this money …Baby!" pleaded the opportunistic **Hustler of the Year.**

The only dancer is ready to perform. *Jazzy* didn't know a Sport Celebrity was just a few feet away from her. She was too busy watching *Q* and *Charmaine's* argument, hoping they just break-up and *"Poppy"* find his way back to her arms.

Jazzy didn't notice the **Platinum-Diamond** chain around **Allen Iverson's** neck, or his fresh Reebok's that's named after him. She's too engulfed in her beloved *"Poppy's"* spat with his spoiled young lover. *Charmaine* knew *Q* would never leave the *"Game."*

All he needed was a **Star Barmaid** with *"MVP"* customer service skills. He desired a *"Superstar"* teammate to reel in this **NBA clientele.** He knew one look at *Charmaine's* ass, and he'll bring all his friends.

"Young Black Millionaires don't just walk in your door every day. "Let's get this money!"

Big Country is the DJ. He cranked up the sound system. *"Blow the whistle"* by **TOO SHORT** started to rattled out of the speakers.

Jazzy started shaking her ass. *A.I.* quietly watched her performance. She's the only dancer in the Club this early on a Monday night. After the five songs were played, she wondered why this so-called star hadn't tipped yet. She summoned her *"Beloved Poppy"* to the stage. *"Why ain't he tipping?"* whispered *Jazzy* in his ear.

Charmaine was busy preparing drinks at the bar, when she noticed *Jazzy* talking too close to her *man.* She's already *lit* from earlier. The weary girlfriend needed his attention. The seven day a week work schedule wore on her nerves. She simply needed a break. The problem with all of this is, it's bad timing.

Charmaine wanted to a have conversation about his cheating rumors. Making matters worse, his number one rumor is whispering in his ear. *"Jazzy! Back up Bitch!"* she warned, shouting across the room from the bar. *Jazzy* is on her *"shit list"* until some answers are given. Those two are just too friendly!

Jazzy wanted to be known, winking a woman-to-woman moment. *Charmaine* realized then, that they do have some history.

The wise *Bar-Maid* is starting to have *baby feelings* of her own. She wondered if they are still fucking. Her only concern is if she's being played. *"Fake Bitches!"* are HER thoughts of any woman that'll *"smile in your face, then Fuck your man."*

"We need to talk" said *Charmaine* to the surprised *Q-Deezy*. He didn't like the bar unattended. She needed to get something off her chest, but he didn't have time for a tantrum. He had to take care of his business. He offered a rain check on their conversation, with a night off. *Charmaine* stormed outside, right in front of their Celebrity guest.

Allen Iverson still hadn't tipped the dancing *Jazzy*. *"Got change for a fifty?"* he asked, watching the soap opera between the *Bar-maid* and the *Boss*. Now it's time to get this party started!

"All you got is fifties?" asked the *Boss,* watching his *Star-barmaid, Charmaine James,* storm off the court. She's on *"baby-feeling reserve,"* needing to evaluate if she needs to retire altogether. The Celebrity laughed at the *Ghetto* drama unfolding. *Q's* getting irked with the basketball Star that jokes about his in-house problems.

He needed some weed to enjoy all the *"drama"* at the *Grindstone*.

"How much is the weed around here?" The answer, *"$50 a half-ounce."*

"How much is the Hennessey?" The answer, *"$50 a pint."*

"How much is the Alize?" The answer, *"$50 a pint."*

"How much is oral sex around here?" The answer, *"$50 for the 'date-room' for every 15 min."*

"See you already have change," answered the *Boss.* He'll be covering the bar for the remainder of the night.

Allen Iverson and his entourage sparked the *"Chocolate Thai."* The mellow groove relaxed the unknown Star, puffing weed at their table. That's prohibited downstairs on the first floor of the *Grindstone,* but he's allowed that privilege with over $10,000 in his pocket. None of the newly arriving patrons recognized the newly crowned *"Prince of*

Philly." His entourage have their fill on the pints of liquor and smoking the finest smelling weed. That's making everybody in the room mellow and friendly.

"How many songs is she going to dance?" asked the Basketball Player, who's getting tired of seeing the *"same"* dancer, *Jazzy's* holding it down while they wait for the other dancers to show up.

The *"Amazon"* wasn't their type at first. She'd danced for 20 songs, without one dollar tipped. She'd sweated out her permed edges, while shaking her ass to the fast reggae beats, giving it her all, moving those powerful legs, twirling on the Brass pole, all performed flawlessly in her high-heel boots. *Jazzy's* endurance alone has won the crowd over!

Allen Iverson started tipping her nothing but $50 bills, out of *"admiration"* of her stamina. As an athlete, he could relate. She was digging deep, performing her heart out, to some of the hardest *"Gangsta"* rap.

DJ *Big Country* played the requested songs. *Jazzy* spoke to the non-tipping crowd through *"Rap."* Her selections were some of the Star's favorites. The Celebrity *Virginia* native began to rain $50 bills on the thugged-out dancer, bobbing his own head to the beat, while *Big Pun's* gangster lyrics put things in the right perspective.

"Bubba Chuck" aka *Allen Iverson* began to feel comfortable with the laughable, Philly *"Go-Go"* Club with one dancer. The weed wasn't too shabby either. He declined the soul food platters, until he saw his cousin fucking one up. *Mrs. B.'s* fried fish, greens and fries, for $50 a platter, almost seemed worth it, and she still demands a tip.

"Welcome to Philadelphia, Hood-style," was better than the fancy welcome party at the *First Union Center,* with whispering fake people, who think he's a convicted *"Felon,"* beating that case in *Newport, Va.* He didn't need the paid super models trying to push his baby-mama *"out the box,"* Nor, did he need the corny *"Live band,"* who's destroying *James Brown's "Super Bad,"* and he definitely did *"Not"* need a smoke-free stadium, serving some nasty-ass gourmet food.

All this *Brother* needed is *"The Grindstone!"*

"I'm faded, it's time to get X-rated!" said the entourage, watching the arriving dancer named *Puddin* walk through the door. She's an 18-year-old, short, Dominican thick'em, with a stacked booty, pushing her way through the hungry, horny crowd of *A.I.s' Crew.* Her ass felt so soft when they groped it. *Puddin* rolled her eyes, thinking *"she should've kept her black-ass home."* Instead, she hurried getting her *"black-ass"* dressed, with the smell of money in the air.

Puddin! Q-Deezy's happy that another dancer has shown up, rushing her to get dressed. He didn't have time to tell her the low-down about the *"new"* Celebrity surprise visitor that only has fifties in his pockets! Dancing on stage wasn't her strong suit anyway.

"I Just started dancing, but I've been tricking for years," said the amateur, too scared to show her muffin top. She rarely hits the stage. Some nights, *Puddin* pays the *MC* not to even mention her name.

Jazzy is exhausted. The *Captain of the Dancers* has danced a 30-song *"set,"* holding their attention until the

Calvary arrived. This one-pony show's muscles burned from the task, and she needs water, and help off the stage, like a heroic marathon runner that just finished the race, passing the baton to the next performer, waiting at the top of the steps.

The Star and his entourage gave **Jazzy** a standing ovation. Her sweat drenched the stage as she excused herself to change out the sweaty outfit. **Big Country** announced the next exotic performer.

"Fellas coming to the stage, it's the Sexy Puddin!"

She receives one clap. **Puddin's** new to dancing, so her dancing outfit is a one- piece bathing suit, with some old high heels. She's a far cry from the fancy, starving models at **Delilah's Den.** The **Grindstone** wasn't living up to its rumored hype. There weren't any legendary **Porn Stars,** famous sexy comediennes or the *"bootylicious"* **Bar-maid.** Just **Puddin.**

She didn't hit the stage as the announcer promised. **Puddin** wanted to give the newly crown *"Prince"* a table dance. Instinctively, she focused on the money man.

Allen Iverson's the man of the hour, like a bachelor on his last night of freedom. He must settle for this make-shift *"Go-Go"* dancer, popping her booty, on this side of the town, where nobody knows his name.

Puddin gave the unrecognizable Star a *"lap-dance,"* instead of a marathon stage performance. She understood that her weak dance skills wouldn't entice this Star, but her soft, fat ass just might do the trick. She knew the first thing you needed for proper a *"lap dance"* is a soft fat ass; arousing the rich young Star with her *one* secret weapon, her extremely *"soft Booty."*

A.I. thought the *"Ghetto lap-dancer"* would be a nice cheap thrill. He's months away from groupie-status fame. Tonight, he's just another regular guy trying bust a nut for 50-bucks. Primed and ready, he asked for a *"date-room."*

Puddin escorted him upstairs. She wanted to show him what she does best. *"Black Butter"* is on full display upstairs, down the hall, pass the dressing room, inside the candle lit *"back-bedroom."*

A.I. paid **DK** the $50 *"date-room"* fee. He told the Star the rules and warned him of the consequences if he didn't follow them. He's another person who didn't know the *"Celebrity."*

A.I. played along with their ignorance about his identity. He wanted to be anonymous anyway. There's no fanfare needed here for a $50 blow job. He gladly entered the bedroom, with the raggedy trick, with the soft ass.

A.I. was on her turf now. She's an *amateur* on stage, but a *beast* in the bedroom. He wanted to know if she was true to her words, feeling all soft and horny.

"Here's your $50 baby girl" he said, instructed to pay in advance by **DK**. *Puddin* looked at the money like an insult, sitting the naïve Celebrity Basketball Star down on the bed. Her explanation said it all:

"Listen man, my boyfriend watches ESPN'S 'Sport-center' every night. Every day I hear that damn theme song... dunna- dunna dunt... dunna-dunna dunt! Mister high school

quarterback AND point guard for Bethel, State Champs for both sports. Am I right? Loved your handling skills at Georgetown, by the way. Welcome to Philly, Mister 1st round draft-pick for the 'Sixers.' I know exactly WHO you are!"

She's going to need $1000 to suck his dick. There wasn't a *"groupie"* in this room. *Puddin* felt both bulges in his pants. The long Basketball Player's dick and $10,000 worth of $50 bills. She's as shrewd as a sport agent, closing a deal. His dick went limp calculating the figures.

A.I. excused himself with his sexy, *Virginian* accent. He hurried downstairs to complain to the *Boss*, who wanted to clown the Star with woman problems. His cover is blown by the lady with the one-piece bathing suit. The idea of busting a load all over her face sounded good for $50, but *"not for a thousand!"* whined the horny athlete.

Groupies and horny super models were just weeks away. He wasn't going to pay this *"Hood rat"* $1000. He whined about *"once he's known around the City,"* services like this would be for free. Tonight, isn't going be one of those nights!

"I'll talk to her" said the *Boss*. He didn't like getting involved in a trick's price. After all, it's her body. He knows *Punany* prices are like gold stock market prices. Prices do flocculate, but *Puddin* was tripping. The whole *"Crew"* has witnessed the raggedy dancer barter the same dick suck for a ride home. Now, suddenly her *"coochie"* doesn't stink!

Q-Deezy hurried upstairs to negotiate a better deal for the horny Star. She's on the bed smoking a cigarette. *"Yo, that Nigga's got money Q!"* she said. The ghetto vixen, with the soft ass is ready to cash in. *Puddin's* cool as ice, waiting for his counter offer. If her *"coochie"* is gold, she wants the highest stock price. They all agreed to $300 for a *Philadelphia* blow job.

Minutes later…

A.I. peeled off six $50-bills. He's reluctant, but realized no other dancers are available. The future Celebrity Basketball Player enters the room. He didn't like being duped to pay extra just because he has it.

"Tricking ain't tricking if you got it!" joked the *"Hood-rat."* She's looking attractive in the dimly lit bedroom. Her lip gloss is popping. *Puddin* looks better as a butt-naked *hoe* with shiny lips than the over-dress dancer with cheap shoes. She quickly dolled up, her body with pineapple body spray.

Puddin wanted to be his welcoming fruit basket. She's smelling like forbidden fruit that likes his skinny 165-pound frame and his long Ball Player's stick. She wanted to autograph his shaft for every would-be female fan. Her skills weren't like *Ménage's* violent touch. She slowly slurped it like water ice, then licked it like a salted pretzel and jerked it like his white home-girls back home. Becky couldn't even compare to her oral master-piece. His body shook from every seductive pull, but he didn't want to cum yet.

Puddin assumed the position and smacked her own ass. She played with her pussy. Spreading her lips so gently calling for his *"balls."* The Star athlete could see the pink end-zone. Clearly, he wants to renegotiate his contract for *"more than oral sex." Allen Iverson* wanted to pound that soft ass like a Hampton Nigga!

She's been coached well. Every *"John"* has a budget when his dick is limp. When it gets hard, all bets are off! She kindly reached down and handed him his pants.

Puddin told him to count out $700 worth of $50-bills. His hard dick was handling the thinking from here on out. He instinctively peeled off 14 more $50 bills, like a Baller under a trance. *Puddin's* surprisingly deep to the scarcely known athlete; juicy *"Black Butter"* that can barely squeeze around his pole, preventing any air from getting in between the friction. Her deep, $1000 *"snatch"* made him climaxed in seconds. Rumor has it, *"she made a thousand dollars for 3 seconds of work."*

Puddin will never watch *Sportcenter* the same. She laughed when she later learned his jersey number was *"The Number 3."*

"Now, when she hears the theme song... *dunna-dunna dunt... dunna-dunna dunt"* her panties get wet."

"Welcome to Philadelphia Mr. Number Three!

CHAPTER TWELVE

"Step into the Light!"

It's 11:30pm., when **Q-Deezy** arrived at the **Grindstone** in his red **Buick,** sporting brand-new *"Pirelli's"* chrome rims, a flashy addition to his vehicle. He's turning some of the **hater's** heads playing catch football right in front the Club, hogging the sidewalk and parking space with their playground shenanigans. The light-skinned, rude one turned his head around when **Q-Deezy** honked his horn.   It's **Munchie** and his boys trying to disrupt some shit by paying a visit.

Q-Deezy and **Munchie** locked eyes when he stepped back on the sidewalk, allowing the **Boss** to park, strapped with his boys that can't fight. **Munchie's** cronies didn't know about their *"Beef,"* they're there to fuck around outside the Chinese store next door.

Charmaine is already inside the Club. She opened the Club minutes ago, coming from hanging out with her homegirl, **Rhonda,** at the **Green Room** bar on **52ⁿᵈ & Girard. Munchie** watched her buy drinks for her main *"dawg,"* then walking to her new man's Club, opening it on her own.

She's ignoring her baby-father's calls, trying to prep the bar for the evening's clientele and warming up tonight's special Chili at $10.00 a bowl, changing the kitchen's name to *"Soul Food Funk"* overnight, offering good pre-made dishes to the crowd. Prepping for tonight's opening, she came in earlier than the rest of the staff.

Q-Deezy sat in his vehicle watching **Munchie** and his boys play in front the Club. He's trying not to jump to conclusions, thinking, *"maybe they're just going to the Chinx."* However, his eyes told it all. This intrusion is intentional; styling and profiling on the *"Old-head's" Strip.*

"Yo! Dude! This ain't a playground!" announced *Q-Deezy*, slamming his car's door, tripping on the young fellas drawing outside the **Grindstone. Munchie's** boys bowed down quickly, embarrassing **Charmaine's** ex by punking his whole *"rift-raft Crew"* off the block.

Munchie couldn't believe his Crew didn't snap back; at least say something slick, hoping they get into some personal *"Beef"* with the Club owner. *Q-Deezy* wasn't having none of that!

"Fuck Outta Here!" personally directed at **Munchie,** hoping he come better than that next time. (Complete with a wink!)

Q-Deezy strolled across the street to use the pay-phone. He's calling **Storm** to get his *"20"* their code word for his location. His friend is 15 minutes away, laughing at him about using a dirty-ass pay-phone… When a gunshot goes off from a moving car! The bullet missed *Q-Deezy's* head by inches, striking the pay-phone.

The fast-moving drive-by car sped down the block and turned left on Media Avenue with no tags. *Q-Deezy* didn't see their faces ducking down behind the parked cars on the block. Most of the people buzzing around the Chinese store thought the gun-shot was a car's backfire, but the intended target knew the bullet was meant for him.

The parked car is great cover, if the shooter returns. Inside the station-wagon, it's **Tracie,** the debunked thick'em that didn't like **Charmaine's** deal. She helped **Q-Deezy** to his feet, dusting off his lapel on his trench coat, hoping he notices she's lost some weight since the last time they've met.

Batting her fake eye-lashes trying to seduce a connection between them, **Tracie** knows there must be an issue in **Q-Deezy's** relationship, seeing **Charmaine** hugged-up tight at the **Copa Bana** on **40th & Spruce,** with his main boy, **Quintin,** sipping on Margaritas, selling his homeboy all the way out.

Tracie tends to have loose lips in situations like these. That's the reason the **"Wrecking Crew"** stopped fucking with her in the first place; telling people's business without all the facts! She thinks his days are numbered with her flighty friend, **Charmaine,** and has switched the script on a few dudes before the birth of her daughter.

The conniving **blabber-mouth** told it all. **Tracie** didn't leave out any details about **Charmaine's** love-life, and that faithful night with **Quintin**. **"Say What?"** asked the frazzled **Boss** scuffling her across the street to his car, pulling the snitching friend inside his vehicle. She likes being man-handled and tossed around, but there's no need to get rough. **Tracie** wants to tell it all!

Payback seasoned this **"Beef." Charmaine** is too full of herself in **Tracie's** eyes, trying to **"Pimp"** her closest friends, thinking she's better than everybody, driving **Q-**

Deezy's car… *"Shit is sickening!"* said *Tracie* like she can taste her own *"HATE"* coming out her mouth.

"You saw this with your eyes?" asked *Q,* wondering if she could see her own reflection with the fake lashes spread across her face, while flashes of jealous rage conjure up visions of a cheating *Charmaine.*

Q-Deezy pulled off into the traffic driving off the block with *Tracie* inside. She's leaving her *Old-head's* station-wagon on the block with the keys in the ignition. *Munchie* watches them sneak off together, thinking *Q-Deezy's* having *"ALL"* the cake!

They don't know that *Munchie* stole *Tracie* friend's station-wagon. They cruised on over to the *Schuylkill River,* parking by the water looking around to see if any familiar faces can see them. He listened to her *"visual accounts"* on re-play and her story didn't have any holes in it.

"Damn! She's telling the truth!" Q-Deezy mumbled his very loud thoughts. *Quintin* knows the rules when it comes to the next man's *"Stable."*

Tracie suggested he deserves better. Dealing with *Charmaine* had half their graduating class contemplating suicide. One poor boy spent $2,000 on a Mink, thinking it might sway her to go the Prom with him. When she stood him up with his own limo, taking the chauffeured ride to "Atlantic City" with another date instead of him, it almost caused the distraught *youngin* to overdose!

"Anwar was her fucking a Back-up Prom date!" claimed the laughing *Tracie*, smoking on *Q-Deezy's* truth-

telling *"Blunt,"* giving all the *"Wrecking Crew's"* secrets ... except hers; the fact that she wouldn't mind fucking with a **Boss**, while rubbing on his **package,** in his **Calvin Klein** underwear **Charmaine** just bought.

Q-Deezy turned down the sexual favor of a pity blow-job. The fact that **Charmaine** might be cheating behind his back didn't piss him off, it's **Quintin's"** betrayal that cuts the most! These *"two"* thought they were being slick the whole time. He expects a *"young girl"* to jump ship... *"that's what they do!"* declared **Q-Deezy**, trying to swallow a *"dis"* going on behind his back, knowing he can serve it right back with best of them.

"It's Cool!" said the calm, cool and collected **Boss,** wondering what kind of friend tells all their business!

"Get the Fuck out my car!" shouted **Q-Deezy**, taking his frustration out on the believable snitch, leaving **Tracie** by the River, two miles from where the station-wagon used to be. It's now in the capable hands of **Munchie's.**

Meanwhile at the *Grindstone*.

Charmaine is cutting-up lemons, trying to get the bar up and running for tonight's crowd. **Quintin** wants to help his new friend. She thinks he's *"drawlin"* coming back there, trying to be known as the secret lover, who got a small taste of **Charmaine's** cookies. She's gotta whisper *"what happened was a mistake."*

On that night at the **Copa Bana**, she slipped up drinking frozen Mango-Margaritas, getting drunk and falling on his dick, when he took her back to his one-bedroom bachelor-pad at **Haverford Courts,** sneaking his friend's inebriated lady in his sexual playground.

      "I'm at work!" said **Charmaine**, swatting his hungry touches for the lust they had just last week. She's reminding him that was *"then,"* immediately thinking she's made a very grave mistake. The one thing she'll always like about **Q-Deezy**, is he never *"Boo-loves"* on the clock, wondering where he's at anyway.

      "Damn, he needs a Cell Phone!" thought **Charmaine,** wanting a better leash on the **Boss-Lover. Quintin's** recorded conversations of **Q-Deezy's** temper tantrums, venting about **Charmaine's** spoiled ass was just *"Tough-Talk."* They're even *"IF"* he's cheating. Unfortunately for **Quintin,** that *"Shit's"* over!

      Charmaine didn't like guys that can't keep their mouths shut, drawing on situations that need to take its natural course. Distracted by the melodrama developing behind the bar, **Jazzy** peeps the *"Casanova"* trying to sweat the *"Star-Maid"* with the fat ass. She was never fooled by **Charmaine's** allegiance to her *"Poppy."*

      Jazzy believes no one can love him like she can, wishing for this day when the *"young-girl"* fuck-up, getting caught with **Quintin's** groping hands behind the bar. **Charmaine** smacked his face in front of everybody watching, spinning the awkward **sexual harassment** around on the **opportunistic business partner.**

      Charmaine plays her part well, running upstairs, away from the **Militant** Partner of **Q-Deezy's.** She calls her baby-father to come and take her home. **Munchie** doesn't need to catch a hack for this, he's got **Tracie's** friend's station wagon. Riding around the neighborhood in a **"Gangsta Lean**," he's there to pick up his baby-mama.

She's spotted riding off by a returning **Q-Deezy**, that's parking down the block. He saw **"his Lady"** climb in the front-seat wearing another cat suit," revealing everything **Munchie** has missed over the past month. They zoom past the **Boss,** who yells from the sidewalk at the car.

Charmaine didn't care who saw her jump into **Munchie's** stolen ride. They'll tell **Q-Deezy** why she left with **Munchie** who's sitting there rubbing his clean-shaven face. She turns up the radio thinking she got everything she needs out those **"Niggas,"** feeling freed from a 7-Night a week grind, playing two friends who's trying to play her against each other. Once again... She's nobody Fool.

Back on the corner of 52nd Street...

The **"drive-by"** car is back, barreling down the block shooting haphazardly at **Q-Deezy**. He's diving out the way of the bullets, that's missing him by inches. The surprise shooter is none other than **Webb.** He's back for the second-time, trying to kill his sister's so-called attacker. Hyped-up on **"Sherm-Sticks,"** he's ready to pop the curb and ram this car up his ass.

Q-Deezy would've followed the fleeing **Charmaine,** if **Webb** wasn't popping off **32-caliber** rounds from a handgun given to him by **Munchie.** He armed the wild

"Nigga" with his Pop's gun. Unlike *Munchie,* the first thing *Webb* did was get some bullets for the six-shooter, needing some protection on his hip since, the *Operation* took his weapon, knowing he'll probably kill *Q-Deezy* early in the *"Game."*

The *Operation* has a truce with the *Grindstone.* They did everything possible to stop *Webb* from killing the *Boss* of the *Grindstone,* but he's coaxed into it by *Charmaine's* conniving baby-father, *Munchie,* who brings the *"Shit"* up while smoking the *"Sherm"* with the thrown-off dope-boy. *Webb* snatched the fire-arm right out *Munchie's* hand, stealing his young boy's weapon to kill a mutual enemy.

Webb's "clappin back" at the fool who raped his sister, knowing *Q-Deezy* has every right to want revenge on the *Operation* for secretly burning his apartment up with a fire-bomb. He's been looking for his missing sister *Emotions* for weeks. It's sending him over the edge, thinking *Q-Deezy* had something to do with her disappearance.

Q-Deezy ran into the *T&D* deli trying to duck out the way of *Webb's* wild shooting, hitting innocent by-standers waiting in line for beer at the counter. *Webb* pulled off after he ran out of bullets, reloading the revolver as he swerved up the street, thinking he shot his target... next stop, *Emotions'* secret hideaway with the crazy security dude from the Club.

"Meanwhile at Bro. Melvin's...

Emotions' body is starting to spoil. *Bro. Melvin* must discard the rotting carcass from his couch. She's nothing but dead, decaying weight. He'd been mourning her death since he snapped her neck in a schizophrenic state; waking up with the so-called love of his life, trying to figure out what the fuck he's done!

"Capital Murder!" said the voices in his head. Blaming her death on his craziness off the prescribed meds, **Bro. Melvin** stopped taking them a year ago, thinking the message should suffice against the crazy thoughts in his brain. He was so wrong.

Emotions laid there motionless, completely stiff and cold to the touch. Putting his mind to purpose, he's trying to figure out how to dispose of *Emotions'* bloated, stinking body. All that thickness was nice when she was alive; now, her thick thighs are the hardest to cut with the hack-saw. He thought her blood was going to be everywhere, he smartly used an old tarp for the drippings.

There wasn't much blood since her heart stopped and the blood began to clot, seeping thick fluid through her back onto the couch. When he turned her over, the stench quickly filled the room. Her fragile, decaying skin's bacteria made it easy for the body to pull apart, making his task of getting rid of a body, even harder.

Webb's pulling up to the rooming-house slowly, watching the neighbors outside complain about a foul-smelling odor in their building. It smells like a dead-dog done crawled up in Melvin's room and died twice. When, they banged on the door with the *Brother* cutting-up a decaying corpse inside, his secret is out. **Bro. Melvin** waited too long to handle this, he was too busy grieving over her body, rocking her for days, crying over the very stupid thing he's done.

Bro. Melvin's not thinking straight. He hasn't eaten in days, looking like a whole **"hot-mess."** He starts hearing the neighbors' car-doors slam outside, making a fuss about the ominous foul odors. They're threatening to call the cops, when **Webb** goes around the back of the rental's room first floor back window, which is covered with houseflies. Though the curtains, he can see an abandoned, dirty kitchenette, crawling with roaches.

Suddenly, the back door opens, by the bloody **Bro. Melvin,** carrying **Webb's** cut-up, dead sister, in kitchen trash bags. He's trying to creep out the rear exit with the gruesome evidence smeared all over his shirt!

"Who's there?" the guilty murderer asked the shadowing figure in the alley, by the trash cans.

"Step into the light!" shouted the **"Militant Soldier"** throwing the last of the trash bags in the driveway dumpster, who fears nothing but Allah!

"Pop-Pop-Pop" goes **Webb's** stolen gun, hitting the **Hack-saw killer** in the chest.

Webb's dead on target this time, being only 3 feet away from the murderous target, holding pieces of his beloved sister in scented glad bags, trying to breathe with three bullets lodged in his chest, shots from **Munchie's** father's stolen gun.

Meanwhile in *Charmaine's* basement bedroom...

Munchie hung around to talk with his weary baby-mother about reconciliation; another male in her life, who wants to know where he stands. Noticing *Q-Deezy's* belongings scattered around the bedroom, he's trying to forget about *Charmaine's* sucking her *Boss'* tool in the same room they're sitting. Shaking his head in disbelief about the last 30 days, *Munchie* screams, *"these fools out here can't Love you like I do!"* still dealing with all this cheating shit!

"I cheated?" asked *Charmaine,* who can't believe the audacity of the ex-boyfriend that cheated on her at least a dozen times. This is turning her completely off, reminding her, in a flash, that he's worse than the *"Old-heads"* she's running from at the bar. *Charmaine* is NOT the victim this time, they are.

"Bye, Munchie thanks for the ride!" said *Charmaine* with a dismissive tone, shoving him up the basement steps. *Munchie* violently shoves her back, remembering how she cracked him over the head in the basement's window that day.

Charmaine's all alone with her abusive ex-boyfriend. Her prison-guard father is doing another double at the prison, and ain't no telling where *Q-Deezy* drifted off to. After hearing *Quintin's* truths and the *Squad's* lies, she just wants to go to sleep and think about all this in the morning!

Munchie's getting more agitated by the second, seeing *Q-Deezy's* underwear folded in the laundry basket. She's been *"playing house with this Pimp? Probably cooking his favorites like a good little girlfriend HUH?"* he asked, remembering the rest of her insults.

"Think you can just use us ... little-dick Nigga's huh?" said the jealous-crazed **Munchie,** bringing her hurtful words back up, smacking **Charmaine** clear across the room, crashing into the same antique lamp she used to crack his head to the white meat, cutting herself on the light-bulb's broken glass.

"I'm gonna get my peoples to kick your ass!" announced his baby-mama, picking glass out her hand. She should've known this would happen... asking his bi-polar ass for a favor. When, they were together he cheated on her almost every week. Now, since the break-up he's a hermit only craving the girlfriend he lost, stripping her clothes off to have forced-sex.

"What you gonna do rape me mother- fucker?" **Charmaine** asked **Munchie,** trying to ward off his deeply disturbed train of thought. Even his crying daughter upstairs didn't stop him from zipping down his fly, trying to penetrate his very dry baby-mama, who's cringing at his touch.

Charmaine put herself into this predicament, trusting this maniac in close quarters, all alone. **Munchie's** dry-humping her because he's so horny from the 30-day drought, spewing his seed all over her stomach. He then runs upstairs, grabs his crying daughter, and darts out the door!

She's still astonished how things have gotten so crazy, holding her trembling hands over her face, crying over the attempted rape. The picky lover never could stand his semen's scent.

Meanwhile at the Grindstone...

The ***Brotherhood*** has arrived at the Club's front door. They're asking questions about ***Debo's*** attacker, a whole three weeks after the assault. They were fresh off tour with ***Guy,*** when the Leader of the ***BBO*** learned ***Bro. Melvin*** aka ***"Fruit"*** put his hands on his youngest brother. Calls were made and once again all roads lead back to the ***Grindstone.***

DJ Irv is the guest disc jockey tonight giving the Club an ambience of a ***"Hip-hop"*** party featuring a 400lbs. ***"Silver-back"*** named ***Big Wayne,*** who strolls through a parting crowd, straight to the bar. ***Quintin's*** the first to speak, knowing each other for some time now, making the introductions between ***Q-Deezy*** and ***Big Wayne's*** very deadly old friends.

He's shaking hands with the 10th degree black-belt Master Booker, pounding fist with the likes of ***Big House,*** the Head of Security at ***Club Moat,*** on ***Broad & Erie.*** They're giving the ***"Salaams"*** to ***Bro. Curt*** and ***Bro. Shamar*** from Insomnia Security, and they never sleep on the ***"Nation,"*** being former members themselves.

"How can I help you brothers?" asked the ***Boss,*** who's noticing his entire team enjoying the Club's sultry sights. Most of the ***Squad*** knows these guys, giving props to these ***"dinosaurs"*** filling the room. ***Big House*** sat on the empty stage using it as a comfortable chair, making it impossible to continue their erotic show.

"You gotta clear the stage my man" said ***Q-Deezy***, still trying to figure out the purpose of their visit, when the gigantic man refused to move, shutting the show all the way down. At the ***Grindstone*** that's the biggest NO-NO.

"My man is he with you?" asked the sharp-dressed *Q-Deezy*, thoroughly strapped with a small *45Cal.* for situations like this! He's been ducking bullets all night, and now this!

"I'm with myself!" answered *Big House,* wishing he gets the cue to knock this nigga out!

Quintin grabbed *Q-Deezy*, who's about to shoot the *"Hippopotamus"* who's acting like he can't move out the way. The man is so massive, bullets probably won't stop the stampede sitting on the stage, who's ready to Bear hug the shit out of him!

Big Wayne chuckled at the scrappy Club owner who's not having none of this *"Brodie-shit."* *Q-Deezy* never liked bullies. Thinking anybody can bleed, he's ready to throw his life away shooting some asshole sitting on a stage in a crowded Club. Maybe the drama in his life triggered this behavior, but fat boy gotta get his ass up!

The leader of the *Brotherhood* put his arms around *Q-Deezy* shoulders calming the entire situation down. They're there for *"Fruit;"* hanging out to have *Debo's* back, just in case the **"Militant Soldier"** returns.

Meanwhile back at *Bro. Melvin's*...

Webb's stepped over his target, who's still breathing and coughing up blood from his bullets. He's slowly dying, confessing a complete lie, describing in a faint voice, that he's just a hired hand cleaning a crime scene. He's blaming a long list of perpetrators for his sister's death. The

Operation for setting this whole thing in motion with a curse, and the *Grindstone* for drawing her back into the *"Game"* while she was pregnant as his intended wife. He's also pointing out the fact that *Charm* ultimately killed her during the fight in the dressing room, and he's just getting rid of the body for her new boyfriend, *Q-Deezy*!

"Oh really?" said the avenging shooter, grabbing at *Bro. Melvin's* collar, discovering the contents in the last *Glad* bag still in his hand… It's his sister's head! *Webb's* whole world snapped in an instant. Now, he's wants to tear this man's head off!

Suddenly, out the shadows, *Bro. Antonio* appears in the driveway's security spotlight saving his fellow *"Fruit,"* by shooting at the delirious dope boy, clipping the zig-zagging hot-head in the shoulder, allowing him to run out the front door. *Bro. Antonio* grabbed the brother and the remaining pieces of his intended wife.

"They don't make Soldiers like this anymore!" said the *"Nation's"* doctor called in to take the bullets out his chest, on the dinette table, while a few other Brothers clean the crime scene. Apparently, the 32Cal. bullets just lodged in his chest muscles, a wonderful side effect from the 1000 push-up daily regiment. The room is cleaned and secured when the Police knocked on the front door asking questions

"You guys hear any gunshots about 6-hours ago?" asked the flat foots, patrolling the area between donut breaks, finally responding to a call about a possible disturbance involving gunshots and the smell of dead flesh. Smelling only Muslim incenses and bleach at this point, the

Police didn't push the issue at the front door. **Bro. Melvin** holds back his screams as he's getting the bullets taken out his chest on dinette table.

"Didn't hear a thing officers" answer the savvy brothers from the *"Nation,"* politely closing the door on the unconcerned Cops.

The drama subsided when they left, leaving The **Good Bro. Doctor** to his work of patching up **Bro. Melvin** from his bullet wounds, pulling out the Quran reciting scripture to wear down the demons cursing his soul!

The one-room efficiency filled with darkness when the sprits came out, spewing its rhetoric of hate for the one true master, the most gracious, merciful ruler of all the worlds. He's pounding the will of Allah back in his mind. All he must do is accept the teachings and recite the *"Al-Fatiha."* Allah has already saved his life. *"Come on home Brother!"* said the **Bro.-Doctor,** hoping he chooses the righteous path laid out for believers that believe.

The Muslim equivalent of an exorcism is being witnessed by the *"Nation's"* Soldiers in the room. The awesome power of God is wiping away all curses made by this so-called **Black Magic.** The true believers, reciting Quranic words, broke the spell out. Ultimately, he's gotta make it stick with prayer and repentance. He's left to sleep on his make-shift bed, bandaged up, healing from **Webb's** non-piercing bullets.

Back at the Grindstone…

Q-Deezy must endure being around his business partner, knowing his secret betrayal about his girl. Pressing matters took more precedence over his personal woes about his relationship, starting with her disappearing ride-along with bi-polar ass *Munchie. Jazzy's* the first one to step-up. She would've told him what's going on, but her new boyfriend, *Debo*, told her to stay out of it!

Suddenly, *Webb* arrives at the Club. *Storm* radios *Q-Deezy* immediately. The *Boss* of the *Grindstone* grabs a *shotgun* and his *45-pound,* passing *Big Country* the pistol, prepping for *Webb's* onslaught of bullets coming their way. He's done with the *32Cal.* popping off shots six at a time, *Webb's* back with a *Tec-9* packed with 32 bullets in the clip!

"I'm Back!" he yelled outside the Club. Even the *Cherokee* across the street didn't have this kind of *"Beef."* They're watching their competition get called out by the *Operation's* corner-boy on his own rampage for blood. *Debo* and the *Brotherhood* left about an hour ago. *Q-Deezy* wouldn't mind their help right about NOW!

The *Boss* stood by the bullet-proof door when the shots rang-out! The entire Club heard the shots smashing though the wall, hitting dodging patrons trying to get out the back-door. They're stampeding over everything in their way. People got trampled escaping the wild gunman's shooting spree, accompanied by his cousin, *"Perk Man,"* blasting 45-pound *hollow-tips* though the brick structure. Bouncing bullets are hitting innocent by-standers by the Chinese store.

Q-Deezy, poking the 12-gauge though the metal flap on the metal door, returns a **Pumpkin Ball** blast from a riot pump shot-gun, giving the Club's shooters something to think about!

"We should've BURNT your ass out again!" confessed the **Tec-9** carrying **Webb,** reloading his murderous weapon behind the parked cars, conjuring a suicidal rage out of **Q-Deezy**, remembering that faithful night when, his family almost died from the **Molotov Cocktail** thrown at the front-door of his family's apartment building, 2-years ago!

Storming out the metal-door releasing the shotgun's blast in their direction, the two Assassins ducked the *"Crazy Man's"* 12-Gauge shotgun assault, missing by inches. **Big Country** follows his lead covering **Q-Deezy's** back, shooting the **45-pound** up the block at the would-be killers, hitting one in the leg!

Meanwhile...

Munchie's sabotaging **Q-Deezy's** Buick parked around the corner, funneling 5lbs. of sugar into his gas tank. He's recruited **Boo,** the third edition of **Charmaine's** flunkies, to burn down the Club later that night, orchestrating a hell-Storm that's exploding all over the place.

"Webb and Perk are some crazy Mother Fuckers!" announced **Munchie** hearing the gunshots in the distance of the Club's shoot-out, making the shit worse by ruining **Q-Deezy's** get-away car! Loathing against everything this man has out of spite, taking his precious things away, will conquer the man that stole his girl.

Q-Deezy and *Big Country* ran off the Club's shooters, while, the rest of the *Crew* lead the patrons away though the maze on alleyways behind the *Grindstone,* protecting the fleeing crowd from the shooter's hot rounds and *Philadelphia's* long arm of the *law.*

Agent Smith, returning to her favorite knuckle-head's *Go-Go"* Club, turns over the guys that got shot at the *Grindstone's* crime scene, thinking they're the *Boss* who's finally got dealt with by the *"Game."* The streets are always watching for the perfect time to strike. *Officer Mack's* collecting the shells out in front of the Club. Knowing the *Grindstone's* taste for *Riot Pumps*, the cartridges must be theirs …piecing the crime scene puzzle's together.

None of the known suspects are at the *Grindstone,* just a few scared dancers hiding upstairs. *Agent Smith* let the hysterical *"Go-Go"* dancers go with a warning.

"I'm gonna lock you up Aquil Bashir!!!"

Rhetoric statement for the *Boss*.

(under the stage at the *Grindstone*, in his secret hiding place.)

To Be Continued…

www.grindstone4life.com

ACKNOWLEDGEMENTS

I would like to take this time to thank my family for enduring countless hours, days, weeks and years of me writing this book. I would like to thank all my fellow witnesses for their interviews and kind words.

REST IN PEACE

Mom-Dukes Sunrise Nov. 16, 1948-Sunset JAN. 6, 2008

"Cha-Cha" Sunset April 14,2014

Big Gene January 9, 1963-April 22,2016

Pimp Gene

Big Wayne, House, Bro Shammar

 Satin*, Sofie, Disco

To the "Love" of my life,

Thank you for the good times and riding though the bad, putting up with my "shenanigans" has probably boggled your mind. I know I'm funny like that, quickly switching up, confusing the natural order of things, but you know I never could hold water. I gots to tell the truth, sometimes sabotaging my own future … but I'm glad you're still here as my biggest fan.

To my babies,

Whitney, Shaq, Khadijah, Siani, Sade, Cynthia this is my testimony of how far I've evolved as a man. "Know your father was the kind of man that made a habit out making something out of nothing!

Luv ya Kids!

Made in the USA
Columbia, SC
17 October 2022

69599069R00146